The

SUTOR

Michael Allegretto

Simon & Schuster

New York London Toronto

Sydney Tokyo Singapore

SIMON & SCHUSTER
Simon & Schuster Building
Rockefeller Center
1230 Avenue of the Americas
New York, New York 10020

Designed by Pei Loi Koay
Manufactured in the United States of America

1   3   5   7   9   10   8   6   4   2

Library of Congress Cataloging-in-Publication Data

Allegretto, Michael.
The suitor / Michael Allegretto.
p.   cm.
I. Title.
PS3551.L385S8   1993
813'.54—dc20   92–33577
CIP

ISBN 0-671-73644-2

My thanks to Steve and Judy Iannacito and Doris Marx,
fine artists and good friends

In memory of Clara Onofrio

THE YOUNG MAN slammed into Valerie Rowe from behind.

He knocked her off balance, yanked the purse from her hand, and ran. It happened so quickly that she felt no fear, only surprise. And a split second later, anger.

Valerie hadn't wanted to come here in the first place. East Colfax, a dozen sun-baked blocks from the capitol building, was an area of porno houses, tape and record shops, liquor stores, bars, and a few blue-collar restaurants. Downtown office workers on their lunch hour mingled, at least temporarily, with seedy street people. The latter group appeared annoyed by the midday invasion of the working class.

Not an area Valerie frequented.

But Brenda had insisted they have lunch at the Sapphire Lounge. After dark the place was a dive, but at noontime it was the source of the best chili rellenos in Denver. Or so said Brenda. And since Brenda Newcomb was the owner of Newcomb's Gallery, and since Valerie's paintings would soon hang there, Valerie thought it prudent to dine wherever Brenda suggested. Even though walking in this part of town had been contrary to her instincts.

And now look what had happened.

"Hey, dammit, stop!" she yelled as the young man raced through the crowd, dodging pedestrians like a running back on his way to the end zone. Valerie ran after him. A futile effort, she knew. After all, the kid was in his teens, while Valerie was a few years over thirty. She was in good shape, sure, but aerobic exercises aside, she was in no condition for a chase through a crowded city street. Besides, she was wearing a skirt and leather-soled flats, and the kid was dressed for action: T-shirt, blue jeans, and athletic shoes.

Still, it was her purse, dammit, with her cash (around thirty dollars, she thought), credit cards, checkbook, driver's license, social security card, photos of her son Matthew, lipstick, gold compact, pen, and who knows what other dear junk she'd never be able to replace. And it was her favorite purse—soft gray leather with plenty of room for everything, everything that damn kid was running away with.

So she ran, leaving Brenda behind, stunned and open-mouthed.

The youth dodged pedestrians, who willingly stepped aside, as if they were his accomplices. Valerie shouted, "Stop him!" But everyone seemed concerned only with avoiding involvement. At least they left a path open for her to follow.

Then, as the thief neared the end of the block, he suddenly ran headlong into a man, bowling him over and landing on top of him. The man struggled with the teenager, both of them prone on the sidewalk, fighting for Valerie's purse.

Valerie hurried forward, amazed that no one was helping. People stared, walking by.

"That kid stole my purse!" she yelled.

The youth saw her approaching and made one final effort for the purse, punching the man in the face and yanking on the strap. When the man refused to yield, the kid scrambled to his feet, ran to the end of the block, and vanished around the corner.

The man stood up, seemingly embarrassed.

"Are you hurt?" Valerie asked, putting a hand on his arm.

He was much taller than she, close to six feet, she guessed, lanky, twenty-five or older. Despite the heat he wore a zippered jacket. He had brown hair and eyes, a pale complexion, and blood at the corner of his mouth. He licked it away with the tip of his tongue.

"No, I'm . . . fine," he said. His eyes flicked nervously from Valerie to the passersby. "I guess this is yours." He handed her the purse.

She noticed that the strap had partially torn free—and that her hand was shaking. Now she could feel her heart thumping in her chest, whether from the exertion of running or the excitement of the chase she wasn't sure.

"Valerie, my God." Brenda hurried toward them. "Are you okay? Should we call the police? Your purse. You got it back."

"Thanks to him," Valerie said, smiling at the man, feeling her heart rate slowing to normal. "How can I thank you?"

"It's . . . all right." He brushed dirt from the sleeve of his jacket.

Brenda said to the man, "There should be more people like you, instead of these, these"— she waved her hand at the pedestrians— "these *zombies,* who couldn't care less about helping out a fellow human being!" She ended with a shout directed at the nearest stranger, who gave her a wide berth.

"I'd like to pay you a reward," Valerie said. She dug into her purse for her wallet.

"That's not necessary." The man shifted his feet, as if anxious to leave, although his eyes had become fixed on Valerie.

"I don't have much cash," she said. "Would you take twenty dollars?"

"Val . . ." Brenda cautioned.

"You don't have to pay me."

"Well, I want to give you *something*. At least let me pay to have your jacket cleaned. My God, you don't know what trouble you saved me—replacing my identification, credit cards. . . ." She opened her wallet.

"Really," the man said, "I don't want any money."

Valerie wondered if she'd insulted him, offering cash for a good deed. "Well, then thank you again," she said, shrugging, "unless . . . listen, we were on our way to eat and—"

"Val . . ."

"—and if you'd like to join us, I'd be glad to buy you lunch." Valerie had spoken quickly, making one last offer, certain the man would politely refuse.

"Well . . ." he said, freezing the smile on Valerie's face.

Brenda cut in: "We'll be talking business. I'm sure you'd be bored stiff."

But the man's attention was focused on Valerie.

"If you insist." His tone was shy. "I'd like that."

Brenda sighed loudly.

"Great," Valerie said, maintaining her smile, trying not to feel like a hypocrite. The truth was, she really *didn't* want to sit with a stranger at lunch. But after all, the man had risked bodily harm to retrieve her purse. The thing now was to make the best of it. "I'm Valerie Rowe," she said, briefly shaking his hand. "And this is Brenda Newcomb."

"Pleased to meet you." The man never took his eyes off Valerie. "I'm Leonard Tully."

Brenda led them through the bar into the crowded restaurant. The place featured Formica table tops, paper napkins, and a linoleum floor. But, Valerie noted with pleasure, the atmosphere was cheerful and the aroma was delicious.

They found an empty table near the back.

After the waitress had taken their orders, Brenda launched into a detailed description of her plans for the opening reception Friday night, just two days from now. Valerie was elated about having her paintings displayed in Brenda's gallery, not only because of the possible, even likely financial gain—although money was certainly important to a single parent raising a young son—but also because she felt this was a step ahead in her career as an artist.

So she listened intently to everything Brenda had to say. And out of politeness she tried not to ignore Leonard.

He was an odd young man, she decided. His haircut, his clothes, everything about him seemed out of date, as if he'd been hiding or locked away somewhere for years. Obviously ill at ease, he kept his hands beneath the table. He was quiet—well, for that matter, they both were—letting Brenda do most of the talking.

Valerie faced Brenda, but she could sense Leonard beside her, staring at her. No, not just staring. Inspecting. She was glad when the food arrived, if only to divide his attention.

"Aren't these rellenos to die for?" Brenda said.

"They're great. What do you think, Leonard?"

Leonard was uncomfortable.

He rarely ate out. Too much noise and commotion and too many people walking past the table, moving *behind* him. He especially hated that. He was used to quiet meals with Mother.

In fact, he was supposed to be on his way home now to fix her lunch. And of course, he was *supposed* to have been scouring flea markets and garage sales for items for their shop—not wallowing in filth on East Colfax.

He would have been driving home at this moment if it hadn't been for the purse snatcher. That stupid kid had run right into him, even after he'd done his best to get out of his way. He'd struggled to push him off, but his arm had become entangled in the purse strap. And then the kid had punched him in the face and run.

He'd felt stupid sitting on the sidewalk holding a purse. But then *she* had appeared, emerging from the crowd like the sun from behind the clouds.

She was beautiful—small and delicate and perfect. He guessed she wasn't more than a few inches over five feet tall, with ripe curves beneath her tan skirt and yellow blouse. He'd never been that close to a woman like her before. Oh, he'd *seen* enough pretty women, strutting with their noses in the air as if they were God's gift to Earth. And he'd seen plenty of the others, the sluts on the street. But this woman, this Valerie with the green eyes and auburn hair . . . she was special.

She'd actually touched him, touched his arm. When that had happened, he hadn't mistaken the look on her face: concern. She genuinely cared about him.

And she'd invited him to lunch.

Although, now that he was here, it wasn't as pleasant as he'd expected. The noise and all. And her loud friend. And these overspiced things on his plate. He'd ordered what they'd ordered, even though he disliked Mexican food. He'd forced himself to eat a small mouthful, and then he'd set his fork aside and pretended to listen to the conversation between Valerie and her friend.

The friend he could do without. She hadn't stopped talking since the three of them entered the restaurant, never giving him and Valerie a chance to get acquainted. He'd occupied himself by watching Valerie. He was careful not to stare, of course, studying her facial expressions, her delicate movements, the curves in her face. . . .

When her shoe brushed his pant leg, he felt the blood rise to his face.

"What do you think, Leonard?"

"What?"

"The rellenos."

"Oh, I guess I'm not too hungry. The fight and all."

Valerie nodded.

"So, Leonard," Brenda said, as if noticing him for the first time, "what line of work are you in? Or do you just hang out on East Colfax?"

"Brenda," Valerie said from the side of her mouth.

"I, I mean we, have an antique store."

"We?"

"Mother and I."

"Ahhh," Brenda said, raising her eyebrows at Valerie. "Mother and I."

Valerie gave her a look, then turned to Leonard. "Antiques. How interesting."

Brenda rolled her eyes.

"You must come by our shop sometime," Leonard said.

Valerie nodded, "Sure," and then automatically repaid the invitation: "And you should visit the gallery."

"Really? Where is it?"

Valerie felt Brenda's hard stare. She winced inwardly and said, "The Newcomb Gallery in Cherry Creek."

"I'm sure it's not to your taste," Brenda told him.

After that both women became intent on their food. Leonard toyed with his fork and tried to think of something to say to Valerie. Then, quite suddenly, it seemed to him, lunch was over. The three of them walked, squinting, into the hot, bright August day.

"Thanks again for what you did," Valerie said.

She shook Leonard's hand. He was reluctant to let go.

"It was my pleasure."

"Right," Brenda said, taking Valerie's arm.

Leonard watched Valerie and Brenda walk down the block, climb into a car, and drive away. His stomach was knotted and his head was spinning. He licked his dry lips and wiped moisture from his palms onto his pants. He'd never felt this way before. But he understood the feeling.

Love.

Chapter

VALERIE DROVE HER TOYOTA EAST ON COLFAX, heading for York Street, with the windows down and the summer heat pouring in.

"God," Brenda said, "don't you have air-conditioning?"

"It's broken."

Brenda fanned herself with her hand. "And I still can't believe you invited that creep to lunch."

Valerie smiled. "Come on, he wasn't that bad. Besides, he risked life and limb for me."

"Yeah, right, he knocked down a kid half his size."

"He got my purse back, didn't he?"

"Listen, all I'm saying is you shouldn't get so friendly with total strangers."

Valerie was about to make a joke about it being a good way to meet men, but when she saw Brenda's serious expression she kept her mouth shut. She'd known the woman for several years, and although their relationship was mainly professional, Valerie considered her a friend. But sometimes Brenda, who was ten years her senior, talked to her like a parent.

"Besides," Brenda said, after Valerie had been silent for a few moments, "I didn't like the look in his eye."

"What look was that?"

"Creepy."

The Newcomb Gallery was nestled among the fashionable, upscale shops on Second Avenue east of University Boulevard. It rested comfortably between a jewelry store and a fur boutique.

Brenda unlocked the glass door and led Valerie inside. She flipped a switch, throwing patterns of light on the barren white walls. They'd been freshly painted in preparation for Valerie's show. The long room was empty, except for one small corner set off with temporary partitions, displaying paintings by several artists.

Valerie followed Brenda across the expanse of neutral gray carpeting to the back room, which doubled as an office and a storeroom. Leaning against the wall beside a paper-strewn desk were more than a dozen flat carrying cases.

As Valerie had learned over the years, each gallery owner had her or his own way of hanging paintings for a new showing. Some of them, particularly owners of small galleries operating on tight budgets, let the artists do it all: select the wall space, decide on the groupings, pound the nails, and hang the frames. At the other end of the scale were the gallery owners who did everything themselves and basically told the artist to stay out of the way.

Brenda was somewhere in between. While she employed several people to help her run the gallery, she preferred the hands-on approach when it came to hanging an artist's works. She also wanted the artist there to help—not only physically, but also to make certain the placement made the most sense, aesthetically.

Brenda briskly rubbed her hands together. "Let's have a look."

The Newcomb Gallery had displayed Valerie's work before, but always in conjunction with other artists. This Friday was the first time that Valerie would be the major artist on display. So as they removed each canvas from its case, Valerie watched Brenda's reaction with a bit of apprehension. Brenda had seen only a few of these paintings before, and she'd seen color slides of half a dozen others. The rest, though, were completely new to her.

"Oh, this is nice," Brenda had leaned the first painting against the desk, then stepped back for a better view. "Have I seen this one?"

"Just a photograph, I think."

The two-by-three-foot painting in acrylic was one of several that Valerie had completed last month for this showing. Like the others in the series it was a swirl of colors suggesting movement and energy, an impressionistic image of a Native American dancer.

Valerie remembered this man—John Her Many Horses, a Cheyenne River Sioux. She'd taken snapshots of him and a dozen other dancers during the March Powwow at the Denver Coliseum.

"I love it," Brenda said, lifting the painting and carrying it toward the doorway. "It will definitely sell."

They unpacked the remaining eighteen paintings—mostly male

dancers, with a few women and children in Native American dress—then carried them into the main room, where they arranged them leaning against the long opposing walls of the gallery, rearranged them until they were both satisfied with the placement, pounded nails, and hung the paintings.

They worked without stopping, and in three hours they were finished with what often could be an all-day job. Valerie was sticky with perspiration. She wished she had dressed for work instead of for a luncheon date.

Now Brenda stood in the exact center of the room, hands on hips. She turned slowly, squinting, stopping, smiling, turning again, as if she were a mighty Sioux hunter who'd crept into the midst of a herd of grazing buffalo.

"Absolutely perfect," she said. "What do you think?"

"I agree."

Brenda nodded, pleased. "Sharon will be in this evening to help me reposition the track lighting."

They began making up tags with the titles and prices, attaching one beside each painting.

Some time ago Valerie had determined the selling price of these paintings by "guesstimate": the minimum amount she would take in payment plus another fifty percent to cover the gallery's one-third commission. But when she'd mentioned her prices to Brenda, the older woman had scoffed.

"You're in a high-rent district here, honey," she'd told Valerie. "Let *me* figure out what we can get."

What she'd figured was more than twice Valerie's estimate. Valerie didn't argue. She knew who was the artist and who the art broker.

"I don't know about you," Brenda said after she'd placed the last tag, "but I'm pooped."

Valerie checked her watch as they moved to the back room. It was nearly four-thirty. "I've got to run or Matthew will think I've forgotten about him."

"How *is* Matthew?"

"Are you kidding? An eight-year-old boy on summer vacation? He's doing great."

"Give him a hug for me."

"I will." Valerie picked up her purse, fingering the torn strap. "That damn thief . . ."

Brenda waved it away. "That can be fixed. Just be glad it wasn't your arm that got ripped loose."

"I suppose you're right."

"Sure I am. Believe me, I know, I lived in New York for twelve years. When something like this happens, you just take it in stride and forget about it. It's history."

Matthew's day-care center was in Lakewood, which meant that Valerie had to drive clear across town to the west side during the height of rush hour. It was five-thirty when she walked into the building, feeling guilty about being late, ready to apologize to her son.

Her guilt dissipated, though, when she found him in the game room in a hotly contested Ping-Pong match with one of the supervisors, Mr. Dawkins.

"Hi, Mom! It's my serve and I'm ahead fourteen to eleven!"

"Don't stop on account of me," she said, although Matthew had already smacked the ball over to Dawkins's side of the table.

Valerie sat in a folding chair against the wall and watched the game. She admired her son's intensity. He always seemed to give himself totally to whatever activity he was engaged in, whether it was playing a game, reading a book, or tossing a ball to their dog. Or now, with his brow furrowed, mouth set, and paddle at the ready.

Valerie smiled. She wondered if she would love him as much if he were more laid-back, even lazy.

No question about it, she thought.

For although painting was a crucial part of her life, Matthew *was* her life. She could barely remember what things had been like, what *she* had been like, before his birth. And she couldn't imagine herself without him.

Finally the game ended, with Dawkins the winner. No surprise, Valerie thought, since he was twenty years older and a couple of feet taller than Matthew.

"Good game," Dawkins told Matthew. "One of these days you're going to beat me."

"Maybe tomorrow," Matthew said, blue eyes shining.

"Maybe."

Valerie exchanged hellos with Dawkins, then said to her son, "How're you doing, kiddo?" She reached out and ruffled his dark blond hair, resisting the urge to pick him right off his feet in a big hug.

But she didn't want to embarrass him in front of "school people," as he called them. Lately he'd become sensitive about displays of affection in public

"I'm not a kid anymore," he'd told her at the beginning of summer vacation. "I'm going to be in the third grade, you know."

She knew he was growing up a little bit every day, changing. But he was still her baby, and she wanted to hug him and kiss him every time they were reunited after a day's absence, no matter where they were.

She waited for Matthew to retrieve his jacket and backpack, then walked him to the car.

"So how was your day?" she asked.

"Cool. This morning we all went swimming, and then after lunch we played T-ball. I got a hit."

"Hey, great."

"And then I almost beat Mr. Dawkins *twice* at Ping-Pong. Well, you saw the last game. Only . . ."

"What, honey?"

"Well, sometimes I think maybe he lets me score some points to keep it a close game."

"Really? Why do you think that?"

"Come on, Mom, he's a lot bigger than me, plus he's really good at sports."

"Oh. Does it bother you that he lets you score?"

Matthew shrugged. "Naw, 'cause some points I win against him and I can tell he's really trying." Valerie smiled, and Matthew asked, "So how was *your* day?"

She told him how she'd spent the morning straightening up the studio, getting ready for her next big project, and about her lunch with Brenda and how they'd hung the gallery and how good it looked. She decided not to tell him about the purse-snatching incident—it was over and done with and best forgotten.

And there was no reason to mention Leonard Tully.

C h a p t e r

3

THEIR HOUSE was on West 32nd Avenue in Wheat Ridge, a suburb west of Denver. The area featured curving lanes, well-tended lawns, and huge old elms. Also here were undeveloped tracts, small gently sloping horse pastures, remnants of times past, islands in the sea of houses.

The two-story house rested amid a flat stretch of mown grass, with a high wooden fence encircling the backyard. All of it sat back fifty yards from the speedy avenue, connected to it by a long, tree-lined gravel driveway. Beyond the trees on either side was pastureland. And beyond that was the press of single-family dwellings.

Valerie raised the garage door with the remote control and drove inside.

Dodger began barking before Valerie had shut off the engine. When she opened the side door of the garage, the black mixed Lab was there to greet them. His legs seemed too short for his body, and when he wagged his tail his rump swung from side to side.

"Hi, Dodger," Matthew said, bending down to give the dog a hug.

As Valerie stepped onto the back patio, she heard the phone ringing in the house. She fumbled with her keys, hurrying, twisting open the dead bolt, fully expecting the caller to hang up before she got there.

The phone sounded shrill in the empty kitchen.

Valerie moved quickly to the end of the counter and lifted the receiver from the wall.

"Hello?" she said, a bit breathless.

When there was no immediate reply, she said "hello" again. There was silence on the line. Then she heard an indrawn breath, as if the caller were about to speak. A click. Then a dial tone.

She made a face. "Thank you *so* much," she said, and hung up.

Matthew and Dodger entered the kitchen.

"I'm hungry, Mom."

20

"Well, why don't you feed Dodger while I take a shower," Valerie said. "Then we'll eat. Okay?"

"Okay." He tossed his backpack and jacket on the kitchen table.

"And put your things away, please."

"*Oh*-kay," he said, retrieving his jacket and pack.

Valerie walked down the hallway, past doorways to the stairway and living room on her left, the guest room, Matthew's bedroom, and the bathroom on her right. She undressed in the master bedroom, put on a robe, and went into the bathroom.

She stood in the shower, letting the hot needle spray play on the back of her neck, melting the stiffness. It wasn't the exertion of hanging her paintings that had tightened her muscles. It was apprehension. Not only for the reception Friday, but also for the West Coast opening in eight weeks.

Valerie felt that her career as an artist had reached a turning point. A lot depended on how well her paintings sold at Brenda's gallery—and whether the paintings she produced during the upcoming weeks were well received on the Coast. It was exciting, but also frightening.

But whether she found success or not, she was happy to be doing what she'd always wanted to do. Ever since childhood she'd loved to draw. Her parents had recognized her talent and encouraged her to pursue it through high school and later at the University of Colorado, where she received a B.F.A. in studio arts. Soon thereafter she'd landed her first job at a small graphic-design company in Denver.

Actually, she landed more than a job.

The owner was Kyle Rowe—tall, blond, and blue-eyed with ruggedly handsome features and a persuasive manner. Several women who worked there had warned Valerie about Kyle's reputation as a ladies' man. But when he turned his charms on her and swore that his days of chasing skirts were over, she found herself succumbing. She was young, barely into her twenties, and falling in love.

A year later, she and Kyle were married.

Exactly ten months after that she gave birth to Matthew. She quit work, stayed home with her son, and began the real work of being a mother. By the time Matthew was a year old, Valerie began to paint again for the first time since college. Of course, her major subject was Matthew. She froze his continuous motion with 35mm. photographs and tacked them beside her easel. Her memories and emotions, her mental image of him as she faced the canvas, provided the feelings necessary to bring the paintings alive.

Kyle viewed her efforts with something less than enthusiasm. "They'll never sell," he said, as if that had been Valerie's intention. "If you did something other than baby portraits," he continued, "you could think about commercial success. I'm just considering your personal satisfaction here. It's not as if we need the money."

That part was true. Kyle's graphic-arts business was growing. He'd hired half a dozen new people, and he was spending more and more time at work, usually coming home very tired—and often late.

It wasn't long before Valerie learned that Kyle's late nights weren't always spent at work. He had revived his activities as a ladies' man. He confessed that it was his one flaw, and that Valerie would have to accept it as a fact of life. Like hell she would. Divorce was inevitable.

Kyle gave her custody of Matthew, plus the house, and he began paying alimony and child support.

Valerie blamed herself for the failed marriage. It wasn't logical, she knew, but that was how she felt. The only two things that kept her from sinking into depression were her son and her painting.

Matthew was three when Kyle moved out—old enough to understand that his father was leaving, but young enough to adapt quickly. Except during the one or two weekends each month that Matthew stayed with Kyle, Valerie did practically everything with her son. She took him to the park, the mall, the zoo, the grocery store, the amusement park, the mountains. . . .

As for her painting, she at least considered Kyle's suggestion about subject matter. She looked at it logically: She lived in the West. Many people were interested in things western. So maybe she should paint western subjects. She took Matthew and her camera to rodeos, stock shows, Indian powwows, and New Mexican pueblos. She painted upstairs in what once had been the master suite but was now her studio, complete with skylights and large windows.

At first she displayed her works at arts and crafts fairs and low-budget galleries, anywhere within driving distance. She'd load up the trunk and the back seat of her Toyota Corolla with canvases, buckle Matthew in the seat beside her, and hit the road.

Eventually, her paintings began to sell.

Now she found Matthew sprawled in front of the TV, watching

cartoon mania, thankfully with the sound turned down. She leaned against the countertop that separated the kitchen from the family room.

"What are you hungry for, hon?"

"I don't know."

"I've got turkey breast, or we could have a green salad with shrimp." It was too hot to cook.

"I don't care."

"Salad with shrimp, then, okay?"

"Okay."

She was removing a head of lettuce from the refrigerator when the phone rang. She thought it might be Greg, since he usually called on the nights when they weren't together.

"Hello?"

No answer.

Valerie wondered if this was the same playful crank or "wrong number" who'd phoned earlier. She pressed the receiver tighter to her ear, listening.

There was faint breathing. And in the background the hollow voice from a television set. Someone preaching religion.

"Who is this?" she asked curtly.

Still no answer.

"Get a life," she said, and was about to hang up when she heard her name.

"V-Valerie?" A man's voice. No one she recognized, but somehow familiar, making her regret her smart-aleck remark.

"Yes. Who is this, please?"

An indrawn breath. A pause.

The line went dead with a soft click.

C h a p t e r

4

AFTER DINNER Matthew helped Valerie wash the dishes.

"What do you feel like doing this evening?" she asked, drying her hands with a towel.

"Watching TV."

"Besides that."

"I don't know."

"How about reading? You still have a library book left that you haven't read."

Matthew made a face and shook his head.

"All right, then, how about a game?"

"Okay." He brightened.

"Which one would—"

"Hangman!"

They sat on the floor in the family room, a writing pad and pencil on the coffee table between them. Dodger curled up next to Matthew.

"Who goes first?"

"Ladies, of course," Valerie said.

Matthew began guessing letters, filling in the blanks. He spelled "baseball," with one arm, both legs, and both feet to spare. Valerie spelled "Dodger." Matthew guessed "orange." Valerie got "television." Then Matthew was hanged by "umbrella."

"That's not fair," he said.

"Why not?"

"It's too hard."

Valerie laughed. "Come on, 'umbrella'? Are you saying you don't know that word?"

"Of course I know it. But how am I supposed to know how you spell it? I'm only a kid."

Valerie grinned. "Don't give me that 'kid' stuff. Besides, think of it this way—you learned how to spell a new word."

"Ooo-kay," Matthew said, giving her a you-asked-for-it-now look, "if that's how you want to play."

He turned the pad to a clean sheet, sketched a crude scaffold, and drew five dashes across the bottom. Soon Valerie had only her feet remaining and she was looking at "s p u r _."

The phone rang.

"Time out," she said, rising, stepping into the kitchen, wondering if it was the crank caller again. As much as she hated answering machines, she almost wished she had one now to screen calls. Instead, she was prepared to hang up at once. But it was Greg.

"How're you doing?" he asked.

"I'm getting hung. I mean hanged."

"Does this mean the relationship is over?"

She laughed. "Fat chance, pal." She stretched the phone cord so that she could look over the counter at Matthew. "We're playing hangman, and Matthew is getting serious about it."

"Tell him hello for me," Greg said.

Valerie spoke away from the phone: "Greg says hello."

Matthew nodded. "Can I turn on the TV?"

"Okay," she said, "but keep it down. And when I get off the phone we'll finish our game, okay?"

"Sure." He reached for the remote control.

"Sorry," Valerie said into the phone, turning away from the family room.

"Should I call later?"

"No, its fine. So how was your day?"

"Busier than hell," he said.

Greg Barryman was the owner-operator of a small printing shop, and Valerie knew that "busy" for him meant nonstop work from 8 A.M. until 6 P.M. or later. She didn't envy him. However, she was glad he was in that particular business, because that was how they'd met.

About a year earlier she'd selected a print shop from the Yellow Pages, the one nearest her house. She'd walked in to get her business cards redesigned. Greg had been behind the counter. A week later her cards were ready, and he asked her out to dinner.

They hit it off immediately, as if they'd been friends for years. And, happily for Valerie, Matthew and Greg got along well, too. For the past six months they had talked about living together—with Greg doing most of the talking. As it was, he spent half his time at her house, sleeping over three or four nights a week. But Valerie resisted further commitment. No, not commitment—complications. She loved Greg, but she was hesitant about another marriage. Another *failed* marriage. She wasn't certain if either she or Matthew were ready for that.

Not that Greg had proposed. But if he moved in with her and Matthew, marriage would be the next logical step.

Now he asked her, "How did it go today at the gallery?"

"Good," she said. "Brenda and I got everything hung in a couple of hours. And it looks great, if I do say so myself."

"Congratulations."

Valerie hesitated. "Something did happen today, though."

"What, babe?"

She lowered her voice so Matthew wouldn't hear. "I got mugged on Colfax."

"What!"

"Well, not exactly 'mugged.' Some kid snatched my purse." She described the theft and recovery.

"Thank God you weren't hurt."

"It all happened so fast I didn't even have time to get scared."

"And this guy, Leonard, he just jumped out of the crowd and grabbed the kid?"

"Knocked him down is more like it," Valerie said. "I offered to pay him, but he wouldn't accept money. So I invited him to lunch with me and Brenda."

"I see," he said, with mock concern. "So this is how you meet men behind my back."

Valerie laughed. "That's right. We're planning to stage the same scene every Wednesday. It's quite arousing."

"Now wait a minute."

"I can't help it," she said, smiling. "I always get turned on by knights in shining armor."

"I wish *I* had come to your rescue."

"Now that *would* have been arousing."

"Hold that thought until tomorrow night."

"Does that mean you're coming over?"

"Absolutely. We can all go out for Mexican food."

"Or I'll fix spaghetti," she offered.

"Whatever," Greg said, "as long as we're together."

"What a sweet talker."

"I mean every word. Listen, I'd better let you get back to your game."

"Okay, see you tomorrow."

"Around seven?"

"Perfect."

"Love you."

"Love you, too." She hung up.

Matthew was engrossed in a sitcom featuring children who talked like adults and adults who acted like children.

"Are you ready to finish our game?"

"Pretty soon, okay?" His eyes were glued to the screen. "This is almost over, and this kid, see the one with the Walkman on, he thinks—"

"That's all right, you don't have to fill me in."

She sat on the floor and looked at the notepad. "s p u r _" was written beneath the gallows. The stick figure dangling from the noose lacked only its feet: two remaining guesses. And she'd already tried "n" and "t," the only letters she could think of that would produce words.

The program ended with adults and children freeze-framed in mid-laugh.

"Is this a real word?" she asked Matthew.

"Course it's real."

"Did you spell it right?"

"I think so."

She sighed and made two wild guesses which she knew were wrong. Matthew drew in the stick feet.

"You're hung!" he said. "I win!"

"Okay, so what's the word?"

"Um," he lowered his eyes and mumbled something.

"What?"

"Sperm," he said quietly.

Valerie didn't know whether to laugh or to be shocked. She was certainly surprised.

"Where did you hear that?' she asked.

Matthew shrugged his shoulders. "At school, I guess."

"From one of the supervisors?"

"No. Some kid called another kid a 'sperm head'."

"That wasn't very nice," she said seriously, suppressing a smile.

He shrugged again. "I guess not."

"You wouldn't call someone that, would you?"

"No. I don't even know what it means."

She stopped herself from saying, *Good.*

"What does it mean, anyway?"

"It, ah, has several meanings." She didn't really want to discuss sex education at this moment. "There's a huge whale called a sperm whale. That's one way it's used. Another way is to name a certain fluid in a man's body."

"A fluid?"

"Yes, it has to do with how babies are born."

"Oh, I know all about that."

"You do?"

"Sure. Intercourse."

Now she was shocked. When she spoke, though, it was calmly. "Who told you about that?"

"No one. I mean, I just heard some kids talking about it and they said that intercourse was this dirty thing a man does to a woman and then she gets pregnant."

Valerie sighed. "What else do you know about it?"

"Nothing. Are we going to play another game, or what?"

"In a minute. First I want you to know that intercourse isn't something dirty. It's something beautiful that a man and a woman do together when they want to have a baby or even if they just love each other. It's how everybody gets born, and the only thing dirty is the way some grown-ups and some kids talk about it. Do you understand?"

"Sure, I guess. Can we play now?"

Valerie sighed again, then smiled. "Okay, well, for one thing, 'sperm' is spelled with an 'e,' not a 'u.' "

"Does that mean I didn't win?"

She laughed. "No, I'll give you credit for originality."

Later, she got Matthew off to bed with Dodger curled up on the floor beside him. She read for a while, watched the late news, then made sure the front and back doors were locked. She turned off all the lights, and went to bed.

Sometime later she dreamed she was walking along a crowded street where everyone tried to steal her purse. She kept telling them that "purse" was spelled with a "u," not an "e."

Across town Leonard Tully slept fitfully and dreamed of having intercourse with Valerie Rowe.

LEONARD AWOKE THURSDAY MORNING with Valerie still on his mind.

He thought of her while he washed, dressed, and fixed breakfast for himself and his mother. In fact, he hadn't stopped thinking about her since noon the day before.

After watching her and her friend drive away, he had gone back inside the restaurant, looking for the phone book. He'd run his finger down the list of "Rowes." There was no "Valerie," but there was a "Rowe, V." He assumed—hoped!—that it was her. He dialed the number immediately, too excited to wait. No one answered.

Of course not, he'd thought, chiding himself. At least give her a chance to get home.

His mother wasn't too pleased when he returned home empty-handed. He explained (lied, really, hating it) that he'd found nothing worth buying at any of the garage sales she'd sent him to.

He spent the rest of the afternoon waiting for a chance to phone Valerie.

The problem was the phone was in the kitchen, right out in the open. He could have used a pay phone, but Mother would have wanted a good reason for his leaving. He didn't have one. And he didn't feel ready yet to tell her about the new woman in his life. He wanted to talk to Valerie first, get to know her better, probably even see her again, before he told Mother.

And so he waited until she was busy with a customer out front in the shop before he quietly dialed Valerie's number.

He let it ring many times. Finally she answered. And then he heard his mother coming, so he hung up without saying a word.

It was half an hour before he had the chance to call again. Again Valerie answered, right there in his hand, right up against his face, her voice soft in his ear. His heart was pounding so hard he could barely speak her name. And he suddenly realized that he was afraid to talk to her. No, not afraid—unprepared. He wanted so much to sound clever. But he hung up, feeling like a fool.

And he'd thought about her all day and all night.

Now, while his mother haggled with a customer out front, he stared at the black phone on the counter, ready to try it again. His palms were sweating. He knew he was torturing himself over this woman.

It made him giddy.

He knew that Valerie was the woman he had been waiting for. He could feel it inside. His mother always said, "There's someone in this world for everyone, Leonard, and somewhere there's a girl for you." God had sent the purse snatcher crashing into him, of that he was certain. Divine intervention had delivered Valerie.

And wasn't it obvious that Valerie liked him? She'd asked him to lunch, hadn't she? And she'd invited him to the gallery for her reception Friday. Or words to that effect. Then, to be sure he hadn't missed the point, she'd brushed against his leg under the table. Well, hadn't she?

He wiped his hands on his pants and reached for the phone.

"Leonard, what are you doing in there?"

He looked up, startled. He hadn't heard his mother approach because of the TV preaching from the countertop.

Francine Tully smoothly wheeled her chair into the kitchen doorway and waited for an answer.

"Nothing, Mother."

"Well, I need you out here." Then she frowned, narrowing her eyes and furrowing her smooth brow, until Leonard could feel her gaze boring into him. They both knew that she had the power to get inside, to tear down his puny defensive front with little more than a look or a word. "What *is* the matter with you?"

"Ah, nothing. W-what do you mean?"

"You act like you wet yourself."

Leonard kept quiet.

"Well?"

"What?"

"Are you going to help me carry a lamp out to the customer's car, or do I have to do it myself, wheelchair and all?"

Without waiting for a reply, Francine backed her chair out of the doorway. She wore a sleeveless print dress that revealed the stringy,

knotted muscles in her arms, muscles developed from handling a wheelchair for nearly two decades. Despite her forty-five years, her face was
almost free of creases, save for frown lines at the corners or her eyes
and mouth. Her hair—once auburn, now mostly gray—was pulled
over her ears and fastened with an elastic band. It fell between her
shoulder blades.

She easily swung her chair around, letting Leonard pass, then followed him into the shop.

The small store once had been the living room and dining area of the
house. The space was crammed with old lamps, radios, vases, dolls,
salt and pepper shakers, clocks, hand mirrors, tin boxes with hinged
lids, plastic madonnas with magnetic bases, pocket knives, cardboard
boxes filled with old issues of *National Geographic,* mismatched cups
and saucers, glass insulators, souvenir spoons, and scores of items of
indeterminate function.

Everything, regardless of its age or state of disrepair, was free of dust
and arranged tightly on tables and shelves. An aisle just wide enough
to accommodate a wheelchair snaked through it all, beginning at the
small counter/display case in back near the kitchen doorway and ending at the front door.

The customer, a corpulent woman in her fifties, opened the door for
Leonard, jangling the overhead bell. Leonard carried out a floor lamp
in one hand and a shade in the other.

"Be careful with that," Francine called after him, her words mingling
with the busy sounds of street traffic.

The woman's car was parked halfway up the block on South Broadway. Leonard followed her past a number of store fronts, many of
them displaying antiques. There were dozens of such shops in this part
of town, although he felt an affinity with none of them—their goods
were all priced astronomically higher than his and Mother's, and the
owners were all snobby and cliquish. He knew they scoffed at his store,
considering it in a class with Goodwill or the Salvation Army.

The hell with them, Leonard thought. If I had my way . . .

"Excuse me, did you say something?" the woman asked. She'd
stopped and turned to face him.

"What? No." Leonard grinned sheepishly.

The woman gave him an odd look, then unlocked her car door.

When Leonard returned to the shop, he found his mother in the
kitchen.

Francine had positioned her chair in its usual place—beside the table and facing the counter where the TV set continually poured forth religious programming. There were three UHF channels for her to choose from, and they never went off the air. She liked to flip between them with the remote control, occasionally stopping at a news show or sitcom just long enough to reassure herself that the networks still spewed out nothing but godless trash.

"I thought we'd have egg-salad sandwiches for lunch," she said, not moving her eyes from the screen.

"There is only one road to salvation." The man held a Bible and pointed his finger at the audience, at Francine.

"Whatever you like, Mother."

Leonard removed a carton of eggs from the refrigerator, then half filled a pot with water.

"Remember," Francine told him, "they should boil for fourteen minutes and not one minute longer."

Otherwise, Leonard knew, the yolks would start to turn green.

"And that road lies in Jesus."

"Otherwise, you get that green stuff around the yolks," Francine said.

Leonard set the table, remembering how Valerie had looked seated next to him in the restaurant. He tried to picture her at the table with Mother, chatting and watching TV while he fixed lunch.

"Rub my shoulders while the eggs are boiling," Francine said. "You know how stiff I get being in the chair all day."

Leonard stood behind his mother and put his hands up under her hair, massaging her neck and shoulders. He knew Valerie expected to see him at her reception. But he felt he should contact her before then, so when they were together Friday night, they'd be at ease with each other. And maybe after the reception, he'd bring her home to meet Mother.

He imagined how it would be with Valerie in his truck, the windows down, the wind blowing her hair, her head thrown back in laughter, her fine, white neck. . . .

Her neck reminded him of the other one, the slut. (Put it out of your mind.)

"Leonard, not so hard, you're hurting me."

"Sorry, Mother."

"I'm not a piece of meat, you know."

Leonard resumed the massage, pushing the slut from his mind, thinking of Valerie. He wondered when he'd get another chance to call her. The more he thought about it, though, the more he wondered if phoning her would be enough. Perhaps he should call on her in person. Or even . . .

Yes, he thought, getting an idea. Perfect. Just the thing for a young man to do who's courting a young lady.

"I hope you've been watching the clock," Francine said. "Is it time, yet?"

Leonard smiled. "Almost."

WHEN VALERIE SAW THE VAN parked beside her house, she stopped short, tugging on Dodger's leash.

Earlier she'd taken Matthew to the day-care center, shopped for groceries, and spent the rest of the morning cleaning house. Sometime after noon she'd had a light lunch, catching her breath, leafing through a magazine. Then she'd taken Dodger for his daily walk.

Now she stood at the far end of her driveway and stared at the unfamiliar van parked near her front door.

A man climbed out.

He wore a white shirt and dark pants. He stepped onto the porch and rang the bell, oblivious to Valerie standing in the distance. She didn't recognize him, but he was too far away to see clearly. She wished she were in the house, facing him with a latched screen door between them.

She considered taking Dodger back along 32nd Avenue and returning later, after the man had left.

Valerie wasn't usually this suspicious. But the purse-snatching incident had made her feel vulnerable. And hadn't she read about a woman being raped not far from here a few months ago? Also, this driveway was isolated, bordered by thick trees, separated from the nearest house by a few hundred yards of horse pasture. And Dodger certainly wouldn't be much help if—

Dodger barked.

The man turned and saw her . . . and waved.

"Miss Rowe?" he called.

She was still wary, but somehow she felt safer that he knew her name.

"Yes," she said, walking hesitantly toward him.

He reached in the door of the van and withdrew a long green bundle. Now Valerie saw the name of the flower store painted on the side of the truck.

"These are for you."

He handed her the bouquet, white carnations wrapped in dark green paper, making her ashamed of her earlier suspicions.

"Thank you. Who are they from?"

"There's a card. Have a nice day." He climbed in his truck and backed down the long driveway.

Valerie led Dodger inside and gently laid the flowers on the kitchen counter. She opened the envelope. There was a small, plain, white card inscribed in feminine handwriting, no doubt belonging to a salesgirl at the flower shop:

> *To a beautiful lady,*
> *From a devoted admirer.*

What a sweetheart, Valerie thought, smiling.

After she put the flowers in a vase and added water, she carried them through the front entryway to the living room and placed them on an end table near the window. She considered phoning Greg at work to thank him. Then she decided to wait—he was coming over tonight.

Valerie inhaled the flowers' sweet scent, then went upstairs to her studio.

She hadn't planned to start her new project until after the reception Friday, perhaps not until after the weekend. She'd been working hard the past few months getting ready for Friday night, and she certainly deserved a break.

But painting was something more to her than a job. It was part of her life. It was what she *did,* and she loved it. When she wasn't working on a painting, she felt edgy, incomplete.

She entered the long studio from the top of the stairs.

The room seemed larger than usual, relatively barren now that most of her canvases were hanging in Brenda's gallery. To her left were a tilt-top drawing table and several color-spattered cabinets filled with paints and brushes. A tall, bare, wooden easel stood vigil over a few spotless white canvases leaning against the wall. At the far end of the long room stood two huge canvases, one of them blank.

On the other one a Navajo medicine man whirled and shook a feathered rattle. He was the reason for Valerie's upcoming project.

The studio felt stuffy, so she cranked the tall windows partially open and let her gaze move across the brown foothills to the west. They were near enough to hide the mountains beyond, but if she leaned close to the glass and looked to her right, she could see beyond the hills to the northward sweep of the Rockies.

Valerie adjusted the easel as low as it would go. Even so, it was awkward to maneuver the blank four-by-six-foot canvas onto it, with the longer sides horizontal. From one of the cabinets she brought out a half-gallon plastic jar of ecru acrylic paint. She dipped in a wide brush and began laying the background on the canvas, remembering how the project had materialized.

A month earlier she had received a phone call from a woman named Katherine Stone, who owned an art gallery in Beverly Hills. Ms. Stone was visiting a friend in Aspen, and the friend owned one of Valerie's paintings. Ms. Stone absolutely loved it. She and Valerie talked at length about Valerie's work, and they arranged a meeting the next day at Valerie's house.

Valerie had already completed most of the paintings for the opening at Brenda's gallery. Ms. Stone liked them all. But she was most impressed with the painting on the huge canvas.

Valerie had explained to her that she'd done the painting many months before, more for herself than to sell, and it had been in her studio ever since.

Ms. Stone said she had several clients who would "jump at the chance to buy this painting." Would Valerie be interested in doing six or seven more with a similar theme and style for a showing in Beverly Hills, say in early October?

Valerie had said yes, knowing offers like that didn't often present themselves. However, she also knew what an enormous project she'd taken on. Just preparing the large canvas had taken her two days— building the oversized frame, stretching the canvas, preparing the surface with boiling water and later with gesso. And she'd worked on the painting (sporadically, it was true) for weeks. Now she was promising to complete seven similar paintings between August 10 (the day of her showing at Brenda's) and early October.

After Katherine Stone had left her house, Valerie wondered if she'd gotten in over her head.

She felt better about it, though, after she'd arranged to have the canvases built by students at the University of Colorado, under the supervision of her former art instructor. They'd built one already—the one that now rested on her easel—and the remaining six were to be done within the week.

No problem, she thought, smiling wryly, seven major paintings in eight weeks.

You can do it, she told herself. Barring complications.

"Forget complications," she said aloud. "Think ecru."

At seven that evening Dodger barked a moment before the doorbell rang. Valerie had already started dinner—pasta with marinara and a green salad—and Matthew had helped her set the table. He ran to answer the door, with Dodger at his heels. A moment later Greg stood in the kitchen doorway. He was a head taller than Valerie, with soft brown eyes and dark brown hair, prematurely graying at the temples.

He smiled at Valerie. "How're you doing?"

"Give me a hug and I'll let you know."

They embraced, and Valerie tilted her head back to kiss him.

"Missed you," she said.

"I missed you, too." He kissed the tip of her nose.

"And thank you for the flowers. They're beautiful."

"Flowers?"

She gave him a gentle poke in the stomach. "You forgot already?"

"I wouldn't think so. Somebody sent you flowers?"

"Very funny. Come here."

Valerie took Greg's hand and led him to the living room and the vase of carnations.

"See? They were delivered this afternoon."

Greg leaned over and sniffed. "Nice. Did this come with them?" He picked up the small white envelope and withdrew the card. His eyebrows went up as he read. "A 'devoted admirer'?"

Valerie frowned. "You really didn't send these?"

Greg shook his head.

"Let me see that again." She took the card from him.

"It looks like a woman's writing to me."

"That's what I thought," she said, puzzled. "I assumed it had been written by a salesgirl at the flower store."

"Maybe they're from Kyle."

Valerie made a face. "My ex-husband is hardly an admirer. Besides, he never gave me flowers when we were *married*."

Greg shrugged. "Maybe from someone who bought one of your paintings."

"Maybe," Valerie said, rereading the card and shaking her head. "It's odd, though."

"Are you guys going to talk about those stupid flowers all night?" Matthew asked.

Greg laughed. "Good point."

After dinner they sat in the family room. Matthew showed Greg what he'd made that day—a large sheet of white paper decorated with water colors, bits of construction paper, and sparkles.

"Hey, that's great." Greg held it at arm's length.

"Do you know what it is?" Matthew asked.

"Well . . ."

"It's Leonardo fighting these two really bad dudes."

"Leonardo da Vinci?"

"Who?" Matthew took the paper from Greg. "It's Leonardo, one of the Teenage Mutant Ninja Turtles."

"Oh, *that* Leonardo."

"So now you know," Valerie said, "why I send my son to one of the finest day-care centers in the area. So—"

The phone rang.

"—so he can paint cartoons." She put her hand on Greg's knee and rose from the couch.

"Well, I kind of like it," Greg said.

"Yeah, Mom, see?"

"I like it, too," she said, crossing the kitchen to the phone. "The technique, that is. It's the subject matter that I'm not crazy about." She lifted the receiver. "Hello?"

"Is, ah, is this Valerie?" A man's voice, one she'd heard before.

"Yes?"

"I wanted to know if you got the flowers."

"Why, yes. Who is this?"

"Leonard."

"Le—" She pictured a pale face, a bashful thin-lipped smile.

"I loved our lunch yesterday," Leonard said shyly. "It was really nice. Nice of you, I mean."

Valerie stared at the phone, not quite believing what she was hearing. Leonard had sent the flowers. And the card.

Devoted admirer.

Tiny hairs rose on the back of her neck.

In the next room Matthew laughed at something Greg said.

"I wanted you to have something to—oops. I have to go now. I'll be seeing you," he said and hung up.

Valerie slowly replaced the receiver in its cradle. She walked back to the family room, feeling slightly off balance.

"Valerie?" Greg looked concerned. "What is it? Bad news?"

"It was Leonard."

"Who?"

"The man who got back my purse. *He* sent the flowers."

"What? How did he get your address?"

"I guess from the phone book."

Greg frowned.

Valerie just shook her head. Then she turned and walked out through the entryway to the living room. She stood for a moment before the table, looking down at the beautiful carnations, recalling how their stems had felt cool and smooth when she'd arranged them in the vase. Their scent, so pleasing before, now seemed sickeningly sweet. The card gaped beside them like a grin. To a beautiful lady.

She picked up the vase and the card and carried them to the front door.

"What're you doing?" Greg asked.

"These don't belong in here."

She went outside and walked up the driveway to the large plastic trash barrel beside the garage. She reread the card.

Devoted admirer.

She dropped the card in the barrel. Then she upended the vase, dumping in the wet-stemmed carnations as if they were putrid.

"WHO WAS THAT?" Francine Tully asked.

She'd wheeled her chair from the bathroom just as Leonard hung up the phone. He stood beside the counter, smiling.

"A young lady," he said.

"Ooo, a young lady, listen to you." She moved her chair to the kitchen table, picked up the remote control, and raised the volume on the TV. She asked absently, "What was she selling?"

The man on the screen pranced across a stage and shook his fist over his head. ". . . the roaring fires of Hell."

"She wasn't selling anything, Mother. I called her."

For the first time that Leonard could remember, Francine looked dumbfounded. Her jaw actually hung open. She did a slow turn from the TV set until she faced him. He fidgeted uncomfortably.

"You called *her?* Do tell."

Leonard shrugged and sat at the table. His face was warm. He'd felt strong and confident talking to Valerie, but his mother could make him feel as if he were still a naughty little boy. He took a deep breath before he spoke, gathering himself.

"She's a young woman I recently met."

"Where'd you meet her?" Francine's voice was suddenly sharp. "What's her name?"

"Her name is Valerie Rowe."

"And?"

"I . . . met her at a Christian singles meeting."

Leonard did not like lying to his mother. But if he had to use a falsehood, this one felt the most comfortable. He'd used it occasionally when he wanted to get out of the house at night . . . to drive around. And after all, the Christian meetings had been her idea.

Francine had begun to mention the singles group about two years ago, soon after Leonard's twenty-fifth birthday.

"A quarter of a century," his mother had chided him, "and still not married." This jab seemed to come out of nowhere, because he'd always taken their relationship for granted: he, the devoted son; she the disabled mother. It had been that way since her accident.

Before that—long before—when Big Ed had still been alive, Leonard recalled little. All he could remember of his father was a giant figure and a booming voice. When he was two years old Big Ed was killed in Vietnam, and Mother . . . changed.

There were continuous beatings for reasons he'd never fathomed. And a host of nameless men, reeking of alcohol, parading through her bedroom. Sometimes she made him watch what they did to her. (Put it out of your mind.) Or else she locked him in the tool shed. That had been the worst, alone in that cramped, cold, dark place for hours, and more than once for a full night and day, having to urinate so badly it hurt, afraid to relieve himself, afraid of what Mother would think of him or what she might do. Mostly afraid that she'd never let him out. He would squeeze himself into a tiny ball, holding so still he could hear the insects skittering about him in the dark, not moving even when they crawled on him. Because if he held extra still and tried very hard, sometimes he could escape.

Then, not long after Leonard's eleventh birthday, his mother drove into a tree on her way home from a bar. She lost the use of her legs, but she found Jesus—an equitable trade. Especially since she had her long-neglected son to care for her.

Leonard was grateful there were no more beatings, no more men, no more shed. Just the two of them at home.

At school he still remained a loner, different from the other kids. But at least at home and in the shop he now felt as if he belonged, as if he'd been accepted by his mother, as if finally he could please her. It had gotten even better after he'd graduated from high school—he could spend more time at home. Life was peaceful. Orderly.

Until he turned twenty-five.

Something about that age had seemed significant to his mother. Perhaps someone had put a bug in her ear—one of her Christian women friends who sometimes came to visit. Or maybe it was one of the innumerable religious brochures she received in the mail. Whatever the reason, she was suddenly and relentlessly on a crusade to get him attached to "some nice, young Christian lady."

He'd tried, he really had.

Less than a year ago he'd finally gone to one of the singles get-togethers she'd been harping about. Well, he hadn't actually talked to anyone. Or even gone inside, for that matter. But he made it to the doorway of the church basement where the function was held. He saw men and women his age and older—talking in small groups, laughing, sipping punch. Mingling. Being sociable. Learning all about each other.

A panic seized him and he got away from there as fast as he could.

He couldn't just go home, though. His mother would demand to know why he wasn't at the meeting. So he drove around the city, killing time, eventually finding himself on East Colfax.

That had been a revelation.

He'd never seen so many colorful, wild-looking people before, all of them just hanging out on the street. He saw a number of women—harlots, his mother would've called them—wearing miniskirts and spike heels, walking alone or in pairs.

When he stopped at a traffic light, one of these women had been bold enough to step off the curb, lean into his truck window, and speak to him. He didn't know how to respond to her, couldn't even remember her words. The light had turned green, and he pulled away so fast he nearly knocked her down. He drove straight home.

His mother wanted to know all about the Christian singles meeting.

He enjoyed it, he said.

She was pleased. Would he go again next week?

Yes, he told her. And he had gone back. To East Colfax.

Sometimes he just drove up and down the street, watching. Sometimes he parked the truck and walked, not talking to anyone, just being close to them, to the women, close enough to smell their heavy perfume. Often, he'd go into one of the adult theaters and watch people on the screen having sex. Sometimes it aroused him. (Put it out of your mind.)

He imagined himself having sex with one of the women on the street. He knew all he had to do was ask. And pay.

Although they were sluts, one thing could be said in their favor—they didn't frighten him or send him into a panic the way the oh-so-perfect women in the church basement had. These women were godless, inferior. Being near them made him feel strong. He knew that eventually he would speak to one of them, tell her what he wanted, and then pay her exactly what she deserved.

And eventually, of course, he had. (Put it out of your mind.)

"Why haven't I heard about this young lady before?" Francine asked him now, pulling him from his thoughts. "You know her well enough to call her on the phone, but you don't want to tell your own mother about her?"

"No, Mother, I just met her. Of course, I was going to tell you."

"She is a God-fearing woman, I assume, not just some strumpet who hangs around church meetings to—"

"Mother, please."

"Well, when do I get to meet her?"

"Soon, I'm sure." He'd been clasping his hands on the table top, and now he dropped them to his lap and wiped the moisture on his pants. "In fact, tomorrow I'm . . . taking her out on a date."

"A *date?* What do you mean?"

Leonard had assumed she'd welcome this news, but he could see he'd been wrong. She sat rigidly in her chair, one hand tightly bunched in her lap.

"I mean we're going out together. It's what young people do. Isn't that what you wa—"

"I know what young people do," she snapped. "I don't need you to tell me. Taking drugs and alcohol and rutting like animals."

"Mother . . ."

"And who is this woman, anyway?" Francine demanded, her voice as sharp as splintered bone. "I've never even seen her. How do I know what she's like?"

"She's very nice. I'm sure you'll like her."

"I'll be the judge of that." She turned back to the television, but for only a moment, hardly long enough for Leonard to relax. "And just where are you going on this *date*." She spat the last word.

"To . . ." He knew if he said "art gallery" she'd fly into a rage. Mother felt that art was antireligion. "To dinner."

"Oh, dinner, is it? And how can we afford this *dinner?*"

Their funds were limited, it was true. However, they weren't exactly broke, what with the life insurance from Leonard's father and the little money his grandfather had left them. To say nothing of the shop. It wasn't a gold mine, but it did show a profit each year.

Still, Leonard wished he'd said something other than "dinner." And he was glad he hadn't mentioned the flowers.

"It's really not very expensive," he said. "I'll probably just have a sandwich."

"Sandwich, indeed." Francine returned her attention to the TV. "I only wish you had talked to me about this first, before you ran off half-cocked. A mother has a right to know."

". . . knows everything," the man on the screen told her. "You can't hide from Jesus."

"I know that," Leonard said.

Later, Leonard helped his mother into bed.

She could undress herself and put on her nightclothes without his help. And she could climb in and out of the wheelchair by herself—as long as she had something solid to grab onto, like the chrome hand-railing he'd bolted to the bathroom wall. But getting in and out of bed was troublesome for her. Oh, she could do it. But it was troublesome. She preferred it if Leonard helped her.

"I believe I'll read for a while," she said.

Leonard arranged her pillows so she could sit up in bed, then straightened the blanket over her. He switched on the lamp beside the bed. The night stand, draped with a paisley cloth, was cluttered with framed pictures of Jesus and photographs of Big Ed, some of them in his Marine uniform. Leonard lifted the Bible from the midst of the pictures and handed it to her. Then he leaned down and kissed her on the forehead.

"Good night, Mother."

"Good night, Leonard."

He paused at the doorway, his hand on the light switch. Francine had put on her glasses, and the reflection from the bedside lamp transformed her eyes into golden disks. The image was at once beautiful and frightening to him, as if she had the power to see into his head.

Leonard turned off the ceiling light, then walked out to the kitchen, switching off a TV evangelist in mid-accusation.

In the bathroom he brushed his teeth, rinsed, flossed, then brushed them again, using only water. He took a mouthful of mouth wash and swished it around for several minutes, making certain to cleanse every enamel surface and crevice. Then he washed his face and rubbed it dry. The towel had a floral print, and the edges were beginning to unravel. Leonard folded it carefully, making sure the corners met, then hung it precisely in the center of the towel bar.

He looked at himself in the mirror over the sink, then leaned forward, focusing on his eyes. They were a pale shade of brown with a scattering of luminous green flecks. He leaned closer still, until he could see the reflection of his face in the mirrored pupils of his eyes. It gave the illusion of a tiny Leonard peering out from inside the head of a giant Leonard.

He smiled.

He remembered how as a child he'd discovered his miniature self residing in the head of a huge body that he controlled from behind the two pale brown windows. He could see out, but no one could see in. Or get in. He was safe in there. They could hurt the body, but they couldn't hurt him.

Leonard switched off the light and went to his room.

He lay in the dark on his narrow bed, staring up at the ceiling, thinking of Valerie.

He pictured them together at the art gallery tomorrow. They'd be standing close, touching, laughing. She'd introduce him to the few other people there and tell them how Leonard had come to her rescue. Afterward he'd bring her back here to meet Mother. They'd all sit and talk for a while, and then he'd drive her home. Maybe she'd invite him in. Of course she would. They'd be alone. She'd turn to him, her lips parted. . . .

Leonard rolled onto his stomach and clutched the pillow to his chest. He could smell the freshness of her hair.

C h a p t e r

VALERIE FELT her body release in orgasm. She clung to him, her fingers in his back, a moan escaping her lips.

"Oh, Greg."

He shuddered, burying his face in her neck. Gradually, his breathing slowed to normal. He moved off her and then, lying on his side, pulled her to him. She laid her head in the crook of his arm. He stroked her bare hip with his free hand.

"I love you," she said.

"I love you, too." He kissed the top of her head, inhaling her scent.

They lay like that for a long time. Then she said, "I'll be right back." She disengaged herself from his limbs, climbed out of bed, and pulled on a robe—not for warmth, but in case Matthew was up. She found her way down the hall and into the bathroom without turning on the lights, her eyes having adjusted to the dark.

When she was finished, she looked in on Matthew. He was in his pajama bottoms, face down, spread-eagle on the bed. The top sheet was tangled around his feet. Valerie gently straightened the sheet and pulled it up to his shoulders. He mumbled something in his sleep and rolled onto his side. She kissed his cheek and said softly, "Sleep tight, baby." Then she moved quietly back to her bedroom.

Greg was already snoring softly. She curled up behind him, thinking how lucky she was to have these two wonderful men in her life. She fell peacefully asleep.

The next morning, there was mild dissension at the breakfast table.

"But why can't I go tonight?" Matthew asked. For the hundredth time, Valerie estimated. The boy had hardly touched his grapefruit half.

"Because, hon, it's just for adults, remember?" Actually, Valerie was torn between taking him to the reception and leaving him home with a sitter. She wanted them to share their lives as much as possible, and she tried hard not to let her work, her art, come between them. But she was fairly certain that after twenty minutes at the gallery, he'd be bored stiff. "You'd be the only kid there," she said.

"So?"

"So, you'll have more fun here with Heather."

"Heather's nerdy."

"Matthew."

Greg laughed. "He's right, though. She is a little nerdy."

Matthew giggled.

Valerie slapped Greg playfully on the shoulder. "You're a big help." She turned to Matthew. "And Heather is not a nerd. She's just . . . studious. Besides which she's responsible, likable, and, ah . . ."

"Available?" Greg put in.

Valerie gave him a look that made him raise his hands defensively. She said to Matthew, "I promise if there's anything good to eat tonight at the reception, like cookies, I'll bring some home, okay?"

"Yeah, I guess." Matthew stared down at his grapefruit.

"And tomorrow, if you want to, I'll take you to the gallery and you can see how it looks with all my paintings."

"Really?"

Valerie nodded.

"You'll be able to see much better tomorrow," Greg said, "because the place won't be jam-packed with a bunch of nerdy grown-ups."

"Excuse me?" Valerie's mouth turned up in a half-grin.

"I was speaking hypothetically."

"What does that mean?" Matthew asked.

"It means," Valerie said, "that you'd better hurry up and finish your grapefruit or you'll be late."

Greg volunteered to take Matthew to the day-care center on his way to work. Valerie kissed them both good-bye at the door, then leashed Dodger and took him for a short, brisk walk. Afterward, she left him in the backyard while she went upstairs to work.

She got out the box of photographs, sorted through the envelopes until she found the right one, and removed a stack of photos. The picture she wanted was on top. She'd used it for the painting that Katherine Stone had seen in Aspen. She would paint basically the same picture again. Except the one in Aspen was twenty-four by eighteen inches, and this painting would be six by four feet.

She moved to the far end of the room in order to see the entire canvas. Now that the background was complete, she imagined how the figure would reside there: a male dancer in beaded buckskin and feathered headdress, back bent, knee raised, right arm thrust forward holding a spear with dangling feathers.

She looked at the photo in her hand, remembering when she'd taken it—two years ago at a Native American festival in Cheyenne. She recalled his name, Eugene Soldierwolf, a Northern Arapaho, and she remembered how he'd danced, with powerful yet fluid movements.

Valerie raised her eyes and saw the man on the canvas. She set the photo aside and then removed jars of paint from the cabinets.

She began with a medium brown, using long, sweeping strokes to indicate the general shape of his back, torso, legs, and extended right arm. It was difficult for her to visualize the proportions of a figure this size, and so she frequently had to stop and step back to the far end of the room to check her progress.

It went slowly. By noon it seemed she'd hardly begun. She wondered if this project might be too much for her. Seven large paintings in eight weeks . . .

"You can do it, dammit," she said aloud.

Valerie picked up Matthew early that afternoon, as she usually did on Fridays. While he and Dodger played outside with a Frisbee, she began going through her closet, deciding what to wear that night. She narrowed it down to two outfits: black pants and a black top with a design of rose and white sequins, or a peach-colored dress. The dress was less formal and more "summery," and if she were attending someone else's reception, she would definitely pick the dress. But the pants and top were more arty, and it was *her* reception.

She hung the dress back in the closet.

She fixed sandwiches for herself and Matthew, but she was too nervous to do more than just nibble. After cleaning up the kitchen she showered and dressed. While she was applying eye shadow, she heard Dodger bark and the doorbell ring.

By the time she reached the entryway Matthew was letting in Heather. The plump girl clutched several textbooks and a notebook to her breast as if they contained her life's secrets. With her free hand she brushed a strand of hair from her shiny forehead.

Matthew said, with some excitement, "Come in here, Heather. I got a new game last week and it's really cool."

Valerie was pleased that her son had forgotten his earlier appraisal of his sitter. She leaned out the front door and waved to Heather's mother, who was already backing her station wagon down the driveway.

Greg arrived shortly thereafter. He wore a sport coat, slacks, and a tie, a rare accessory for him. He kept his hand behind his back as he leaned forward to kiss Valerie. Then he produced a single, long-stemmed red rose.

"For the artist," he said.

"Thank you, sir." She had a brief, unpleasant memory of Leonard's flowers.

"By the way, you look terrific."

"You look pretty spiffy yourself." She kissed him again and fingered his tie. "Have I seen this before?"

He shook his head. "I bought it today."

"You're kidding."

"Why? Don't you like it?"

"No, I love it." She smiled. "It's just that—*you* buying a *tie?*"

"I'm not totally out of the mainstream of fashion, you know. Besides, tonight is a special occasion. I even shined my shoes."

"What a guy."

Before they left, Valerie told Heather there was ice cream in the freezer and strawberries in the fridge. Then she wrote down the number of the gallery.

"We should be home well before midnight," she said. "But if you need to, you can reach us here."

She kissed Matthew on the cheek. "You be good, okay?"

"Okay. And you know something?"

"What, hon?"

"Well, um, none of the other kids I know have moms that have receptions, and . . ."

"Yes?"

"Well . . . I'm real proud of you."

The remark caught Valerie off guard. She felt her eyes mist, and she gave him a big hug. "Thank you, baby. That means a lot to me."

On the way to the gallery Valerie told Greg what Matthew had said. He smiled and shook his head.

"He's a good kid."

"I know. I'm lucky."

"So is he," Greg said. "So am I, for that matter." He reached over and put his hand on her leg, and she laid her hand on top of his.

They rode for a few moments in silence, Greg keeping the car in the flow of traffic.

"Are you nervous about tonight?" he asked.

"Not really. Well, a little. I'd be more nervous if it weren't for you."

"What'd I do?"

"Just being with you," she said, squeezing his hand. "And bringing me a rose. That was sweet."

"You're welcome. I didn't want . . ."

She looked at him. "Didn't want what?"

He sighed. "I mean, I'd planned on bringing you a flower anyway. But doubly so after yesterday."

Valerie knew what he meant before he said it.

"I didn't want the carnations from that goofball Leonard to be the last flowers you'd received before tonight, before your reception. I know it's silly, but—"

"No," she said, putting her hand on his arm. "It's not silly. I feel the same way."

Receiving flowers from Leonard had seemed unnatural to Valerie . . . obscene, in a way. She'd even been bothered by his final words to her on the phone: "I'll be seeing you." She knew it had been only a figure of speech, but she didn't like the idea—even the possibility—of ever seeing him again.

She pulled Greg's arm toward her, palm up. "The rose was perfect," she said and kissed the palm of his hand. Then her tongue flicked out, tickling.

"Hey!" He grinned. "I'm trying to drive."

A short time later Greg found a parking slot near the front of the gallery. He stopped Valerie from climbing out.

"Wait till I open the door for you."

"Get real," she said, smiling.

"I am. This is your night, so just keep your butt in the seat until I get over there."

He walked around the car, opened her door, and extended his arm for her. "My lady."

"Now you *are* being silly."

She stood on the sidewalk, and he kissed her.
"You know what?" he said.
"What?"
"I'm proud of you, too."
They walked hand-in-hand into the gallery.

Chapter

WHEN VALERIE AND GREG WALKED IN, Brenda and her assistants were setting up a table at the far end of the gallery with bottles of wine, a bowl of punch, cheese, strawberries, and melon slices. There were already several guests, sipping wine from plastic glasses and browsing among the paintings.

Brenda wore diamonds and a white silk dress. She strode across the room to greet them, smiling broadly, arms extended.

"Hi, kids. Isn't this exciting?" She took Valerie's hands and kissed her cheek, then turned and kissed Greg's. "How've you been? I haven't seen you for a while."

"Fine, thanks," Greg said. "And you look fantastic."

Brenda raised her eyebrows at Valerie. "Still the charmer, I see."

"He has his moments."

"Come on," Brenda said, moving between them. She hooked her arms through theirs and led them toward the back. "Let's get some wine before the buying public arrives."

"I *hope* there will be buyers."

"Don't worry," Brenda said. "In fact, I've already sold one of your paintings."

"You're kidding."

"Nope." She nodded toward a canvas on the wall. A round red sticker had been pasted over the price. "I opened the door not thirty minutes ago, and a couple walked in, said, 'We'll take it,' and wrote me a check. Also, there's a woman coming tonight, a friend of mine, who wants to meet you. I *know* she'll buy something."

By eight the gallery was crowded. Some people had viewed the paintings and left, but the majority of guests remained to talk in small groups.

Brenda pulled Valerie away from Greg to introduce her to Mrs. Hadley, an elderly woman who wore earrings with large colored stones. Valerie decided they were too gaudy to be fake.

"I wanted to meet you before I left," Mrs. Hadley said. "I simply love your work."

"Thank you." Valerie knew the compliment was sincere. And although she was proud of her own paintings, she couldn't help feeling slightly embarrassed whenever she received high praise from strangers.

"Mrs. Hadley purchased one of your paintings tonight," Brenda said, "and she'd like to commission another."

"Would you be interested?"

"Why, of course," Valerie said.

"Excellent." Mrs. Hadley removed a card from her purse and handed it to Valerie. "I'll be traveling abroad for the next month. When I return I'd like you to call me."

"I certainly will."

As Brenda led Mrs. Hadley toward the front of the gallery, she turned and winked. Valerie silently mouthed, "Thank you." Then she scanned the faces in the crowd, searching for Greg.

"Nice turnout."

The man's voice came from behind her, but she recognized it at once.

"Hello, Kyle," she said, turning to face her ex-husband.

He looked, she thought, as handsome as ever—cobalt-blue eyes, rugged features, and curly blond hair. He wore a linen sport coat with the sleeves pushed up over his forearms.

"I'm glad you could come."

"Wouldn't miss it." He flashed a too-brilliant smile. "I'm one of your biggest fans, remember?"

Valerie merely nodded and smiled. She knew he was full of bullshit about ninety percent of the time. But she also knew he was trying his best to be nice.

"So," Kyle said, "it looks as if your popularity has reached dizzying heights."

"I should be so lucky," she said. "Actually, though, things are going pretty well."

"If anyone deserves it, you do."

"Yeah, right."

"Don't be so self-deprecating. You've worked hard and you've earned whatever rewards come your way."

"Well, thanks."

"You're welcome. And I really am happy for you," he said with feeling. "I mean it."

Valerie nodded again. "I appreciate your saying that."

They were silent for a moment, and then they both spoke at once:

"Where's—"

"Where's—"

Valerie laughed. "You go first."

"Where's Matthew? I thought I might see him tonight."

"He's home with a sitter. I considered bringing him, but I was afraid boredom would set in before he finished his second glass of punch."

"You're probably right."

"Where's Alyce?" With a "y," Valerie said to herself.

"She . . . had something else to do tonight. In fact, I can't stay long. I'm supposed to . . . meet her."

"Oh." Valerie saw a brief cloud pass behind Kyle's eyes. She'd heard from a friend who still worked for Kyle that his new marriage was already shaky. She felt the urge to ask him about it, to console him, if necessary. Although Kyle had his faults, in particular a roving eye, Valerie knew that deep down he was a good person and that he would never consciously hurt anyone. She believed that his biggest problem was he'd never completely grown up. For all his social acumen and economic success, he was in some ways still a little boy, not willing to take full responsibility for the consequences of his actions.

"Well," Valerie said, "be sure to tell her I said hello."

"I will."

"Hello."

Valerie felt cold fingers touch her elbow. She looked back and the smile froze on her face.

Leonard Tully stood behind her. He wore a rumpled brown corduroy coat and a sheepish grin. The knot in his wide green knit tie was as big as a child's fist. There was a sheen of perspiration on his pale forehead, and his eyes darted about as if he were surrounded by enemies.

Valerie was disconcerted by his presence. But he looked so out of place that she almost felt sorry for him.

"Oh . . . hi," was all she could manage.

"I made it." He spread his hands. "I mean, here I am."

"Well . . . thank you for coming."

"Are all these paintings yours?"

"Most of them."

"You're very talented."

"Yes, she is," Kyle said.

"Oh, I'm sorry, Kyle, this is Leonard, ah . . ."

"Tully."

"Yes, and Leonard, this is Kyle Rowe, my former husband."

Kyle frowned at her and smiled at Leonard, shaking his hand. Valerie understood Kyle's look, realizing how ridiculous she had sounded. She'd never introduced him to anyone as "my former husband." It had been a feeble attempt to insulate herself from Leonard.

"How do you do," Kyle said.

Leonard simply nodded and withdrew his hand.

"Are you an old friend of Valerie's?" Kyle asked with mild sarcasm.

"We met Wednesday."

"Not so old, then."

Valerie saw that Kyle was sizing Leonard up, the way he always did when he met someone for the first time—looking for weaknesses, preparing verbal darts.

"Leonard came to my rescue," Valerie said suddenly.

"He what?"

"He stopped a purse snatcher."

Kyle looked at Leonard with a mixture of surprise and disbelief. Leonard averted his eyes, embarrassed.

"Um, go ahead, Leonard, tell him about it."

"Well, I don't know. . . ."

"Please," Valerie insisted.

"Yes, well, first I saw this kid running toward me. . . ."

While Leonard hesitatingly recounted the incident, Valerie scanned the crowd, looking for Greg. She wanted him here, now, an ally. The two men flanking her, although they couldn't have been more different from one another, shared one thing in common: neither of them seemed to communicate on her frequency. She spotted Greg standing with Brenda in a small group, and she willed him to look this way. She desperately wanted to wave him over.

"Earth to Valerie," Kyle said.

"Excuse me?"

"I was just about to tell Leonard here that you have an uncanny way of meeting some really *interesting* people." His voice dripped with sarcasm.

"I suppose," she said. "I met you, didn't I?"

Kyle smiled. "Good point. And on that I believe I'll take my leave."

He held her hand in both of his. "Congratulations on all this," he said. "You've done some really good work."

"Thanks."

"And, Leonard," he said brightly, dropping Valerie's hand and slapping Leonard on the shoulder, "it's been enlightening."

Kyle moved away, threading his way through the crowd. Valerie saw him stop and exchange a few words with Greg and Brenda. Brenda shook his hand and waved good-bye.

"I didn't know you'd been married," Leonard said, as if he should have known.

"What?" She looked up at him and noticed tiny, tight lines at the corners of his eyes and mouth.

"I can see why you'd want to divorce someone like that." One close friend to another. "He thinks he's pretty smart, doesn't he?"

Leonard's intimate manner chilled Valerie. She had the urge to flee from him, but there was nowhere to go. Perhaps she could pry him loose another way.

"There's someone I'd like you to meet," she said and started to lead him toward Greg.

Leonard touched her arm, little more than a brushing of his fingers across her skin just above the elbow. But it was enough to stop her.

"Couldn't we talk together for a while, just you and I?"

"Ah, you should meet Greg first."

He stared down at her, unblinking. It was the first time she'd noticed his eyes—pale brown, translucent, as if she could see right through them into his mind, as if he could see into hers.

"All right," he said, narrowing his eyelids, smiling thinly. "If that's what you'd like."

Valerie made her way between clusters of friends and strangers. She sensed Leonard close behind in pursuit. When she reached Greg, he and Brenda were just detaching themselves from several other people.

"Hi," she said, grabbing Greg's arm.

"There you are." He smiled, then glanced over the top her head at Leonard.

"This is someone I want you to meet," she said, giving him a knowing look. She stood directly between them now, and she realized with some surprise that Greg and Leonard were the same height. She would have guessed that Leonard was inches taller than Greg. Perhaps it was because Leonard was stringy, raw-boned. Or maybe he was slouching, perhaps defensively, feeling threatened.

"Well, well," Brenda said loudly, making Leonard wince. "Look who found his way into my gallery. Leonard, isn't it?"

"Len—" Greg frowned, looking down at Valerie, who barely nodded her head.

"Did you come here to buy a painting or two, Lenny?" Brenda asked with a wicked smile. "Or were you just hoping for another free lunch?"

"Brenda, please," Valerie said, admonishing her.

"No, I . . . came to see Valerie."

Brenda pursed her lips and turned to Valerie. "You see what I mean?" she said. "I warned you about this the other day. You can't be socializing with just anyone you bump into on the street."

"Brenda, for God's sake." Valerie felt her ears redden in embarrassment. She'd wanted Leonard to meet Greg so he'd understand that she was involved with someone. But she hadn't intended for him to be attacked. She looked at Brenda and spoke softly, but forcefully: "There's no need to—"

"You see, Len, it's like this," Brenda went on, ignoring Valerie. "Valerie is leading a full and busy life and she doesn't have time to be harassed by you. She doesn't want you hanging around, and neither do I. So why don't you just run along." She made a brushing motion with her fingertips.

"Jesus, Brenda," Greg said.

Valerie could see that Greg wasn't sure if Brenda was serious or kidding. But she could tell that he, too, disapproved of her rudeness. He turned toward Leonard and offered his hand.

"We haven't been introduced." His tone was formal. "I'm Greg Barryman."

Leonard seemed not to notice him. He stared at Valerie, puzzled and hurt. He opened his mouth as if to speak, but no words came. Suddenly, he pushed aside Greg's hand and strode toward the door.

"Leonard, wait." Valerie took a step in his direction, but Brenda stopped her with a hand on her arm.

"Let him go," Brenda said.

Valerie knew it wouldn't do to get in an argument with Brenda, but she had a difficult time reining in her anger.

"That was a bit strong, don't you think?" she asked pointedly.

Brenda raised her eyebrows and spread her hands. "Tossing a creep out of my gallery? Not at all. Listen, hon," she said, patting Valerie on the arm, "every time I lay out free wine and cheese, one or two deadbeats stumble in here off the street looking for a handout. You should be thanking me for the favor. That's the last you'll see of that character. I'm going to mingle."

After she'd left them, Valerie told Greg, "Sometimes she really pisses me off."

"I can see why."

She squeezed his hand. "I mean, God knows the guy is weird. But he didn't mean any harm. And he certainly didn't deserve to get thrown out."

"I suppose."

Valerie sighed and shook her head. "I'll bet it was hard for him to come here tonight. I mean, he looked scared to death."

"Hey, he's a grown-up. You don't have to feel *too* sorry for him." He put his arm around her. "Come on, let's get another glass of wine."

Valerie nodded. But she couldn't help glancing at the empty front doorway.

"And you know," Greg said, steering her toward the rear of the gallery, "Brenda is right about one thing."

"What's that?"

"We'll never see him again."

C h a p t e r

LEONARD STRODE DOWN THE SIDEWALK, fists clenched at his sides.

He heard a woman laugh, and his head snapped around. He half expected to see Valerie across the street, laughing at him. No, not Valerie—Brenda. But of course it was neither, just a young woman, walking hand in hand with her man, out on a date. Or perhaps they were going home now, to be alone.

Leonard stopped suddenly and turned. The sidewalk was well lighted but empty—all the shops and boutiques had closed for the night, except for the gallery at the far end of the block. He could go back now and make things right, explain to Valerie that he'd felt sick for a moment, that's why he'd rushed out, but he was fine now and—

Three people emerged from the gallery and climbed in a car parked at a curb. Leonard saw them smiling as they drove past.

He imagined what it must be like inside the building now, all of them talking about him, having a good laugh. And poor Valerie. How embarrassed she must be. All because of Brenda.

Leonard spun on his heel and walked away from the gallery, feeling like a coward for running away. His truck was waiting faithfully for him around the corner. He climbed in and slammed the door solidly, reassuringly. Safe. He started the engine and let it idle, listening to the muted power, feeling it vibrate through the seat and floorboards.

Leonard began to relax, his hands on the wheel, his mind producing images of what should have happened, what could still happen. He grinned at one scenario: He'd speed around the block, and at the right moment he'd jerk the wheel, jump the curb, and crash through the gallery's front window, laughing at the looks on their faces just before he plowed into them.

His jaw muscles tightened. He eased the truck into gear and slowly pulled away from the curb.

He should drive home now, he knew. Before something happened.

But when he reached University Boulevard, instead of continuing west, he turned right and headed north toward Colfax.

He cruised up and down the avenue, watching the street people. It was easy to pick out the sluts: bare arms and shoulders, brief skirts or shorts, heels, painted faces.

I could have one any time I want, he thought. Right now. That one. I could make her do whatever I wanted, show her who's better, show them all, Brenda and her oh-so-pleased-with-themselves friends.

He passed by the Sapphire Lounge, where he'd shared that wonderful lunch with Valerie. As if on cue, a car pulled away from the curb, leaving a single parking place. Leonard swung his truck into it.

The lounge was just as crowded and noisy as it had been during that noon hour two days ago. But this was a different crowd, a different noise, a different smell. People were jammed elbow to elbow along the bar, laughing raucously and shouting at each other through a reeking fog of smoke. All the tables were filled, too. But unlike last Wednesday afternoon, there was no food in sight, only smudged glasses, beer bottles, and ashtrays choked with cigarettes.

Leonard tried to pick out the table where he'd sat with Valerie. Their table. It was presently occupied by a fat man with a mustache and a woman with a red dress, both drunk, fondling each other.

Leonard wished they would stop, wished they would get up and leave so that he could sit there. He'd take the chair on the far side of the table, just as he'd done on Wednesday, and Valerie would be on his right and . . .

He turned and elbowed his way toward the door. The room had suddenly become too warm, and he felt suffocated by the smoke.

Outside, he drew in a long breath and let it out slowly, allowing the panic to leave him.

You're making a fool of yourself, he thought. You can't simply wish for her. *Act.*

And he knew what had to be done. The first thing, anyway.

Leonard got in his truck and headed back to the gallery. He drove slowly past the building, peering through the front window. The reception was still going on, but there were fewer people. For a moment he thought he saw Valerie, but he couldn't be sure. He parked the truck a few blocks away, then walked back. He found a good observation post in the shadows across the street, a few doors up from the gallery.

He waited.

By ten-thirty the last of the guests had departed. The only people left there were Valerie, Brenda, another woman, and a man.

Leonard couldn't see the man's face. He wondered if it was Kyle Rowe. He hoped not, because he didn't like the idea of an ex-husband hanging around. In fact, he didn't like it that Valerie *had* an ex-husband. Somehow having been married and divorced made her seem less . . . wholesome. However, he was ready to forgive and forget, because obviously their marriage had been Kyle's idea, not hers. She'd been innocent and gullible, and Kyle had taken advantage of her, talking her into it. And as soon as she'd come to her senses, she'd kicked him out and gotten a divorce.

Everyone makes mistakes, Leonard thought. She's entitled to one.

Then Valerie, Brenda, and the man came to the front door. Now Leonard recognized him as the one who'd introduced himself—Greg Barryman. He felt relieved that it wasn't Kyle Rowe.

Brenda kissed them both goodnight. Leonard couldn't quite hear their voices. Brenda went back inside, and Greg and Valerie walked toward the lone car on the street.

What's she doing with *him?* he wondered.

Probably just getting a ride home, he reassured himself.

He watched closely to see if they touched. No. Good. Obviously, just a ride home. Greg unlocked the door for Valerie, then walked around the car, got in, and drove away. Soon Brenda and the other woman came out, and Brenda locked the gallery's front door. They exchanged a few words. The woman walked away.

Now Brenda angled across the street, coming directly toward him.

Leonard moved farther back in the shadows, ready to bolt, thinking she must have seen him. But no, she merely walked along the sidewalk to the end of the block and turned the corner, her heels clicking on the concrete.

Leonard went after her, silent in his crepe-soled shoes.

She'd interfered from the start, yammering away at lunch, not letting him say more than a few words to Valerie, then practically dragging her out of the restaurant. And tonight, the same thing only worse, butting in, humiliating him, keeping him away from Valerie, forcing him out of her gallery. Well, they were *both* out of the gallery now.

Leonard paused at the corner and watched Brenda walk through the yawning opening of a parking garage. He hurried after her.

There was no attendant in the glass booth, and the striped barricade arm was raised. Brenda was not in sight. Leonard stopped and held his breath for a moment, listening. Silence, except for the pulse in his temples. Then he heard the faint click of her heels. He walked quickly up a ramp, passing beneath a sign: Parking By Monthly Permit Only. When he reached the next level he saw Brenda moving away from him along a wide aisle that ran between a scattering of cars. There was no one else around.

Leonard hurried quietly after her, loosening the knot in his tie, whipping it from his collar with a whisper.

Brenda was between two cars now, digging in her purse for her keys, her back to the aisle. Leonard came up behind her with his arms raised, the tie wrapped around his fists. Brenda either heard or sensed him there, because she started to turn just as Leonard brought the tie over her head. In an instant it was under her chin and tight around her throat.

Brenda went wild.

Instead of struggling feebly for the tie, as Leonard had expected her to do, she twisted from side to side, swinging her elbows, catching him under the ribs. And she kicked back, raking her heel on his shin, causing him to cry out.

Surprised and angered, he tightened his grip and yanked her off her feet, then swung her viciously to the side, banging her head against the door of her car just below the window. He swung her the other way, and her head bounced off the door of the other car. Suddenly, she went limp in his hands. Leonard gripped the tie even tighter and swung her again, hard to his right, then to his left, then to his right. Her head made dull, sickening thuds against the sheet metal.

Leonard stopped, panting, hunched over. His arms were straight down, and Brenda's head hung limply a few inches above the concrete.

Leonard nervously peered over the tops of the cars and scanned the parking garage. No one. He unwrapped one hand from the tie and let Brenda settle to the floor. Her dress was hiked up and her legs were spread in an obscene fashion. She looked silly to Leonard, like someone who'd just slipped on a banana peel. He nearly giggled. Then he saw blood smeared on the door and window of her car.

Just like the other time, he thought.

And at once he knew what he had to do with the body.

He backed away from her, examining himself for blood. Some had gotten on his hands and his tie, but thankfully not on his jacket. He made a face and wiped the blood from himself with a clean portion of the tie, then carefully rolled it up and put it in his jacket pocket. He smoothed back his hair and walked quickly to the ramp.

Once outside, Leonard breathed in the mild night air. He walked with his head up, a man with a purpose, confident. From this point on his course was clear. He would take the body to the same place he'd taken the other one. The cabin. Of course, the circumstances had been different then, but the results would be the same: no body, no guilt.

But after he'd reached his truck, he began to rethink the situation.

He was lucky no one had been around. Anyone could have come up the ramp while he was struggling with Brenda. Even the person who'd parked next to her. Maybe that person was there now, shocked, ready to call the police. Or what if someone showed up while he was loading her into the truck?

No, he couldn't go back. He'd have to leave the body where it was. But he was safe. There were no witnesses, no evidence of his being there. He could put it out of his mind.

He drove west toward Broadway, then south toward home.

He turned down the alley and parked behind the house. As quietly as possible he unlocked the back door and walked along the hallway to his room, not wishing to awaken his mother. He couldn't face her now. He needed time to make up a story about—

"Leonard?"

The lamp beside her bed clicked on, sending a shaft of light through the open doorway, spotlighting him in the hall.

"Yes, Mother?"

"How was your evening?"

"It was . . . very nice." (Put it out of your mind.)

"Well, come in here and tell me all about it."

Leonard's palms were wet and his feet were leaden. He moved awkwardly toward his mother's bedroom, desperately trying to imagine how things might have been tonight with Valerie. He could've picked her up in his truck and taken her someplace nice, someplace his mother would approve of.

He entered the bedroom, where his mother lay waiting, while his mind formed images of what might have been.

ON SATURDAY VALERIE OPENED THE DRAPES, filling Matthew's room with morning light. Her son yawned expansively. She sat on the edge of his bed, brushed back his hair with her hand, and kissed him on the forehead.

"Good morning, sleepyhead."

"Mornin'."

"Were you planning on spending all day in bed, or do you want to have breakfast with me and Greg?"

"Breakfast, I guess."

"You guess, huh," she said, touching his cheek with the back of her hand.

His eyes brightened, as if he'd just remembered something. "What did you bring me from your party last night?"

She shook her head sadly. "There wasn't anything you would've liked, just cheese and wine and things like that."

"Yuck."

"I guess Brenda wasn't expecting any kids."

"Dumb old Brenda."

"But we'll get ice-cream cones today to make up for it."

"Okay!"

"And don't be too hard on Brenda. You know what she did for me last night?"

"What?"

"She sold four of my paintings."

"Really? Wow, neat."

"So, did you and Heather have fun last night?"

"Yeah," he said, sitting up in bed. "We did a jigsaw puzzle and played some of my games."

"Sounds like a good time." She ruffled his hair. "Now why don't you get washed up and dressed and we'll have breakfast. Then we can talk about what we're going to do today."

"We're going to the gallery. You promised."

"I remember. But that won't take long, and we can think of something more fun to do after that, okay?"

"Yeah."

What they thought of was the City Park zoo. Greg said he'd meet them at the gallery at one. He had to work at the print shop all morning, and the gallery was more or less on his way to the zoo.

Valerie kissed him good-bye at the door. He held her with one arm, his jacket and tie draped over the other.

"Love you."

"Love you, too," he said. "And last night was great."

"I know, but it was as much Brenda's doing as mine."

"I'm not talking about the reception," he said, sliding his hand down to her rump.

"You've got a dirty mind, you know that?"

"You love it."

"Could be." She kissed him again. "See you at one."

After Greg left, Valerie and Matthew took Dodger out for a walk. Matthew led them within hailing distance of a friend's house. In fact, Jerry Lawson and his younger brother called out to him from the front yard.

"Can I go?"

"Okay, but—hey! Come back here a minute."

He did so, pawing the ground like a colt.

"You stay close by their house, and I'll pick you up at noon, okay?"

"Okay, bye." And he was away, showing her the bottoms of his white sneakers. She watched him join the other boys—immediate kinship, as if he'd been away for only a few minutes. The three of them put their heads together for a moment, then ran around the side of the house toward the backyard, where adventure lay.

Dodger barked once and tugged on the leash.

"Sorry, boy, we've both been abandoned."

After their walk, Valerie put Dodger in the backyard, then cleaned up the kitchen. She'd planned on doing some housework, but with Matthew gone and the house quiet, her thoughts rose to the studio.

The hell with dusting, she thought, and climbed the stairs, eager to paint. However, the sight of the enormous canvas, barely begun, was enough to take her aback. She experienced the barest hint of panic. A tiny voice calling from one shadowy corner of her mind suggested that perhaps she'd taken on more than she could handle and that it would be impossible for her to complete all the paintings on time and—

Bullshit, she thought and picked up a brush.

Valerie and Matthew arrived at the gallery just before one. Surprisingly, the front door was locked. Valerie peered through the window and saw Sharon seated at the desk in the rear. She rapped on the glass, then waved. Sharon came forward and unlocked the door.

"Hi. I thought you'd be open."

"Come in," Sharon said dully. She was a young woman with long black hair, dressed in a beige skirt and white blouse. She moved stiffly out of the doorway, a somber look on her face.

Matthew pulled Valerie into the long room. "Wow, this is neat! Did you paint all of these?"

"All except the ones in that corner."

"Wow, those are *really* neat!"

"Hey, thanks a lot." She smiled and turned to Sharon. "Have you met my son? Matthew, this is Sharon. She helps Brenda run the gallery."

"Hello," Matthew said.

Sharon nodded, forcing a smile, and Valerie knew that something was wrong.

"Where's Brenda? I expected to see her here today."

"Then . . . you haven't heard?"

Valerie felt her stomach tighten. "Heard what?"

Sharon glanced down at Matthew, who was already looking around for something to do.

Valerie suggested, "Matthew, why don't you walk around and see all the paintings, then tell me which one you like best."

The moment he moved out of hearing, Valerie turned to Sharon. "What's wrong?"

"Brenda was assaulted last night."

Valerie was stunned. "My God. What happened? Is she all right?"

Sharon shook her head. There were tears in her eyes. "She's in a coma at St. Joe's hospital."

"Oh, no." Valerie felt as if she'd been kicked in the stomach. She tasted bile in her throat.

"It must have happened right after we locked up the gallery last night," Sharon said. "I said goodnight to her at the door, and we went our separate ways. She . . . she told *me* to be careful." Sharon looked away, shaking her head. "She walked to the parking garage and that's where he jumped her."

"He? Did the police catch him?"

"No. I say 'he' because the police think it might have been an attempted rape. Her purse was lying beside her, and she still had her money and jewelry, so it wasn't robbery. A man and a woman found—" Sharon made a pained sound and looked away. "They found her and called an ambulance. The police notified me this morning. My name and number were in Brenda's purse."

"Oh God." Valerie put her hand on Sharon's arm, then withdrew it.

"They asked me about her relatives. There's only her brother, you know. I phoned him, and he's flying in from Tuscon later today."

Valerie felt dizzy, nauseated, as if the planet had shifted on its axis and her inner ear hadn't yet adjusted. Her last image of Brenda was of her standing in the doorway of the gallery, waving good-bye to her and Greg, laughing, looking radiant. And now . . .

"Have you been to the hospital?"

Sharon nodded, eyes downcast. Valerie wondered if she were somehow blaming herself for what had happened. "She's . . . not good," Sharon said. "She's in intensive care."

Valerie saw Greg enter the gallery. Matthew ran to him.

"Hey, Greg, look at all my mom's paintings!"

Greg waved at them from across the room, smiling, letting Matthew tug him by the hand.

"Are you going to be all right?" Sharon nodded, and Valerie said, "We'll go see her now."

"Let me know if, well, if anything."

"I will," Valerie said. "I'll call you later."

She met Greg in the center of the room. He studied her face for a moment before he asked, "What is it?"

"Brenda's in the hospital. We should go there."

Along the way, Valerie related Sharon's story. Greg drove in silence, his look grim.

"I wonder . . ."

"What?"

He looked vaguely startled, as if he hadn't known that he'd spoken aloud. "Nothing," he said.

After checking at the admissions desk, they rode the elevator up to the intensive care unit. The round, open central room, with its video monitors and digital readouts looked disturbingly high tech to Valerie—cold and sterile. Behind the curving counter a few white-clad men and women spoke in hushed tones, checked monitors, and made notes on clipboards. Valerie left Matthew in an adjoining waiting room where there was a stack of comic books on a table. Then she and Greg asked a male nurse to show them to Brenda's room, one of eight radiating from the central area like petals on a flower.

The walls were painted sunflower yellow, but there was nothing cheerful about the room. Stainless-steel machines and TV stands flanked Brenda's bed. A breathing tube trailed from her throat. Her neck was a mass of purple and green bruises, and her eyes were closed and blackened.

"She's still in a coma," the nurse said. "She's suffered a severe concussion and her trachea was partially collapsed."

"What's the prognosis?" Greg asked quietly.

"We're hopeful she'll recover."

"Who is her doctor?" Valerie asked.

"Dr. Jeffries. He's due up here in," he checked his watch, "about half an hour."

Valerie nodded. "When do you expect her to regain consciousness."

"We don't know."

"Will she ever?" Greg asked suddenly.

The man was silent for one count too long, Valerie thought. She looked at his face: no expression.

"As I said, we're hopeful."

Valerie and Greg sat with Matthew in the waiting room. After Dr. Jeffries arrived and checked on his patients, he spoke for a few minutes with them, telling them little more than the nurse.

On their way out of the hospital Matthew wanted to know, "Are we going to the zoo now?"

"Honey, I don't know. . . ."

"I think we should," Greg said. "It won't do any of us any good to sit around. Brenda's getting the best care possible. All we can do is wait and, well, pray."

"I want to see the tigers first, okay?"

Valerie smiled weakly, feeling sick to her stomach. She knew the image of Brenda in that room would never leave her, even if—even *when,* she screamed internally—Brenda was eventually released from the hospital.

"Sure, hon, that'll be fine."

It was after they'd been at the zoo awhile, when Matthew had run far ahead of them to peer through the fence at the zebras, that Greg finished the sentence he'd begun hours before: "I wonder if Leonard Tully is the one who attacked Brenda."

"What?" Valerie stopped walking, forcing Greg to halt and turn to face her. "You're not serious."

Greg shrugged, his expression somewhere between sadness and anger. "I don't know. I'm just wondering."

"But why? I mean, why would he?"

"Well, for one thing, when he left the gallery last night he was plenty pissed off at her."

"He was? He just looked embarrassed to me."

"Same thing," he said.

Valerie shook her head slowly. "Jesus, Greg, *Leonard?* He seems, I don't know, so quiet and shy. I mean, he's weird, yes. But violent?"

Greg looked away, watching Matthew in the distance.

After a moment Valerie asked, "What . . . should we do?"

"Maybe I'll call the police tomorrow, and see what progress they've made."

"But you can't just accuse Leonard because of—"

"I'm not going to accuse him."

"Then what?"

"I'm just going to talk to the police, Val, that's all. Come on, let's go see the zebras."

C h a p t e r

LEONARD AWOKE THAT SATURDAY MORNING thinking of Valerie. The story he'd told his mother last night about their dinner date was nearly as vivid in his mind as what actually had happened at the gallery reception . . . and afterward.

He washed, dressed, then drove to Winchell's to buy doughnuts, the one sinful indulgence that his mother allowed herself on weekends. A copy of the *Rocky Mountain News* was lying on a table near the display counter. Leonard began turning pages out of curiosity, to see if Brenda Newcomb's death had warranted any ink. When he found the article, his face turned white.

WOMAN BRUTALLY ASSAULTED

A woman was severely beaten late last night in a parking structure near the Cherry Creek shopping center. Brenda Newcomb, 46, of Denver, owner of Newcomb's art gallery, had closed the gallery about 11:00 P.M. and apparently was walking to her car when the attack occurred. Police have no suspects in the beating and say it may have been an attempted rape. Ms. Newcomb remains in critical condition at St. Joseph's hospital.

Critical condition, Leonard thought, only critical. Not dead. Panic constricted his chest, bowed his head, and hunched his shoulders. Not dead.

"Hey, buddy, you okay?"

"What?" Leonard looked around, startled, faint.

The man who'd sold him the doughnuts was staring at him. His paper hat was cocked over one eye and his flour-speckled arms were crossed over his ample belly.

"You look sick," he said, his voice a mixture of concern and irritation. "You're not going to get sick in here, are you?"

"N-no. I just feel a little dizzy, that's all."

"Maybe you should take your paper and leave."

Leonard walked stiffly outside. The sunlight seemed much warmer than before, and the light hurt his eyes. He sat in his truck and took deep breaths, forcing himself to relax. He reread the article. No suspects, it said, so Brenda hadn't told. Not yet, anyway. Maybe she was too weak to talk, at least for the time being. But by tonight or tomorrow or the day after that she might recover and tell the police about him.

Now, wait . . .

He'd come up behind Brenda in the garage without her noticing. Had she seen his face during the struggle? He didn't think so. But what if she had?

Leonard started the engine. He had to get away, at least temporarily. He had to go somewhere free of distractions, someplace where he could be alone to sort things out.

The cabin.

When he got home his mother had already made coffee and set out plates and napkins. A man in a purple-and-black robe murmured from the countertop about the discrepancies of science and the validity of faith.

"Did they have chocolate glaze?"

"Yes, I got you three."

She gave him an impish grin. "Leonard, are you trying to make me fat?"

She'd asked for three. "Of course not," he said.

He poured them coffee, then bit into a bear claw. When he spoke again, he tried to sound nonchalant.

"I think I'll go to the cabin today."

"Oh?"

Just that one word, but it entered his chest like a thin blade. It wasn't that she denied him going there. After all, it was The Cabin, a shrine, and he was the caretaker. But he always let her know days in advance when he was going. This was sudden, and she wanted to know why. Moreover, she didn't like his going on Saturday, one of their busiest days. She was displeased and she'd be listening carefully to his explanation, so it had better be good, young man. He'd heard all of this in her "oh."

"I heard on the truck radio that there was hail last night in the mountains." He didn't like lying to her, but there it was. "I thought I'd better check for damage."

"Just from hail?"

"You know, the roof."

She looked hard at him, as if she were trying to see beneath his skin. He stared back, unflinching.

"You won't be all day, will you?"

"No, Mother."

She looked at him a moment longer. Then she added and picked up another doughnut. "Just don't be too late. I don't like being here alone."

"I know, and I won't."

She turned toward the TV set. "I really should get up to the cabin myself. It's been months and months."

Years, Leonard thought.

Fifteen miles south of Denver, at the tiny town of Sedalia, Leonard turned west onto state highway 67. He'd put his tools in the bed of the truck and he'd changed into blue jeans and work boots—partly to convince his mother of his motive for leaving and partly because the cabin might actually need repairs.

The two-lane blacktop took him into the wooded foothills. After a few miles he turned onto a snaking, county-maintained dirt road. Twenty minutes later he left the road and followed a pair of parallel ruts that twisted through dense blue-green pines and green and white aspens.

The cabin lay in a clearing, waiting for him like a friend. He parked near it, shut off the engine, and climbed out.

For a time he stood leaning against the truck, his eyes closed, his face turned up to the warm morning sun. At first the only sound was the ticking of the cooling engine. He breathed in fresh pine air and listened. A bird twittered in the trees beyond the clearing. Aspen leaves rustled in the mild breeze. Leonard felt his soul fill with calmness and strength.

So different from in the city. Too many roles to play there: son, shopkeeper, suitor. Here he was simply Leonard Tully, and that was enough.

He undid the heavy padlock and pushed open the cabin's stout, wooden door.

The interior consisted of a single square room with a pair of cots by the far wall. To the left of the door was a box of firewood and a Franklin stove, its black metal flue pushing up through the sloping ceiling. Against the right-hand wall was a wooden table and three chairs. The table top was bare, except for a clear-glass oil-filled hurricane lamp. Between the table and the cots was a crude arrangement of shelves and drawers for cookware. Leonard kept the plates and silverware clean and neatly arranged, although they hadn't been used since Big Ed had been alive.

Francine's husband, Ed, and her father had used the cabin during their fishing weekends. After Francine's father died, Big Ed had brought her and Leonard here a few times (or so Leonard had been told; he'd been too young to remember), but Francine didn't like it, especially since there was no electricity, tap water, or bathroom. Especially that. Oh, there was an outhouse near the edge of the clearing, but it was too disgusting to even think about, much less use.

Then Big Ed died in Vietnam. The cabin lay abandoned.

It wasn't until years later, after Francine's accident and rebirth in Jesus, and after Leonard had grown big enough for physical labor and old enough to drive, that Francine began to think about the cabin. It should be maintained, she'd told Leonard, in memory of her father and Big Ed.

Among the improvements Francine demanded were heavy wire-mesh screens over the windows and a new door. "To keep out trespassers," she'd said. At first she'd supervised Leonard. But once she'd seen that he was capable of doing the work—he was, after all, a handy young man—she let him come here by himself. Besides, she still didn't like the lack of electricity or running water, and now, wheelchair bound, she found the place even less appealing than before. And really, it wasn't necessary for her to be there. As long as the work was done and the cabin maintained. As long as her father and Big Ed could look down from Heaven and see that she hadn't forgotten them.

For all Leonard knew, his father and grandfather might be roasting in Hell. But he took care of the cabin because that's what his mother wanted. Besides, it was his cabin, too.

He retrieved the broom from the corner and began sweeping out a fine layer of dust. He used a rag to wipe off the table, chairs, and shelves. Then he removed the blankets from the cots and shook them outside. Only after he'd remade the cots and washed the dusty plates and forks did he walk around the outside of the cabin, looking for weather damage. He found none.

His duties completed, he walked away from the cabin and entered the woods. A hundred yards later he stepped into a small opening in the trees, his special, private place.

The place with the grave.

It was near the center of a small clearing, but the ground looked undisturbed. Leonard had done a meticulous job of camouflage—smoothing dirt, scattering rocks and branches. Now he circled the clearing, keeping the open area free of his footprints, looking for signs that anyone had been here—a lost hiker or stray hunter—or that an animal might have somehow picked up the scent through the plastic wrapping and two feet of dirt. But everything looked fine, natural.

Content now, Leonard sat on his haunches with his back to a tree, crossed his arms over his knees, and closed his eyes.

It was clear that he had three alternatives.

First, he could simply forget about Brenda and continue with his plans for Valerie. This would be all right so long as Brenda remained in critical condition or if she died—or even if she recovered, assuming she couldn't identify him. However, it would be dangerous to rely on that. So assuming she recovered . . .

Second, he could run while he still had the chance. By the time Brenda recovered and sent the police to get him, he could be a thousand miles away. His mother, though, would be left alone. Could she manage without him? Possibly. But what would she think of him? At the worst, she'd hate him; at best, her heart would be broken. Of course, this all depended on Brenda's survival. Therefore . . .

Third, he could kill Brenda. And this time, he'd make sure she was dead before he walked away. But it would be difficult to get to her in the hospital. Perhaps impossible.

If only he'd gone back for her last night, loaded her in his truck, and driven her up here like the other one, the slut. Then he wouldn't have this problem.

He thought back to that other time, several months ago.

He'd been cruising Colfax at night, while his mother sat home, imagining him at a Christian singles meeting. He'd stopped for a red light. The woman had come right up to his truck and poked her head in the window.

"You want to party?" she asked.

He could see that she was young, even through the makeup, probably still in her teens. He felt in a daze, the blood pounding in his
temples, too nervous to say anything. But he must have nodded, because she opened the door and climbed up on the seat beside him.

"Twenty for head, forty for half and half," she said, as the light
turned green, "in advance."

"Twenty," he said, partly because he wasn't certain of what she'd
meant by "half and half," but mostly because he only had twenty-five
dollars in his wallet.

"Turn right and drive to the park," she said, reaching over and
unzipping his fly.

Several blocks later they were parked beneath a tree between two
distant arc lights. There were a few other parked cars, none of them
nearby. Her face was in his lap, and he could feel himself in her mouth.
He'd never felt anything like this. It was like a warm, soft electric
current passing through his entire body. He clenched his teeth and
gripped the steering wheel with both hands. He knew it was wrong.

He looked down and saw her burrowing there, like some filthy
animal, gnawing at him.

Suddenly, he was filled with loathing. He grabbed a handful of her
hair and yanked her off him.

"Hey, what the fuck!"

"Get out!" he yelled, putting his hand in her face and shoving her
hard against the door.

She struck out defensively, raking her nails along his forearm. They'd
sliced his skin like razor blades. The inside of the truck seemed to fill
with a hot red mist, and he watched himself grab her neck with both
hands and squeeze until his thumbs were white and bang her head
again and again on the steel window frame of the truck.

He stopped as quickly as he'd begun, and sat back, breathing hard,
staring, unbelieving. She was slumped in the seat, dead.

He reached over her, ready to open the door and dump her out like
a bag of trash. But he froze as the glare of headlights caught him
through the rear window. Another pair of lovers parked fifty feet behind him.

Leonard forced himself to calm down. He had to get rid of the body
where no one would see him. One place came to mind: the cabin. But
it was too late to drive up there that night.

So he'd shoved the body down on the floorboards and driven home.

After he'd parked behind the house, he'd retrieved a tarp from the rear of the truck and draped it over the body.

That night he'd slept the sleep of the innocent. The next morning he'd driven here. . . .

Leonard's legs began to cramp, bringing him out of his reverie. He stood and stretched, feeling refreshed, as if all of his problems were solved. Although he still wasn't sure what to do about Brenda.

Perhaps he should just put her out of his mind.

He took a last look around the clearing, then made his way back toward the cabin, thinking more pleasant thoughts.

Valerie.

He could hardly wait to see her again.

13

ON SUNDAY MORNING Valerie returned to the hospital.

Dr. Jeffries was not there, but a nurse informed her that Brenda's condition had not changed. Valerie tried to take that as a positive sign. However, when she stepped into Brenda's room her faint hope vanished. Brenda's eyes seemed sunken in her head, and her face, where it wasn't covered with bandages or purple bruises, was a sickly grayish white.

Outside, Valerie leaned against a concrete pillar by the entrance and let the sun dry the cold sweat on her forehead.

She'll be okay, she told herself, walking unsteadily toward her car. She'll be okay.

When she got home, Greg was waiting for her at the front door.

"How is she?" he asked.

Valerie saw that he and Matthew had already fixed sandwiches and laid out their backpacks. She felt a spasm of guilt about leaving for the mountains to have fun while her friend lay in a hospital bed. And she wasn't sure she should take a full day away from painting. On the other hand, she knew it would do her good to get out of the city, away from everything, if only for a little while.

"She's the same," Valerie said. "At least that's what they told me. But I think she looks worse."

Greg laid his hand on her shoulder. She moved closer, and he put his arm around her. "She'll pull out of it," he said. "I'm sure she will. She's a tough gal."

"I hope you're right."

"Are we going pretty soon?" Matthew looked at them expectantly. He wore blue jeans, a Bart Simpson T-shirt, hiking boots with red laces, and a blue baseball cap.

"Pretty soon," Valerie said. She gently tugged the bill of his cap down over his eyes.

"Hey!"

"As soon as I get changed, okay?"

An hour later they were climbing out of Greg's car at a trail head in Golden Gate Canyon state park. They'd stopped at the visitors center for a map, and now Greg spread it on the hood of the car, while Valerie and Matthew leaned in on either side of him.

There were about a dozen foot trails shown on the map, categorized by degree of difficulty. Most were "easy."

"We could start on Coyote Trail," Greg said. He traced a path with his finger. "This looks like four or five miles. What do you think?"

"Let's go!" Matthew cried.

"Valerie?"

"Hey, I'm ready if you are."

The trail through the trees was easy to follow, so they let Matthew lead the way. Every few hundred yards they came upon a wooden post with a small emblem, a stylized footprint of a coyote, to let them know they were still on the correct path. Despite these minor signs of civilization (and an occasional party of hikers), Valerie felt as if they were alone in the wilderness. Her responsibilities in the city seemed remote and artificial. Here everything was real—trees, wildflowers, ground squirrels, hawks—each living exactly as it should.

Later, they stopped to rest and have lunch in a small clearing just off the trail.

After they'd eaten, Matthew wandered away, poking under rocks with a stick.

"Stay in sight," Valerie called after him.

Greg peeled an orange, dropping the pieces in a paper bag. He offered Valerie a slice. She bit it in two, then chewed thoughtfully, listening to the sounds of the woods.

"I always forget how peaceful it is up here."

Greg nodded, saying nothing, munching a slice of orange.

"You're being awfully quiet," she said.

"I'm just . . ." He shrugged and smiled wanly.

"Is something wrong?"

He turned his head to watch Matthew for a moment. The boy was thirty yards from them, kneeling on the ground, arranging small stones and twigs in an arcane pattern.

"I was going to wait till we got back to tell you."

"Tell me what?" Valerie asked.

"I phoned the police while you were at the hospital."

Valerie stared at him.

"I wanted to know if they'd found whoever attacked Brenda."

"I take it they haven't," Valerie said.

"No."

"Did you tell them about Leonard?"

"No."

"Good, because I don't think—"

"I'd planned to," he said, interrupting her, "but the detective in charge of the case was off duty. I left my number and asked that he call me tomorrow."

"What will you tell him?"

Greg shrugged. "About Leonard."

"Yes, but *what* will you tell him?" There was concern in Valerie's voice.

Greg paused. "You sound as if you want to protect him."

"No, I don't. Well, maybe I do. I mean, what has he done?"

"He's a weird character, Val. Who knows what he could do?"

"Just because he sent me flowers doesn't—"

"It's not just the flowers and you know it." He exhaled. "I don't want us to argue about this. It's obvious that this guy is operating on his own wavelength. We don't know what he's capable of. Besides, do you think it was just a coincidence that Brenda was attacked only hours after she threw him out of her gallery?"

"Why *couldn't* it be a coincidence?" Valerie wasn't so much defending Leonard as playing Devil's advocate.

"Val, come on."

"I'm serious. I don't see any connection. Not really."

They were silent for a moment. The only sounds were a few twittering birds and the whisper of the breeze through pine needles.

"All I'm saying," Valerie went on quietly, "is that you should be careful when you talk to the detective. If Leonard really didn't do anything, you'd be accusing an innocent man."

"I'm not going to accuse him. I'm simply going to describe what happened and let the cops take it from there. Okay?"

Valerie turned away and watched her son admire his design of sticks and stones. . . .

. . . May break my bones, she thought, remembering the children's rhyme. But names will never harm me.

"I suppose," she said at last.

After they'd picked up their gear and trash, they reshouldered the packs and resumed their hike. When they finally arrived back at Greg's car, the sun was casting long shadows, and they were sweaty and tired. They drove home and found Dodger mad with excitement.

"Hiya, boy, did you miss us?"

Matthew barely got the words out before the dog was all over him, trying to lick his face.

"I'd say just a little," Valerie said. She dropped her pack on the kitchen floor and plopped down in a chair. "I'm beat. I feel like we climbed a mountain."

"I'm hungry, Mom." Matthew entered the kitchen with Dodger at his side.

"I'm hungry, too," Greg added. But when he saw the look on Valerie's face, he added, "Kind of."

"What would you like?" Valerie tried to muster enthusiasm, not quite making it.

"Didn't I see some ground beef in the fridge?"

"I think so."

"And buns?"

She nodded, starting to rise. Greg leaned over, put his hand on her shoulder, and gently pushed her back into the chair.

"Then why don't I start the coals," he said, "and you just sit here and rest?"

"Can I take a shower instead?"

They ate at the round wooden table on the patio as dusk descended about them. The sky beyond the foothills was deep blue, turning purple. Directly above it was already dark enough to see the first star of the evening.

"You see it?" Valerie asked, pointing.

"I do now. You saw it first, though, so you get to make a wish."

"I wish that—"

"Don't say it out loud, Mom, or it won't come true."

"He's right."

"Okay, I wish . . ." She put a finger to her bottom lip and gazed up at the star.

The phone rang.

Valerie sighed and rose from her chair.

"Come on, Matthew," Greg said, standing, "help me clear the table while your mom chats on the phone."

"Hey," Valerie said, holding open the screen door, "I got my wish."

"What?" Matthew looked confused.

"She's just kidding us," Greg said, smiling.

"Don't be too sure." She crossed the kitchen and picked up the phone. "Hi, Valerie."

She felt a sudden chill.

"Is this . . . Leonard?" She looked at Greg. He'd just come in with a stack of plates in one hand and three glasses in the other. Now he stopped dead in his tracks, staring at her. She turned the earpiece slightly away from her head. Greg set down the plates and glasses and stood beside her, his head near hers, the receiver between them.

"Yes, how are you?" Leonard asked pleasantly.

"What do you want?" Valerie kept her voice neutral. She did not wish to encourage Leonard with friendliness nor anger him with antagonism. Her heart was pounding.

"Just to talk," he said. "And to apologize."

"For what?"

"You know. For Friday night."

Valerie exchanged a glance with Greg.

"What do you mean?" she asked.

"For leaving your reception so abruptly," Leonard said in her ear. "I was upset, have been upset. It's my mother, you see. She hasn't been well, and, ah, I behaved badly Friday and I apologize."

"I see."

"I hope I didn't embarrass you."

"No, you didn't."

Valerie hated this, conversing with Leonard as if they were friends. She could feel Greg beside her, tense, his breath on her cheek.

"I phoned you several times today, but I guess you weren't home."

"No. We were out."

"We?"

"My son and Greg and I," Valerie said emphatically. She wanted Leonard to take the hint, to hang up and never call back.

"Greg Barryman?"

"That's right."

"Give me the phone," Greg said softly putting his hand on the receiver.

Valerie pulled away. Greg stood back with his jaws clenched, territorial.

"Listen, Leonard, I'm going to hang up now, and I don't think you should call here anymore."

"I understand."

"You do?"

"Yes."

"Good, then, good-bye."

"Wait. Please."

"I mean it, I'm—"

"I just wanted to ask you about Brenda."

Valerie's chest tightened. "Brenda?"

"Yes," Leonard said. "Wasn't that terrible?"

"How . . . do you know about Brenda?"

"I read it in yesterday's paper. I was shocked," he said sincerely. "What an awful thing."

Valerie had a clear image of Brenda lying in intensive care. She felt dizzy.

"Have you talked to her?" Leonard asked carefully.

"No."

"Haven't you visited her in the hospital?"

"Why are you asking me this?" Valerie voice was tight, higher-pitched than before. "What do you *want?*"

"I'm concerned, that's all," Leonard said calmly. "When I spoke to a nurse on the phone, she said Brenda hadn't regained consciousness. I just wondered if—"

Valerie hung up. She could take no more of this. She leaned on the phone for support.

"What did he say?" Greg asked angrily.

"That he'd read about Brenda's attack. He wanted to know if I'd seen her in the hospital. He said he called there to check on her."

"That son of a bitch."

Valerie said nothing.

"I'm definitely talking to that detective tomorrow."

Valerie nodded. "Yes, I think you should."

14

ON MONDAY MORNING, after taking Matthew to day care and walking Dodger, Valerie tried to immerse herself in her painting. It wasn't easy.

Her mind kept replaying the previous night's phone call from Leonard. She tried to remember not only his words but also the inflections in his voice. Had he implied that he'd attacked Brenda? Not really. In fact, he'd sounded genuinely concerned about her. Too concerned? she wondered. He barely knew Brenda, yet he'd called the hospital about her. Was he afraid of what she might say if she recovered?

When she recovered, Valerie told herself.

She put down her brush, stepped away from the large canvas, and stood at the window. Before her lay the sweep of the foothills. In her mind's eye, though, she saw Brenda lying in the hospital bed, tubes and wires attached to her. Valerie was not sure she believed in God, but she found herself praying that Brenda would recuperate.

After a time she returned to the canvas.

By early afternoon she'd roughly defined the arms, legs, torso, and head of the dancer. A vast amount of detail still had to be added, but she'd done enough of the painting now to believe that she could finish it this week.

She smiled. Eight weeks, seven paintings. Hey, no problem. Providing there were no major distractions.

The phone rang, distracting her.

She went downstairs to answer it. Then she hesitated, her hand hovering above the receiver. What if it was Leonard?

No, she thought. I told him last night not to call me again. I hung up on him. He got the message.

Still, she was relieved when she heard Greg's voice.

"I hope I didn't interrupt your work."

"It's okay," she said. "I needed a break, anyway."

"Good. The reason I called is I just got off the phone with Detective Gianelli from the Denver police. He's the one investigating Brenda's attack. He wants to talk to me in person. And he, ah, also wants to talk to you."

"Me? Why?"

"I explained a little to him over the phone, and he asked if anyone could corroborate it. And, well, I said you could."

"Corroborate what?" Valerie felt as if she were being forced into something against her will. "I mean, what are you going to tell him?"

"Only what happened at the reception. And Leonard's calling you last night."

"But what does that prove?" Valerie realized why all this was upsetting her. She'd be helping Greg send the police to question Leonard. What if he found out about it? Guilty or innocent, he wouldn't like it.

"I don't know that it proves anything, Val. But didn't we agree last night that we should call the police—in case there is a connection?"

She drew in her breath and let it out. "Yes."

"Okay. Gianelli said he'd meet us at my shop or your house, whichever we'd prefer."

Valerie wasn't sure why, but she didn't want the police in her house. Not for this, anyway.

"I'll come there," she said. "See you in half an hour."

She washed up and changed from her shorts to a blue-and-white print summer dress. Her stomach was growling, but she felt too nervous to eat. Besides, there wasn't time. She chewed an apple while she drove to Greg's print shop.

The building was part of a small shopping complex in Lakewood, just off Wadsworth Boulevard. When Valerie pushed through the door, she found the place alive with activity.

Greg stood behind the counter helping one of three waiting customers. He barely had time to give her a wink and a smile. Behind him, Janice was furiously writing down a phone order, the receiver tucked between her shoulder and ear. A wisp of blue-gray hair, which had somehow managed to escape that morning's blast of hair spray, dangled onto her forehead.

Beyond the end of the counter, in the depths of the fluorescent-lit shop, a malevolent-looking print machine was churning out brochures on colored paper under the watchful eye of Mitch, the ponytailed young printer. A middle-aged man, recently hired, whom Valerie had not yet met, was making an adjustment on the paper cutter.

Valerie stepped aside to let in another customer. Greg looked at her sheepishly, as if to apologize for putting her through this inconvenience. She shrugged to let him know it was okay. In fact, she was beginning to feel at ease in the familiar, bustling surroundings.

But her stomach tightened when the man she'd let in introduced himself to Greg as Detective Gianelli.

The policeman was about Greg's height, but broader through the shoulders. He was good-looking, Valerie thought, with black wavy hair and dark eyes. He wore a tie, but in the heat of the day the knot was loosened and his collar was unbuttoned.

Greg asked Janice to take over, then he led Valerie and the detective down the aisle between printing equipment and shelves of paper.

At the rear of the shop was a small office with two chairs and a metal desk. The desk top was crowded with a computer console and printer. Cardboard boxes pressed in from three walls.

"Please sit down," Gianelli said, as if this were his office. He rested one haunch on the desk and waited for Greg and Valerie to take their seats.

"From what you told me on the phone," he said, "I understand that both of you are friends of Brenda Newcomb and that you were both at the gallery on the night of her assault, last Friday. Is that correct?"

"Yes," Greg answered. "The reception Friday was for Valerie."

Gianelli turned to her, eyebrows raised. "Those are your paintings?"

Valerie nodded. "Most of them."

"You're very good. I liked them a lot."

"Thank you."

"Have you been painting a long time?"

"For a number of years," Valerie said, feeling extremely uncomfortable. She didn't like this situation to begin with, and she definitely wasn't in the mood to chat about art.

"I'm something of a painter myself," Gianelli said, smiling. "Not very good, you understand, but I find it relaxing. Do you? Or is it more like work?"

"I . . . guess a little of both."

"I suppose it would be." Gianelli's smile faded. "Yes, well, back to business. Who do you think assaulted Ms. Newcomb last Friday night?"

Valerie was taken aback by the directness of Gianelli's question. "I, ah . . ."

"Leonard Tully," Greg said evenly.

Gianelli nodded, withdrew a notebook, and wrote down the name. "Address? Phone number?"

Greg shook his head. "No, we don't know where he lives. But he did mention that he owns an antique store."

"In Denver?"

Greg shrugged and looked at Valerie. "Did he say where?"

"I . . . no."

"Why do you think Mr. Tully attacked Ms. Newcomb?"

"Because of what happened Friday at the gallery," Greg said. He described the scene between Leonard and Brenda and how Leonard had rushed out.

"Did he return to the gallery after that?"

"No."

"Did you notice which direction he went when he left?"

"No. Val?"

She shook her head no.

"When Mr. Tully was at the gallery did he threaten Ms. Newcomb?"

"Not in so many words," Greg said.

"No?" Gianelli raised his eyebrows.

Greg chewed his lip. "He didn't exactly threaten her."

"Well, what exactly did you hear him say?"

"Actually, nothing," Greg said, beginning to fidget in his chair. "He just walked out."

"Just walked out," Gianelli repeated. "I see. Did *anyone* at the reception hear him threaten her?"

Greg shook his head impatiently. "I don't know, but look, this guy is definitely weird. I think you should go talk to him, question him. I've got a feeling he's the one who did it."

"A feeling," Gianelli repeated. "Can you tell me about the relationship between Ms. Newcomb and Mr. Tully?"

"Relationship?"

"Yes, how do they know each other? Or did they meet Friday night for the first time?"

"No, they met last Wednesday," Greg said. "Valerie was there."

Gianelli turned to Valerie and waited.

"Brenda and I were going to lunch," she said, "and then some kid grabbed my purse. . . ." She described how Leonard had knocked down the man and rescued her purse, how she'd asked him to lunch, invited him to the gallery.

"Was there any antagonism between Ms. Newcomb and Mr. Tully that day?" Gianelli asked.

"No."

"Did they meet or speak to one another between Wednesday noon and Friday evening?"

"Not that I know of," Valerie said.

"But he's phoned Valerie several times," Greg said with obvious distaste. "He even sent her flowers."

Gianelli looked at Valerie with interest. "Is that correct?"

"Yes," Valerie said.

"Has he threatened *you* in any way?"

"No, not at all."

"Has he made any sexual advances toward you?"

"No," Valerie said firmly.

"There was a note with the flowers," Greg said. "Tell him about the note."

"It just said something like 'from an admirer.' "

" 'From a *devoted* admirer,' " Greg said.

Gianelli studied Greg's face for a moment before turning to Valerie. "When did Mr. Tully phone you last?"

"Last night."

"What did he say?"

"Nothing much. But then . . . he asked about Brenda."

"Oh?"

"He said he'd read about her attack and phoned the hospital. He sounded, well, concerned about her."

"I'll *bet* he's concerned," Greg put in.

Gianelli asked Valerie, "What else did he say?"

"Nothing. I mean, he was only on the line for a few minutes."

"Did it bother you that he called?"

"A little, yes. I told him not to call back."

"And what did he say to that?"

"He said he wouldn't."

"Mm-hm. Now on Friday night at the reception, did you speak to Mr. Tully?"

"Yes."

"Did he say anything about Ms. Newcomb then?"

"No."

"What did you talk about?"

"We only spoke briefly," Valerie said. "He complimented me on my paintings. That's all."

"I see." Gianelli rubbed his chin, then lowered his hand. "Is there anything else either of you would like to add?"

Valerie shook her head no.

"What are you going to do?" Greg wanted to know.

Gianelli closed his notebook. "Find Mr. Tully and question him. But that's about all I can do. At this point, anyway. Unless . . ."

"What?"

"Unless you'd like to file a harassment complaint."

Greg opened his mouth, then closed it.

"I'll be honest with you," Gianelli said. "It doesn't sound as if you have any basis for a complaint. After all, what has Mr. Tully done? He helped Ms. Rowe recover her purse. He was polite at lunch. He sent flowers. He was soft-spoken at the reception. When Ms. Newcomb asked him to leave, he did so. And when Ms. Rowe asked him not to phone anymore, he said he wouldn't."

Greg started to speak. Gianelli raised his hand to stop him.

"As I said, I'll question Mr. Tully. And everyone else who signed the book at the reception." He looked from Greg to Valerie, waiting for a response. When none came, he stood from the desk. "I guess that's all for now," he said pleasantly. "Thanks for your time. I can find my way out."

He left Valerie and Greg alone in the room.

"Terrific," Greg said. "Gianelli thinks I'm accusing Leonard because I'm jealous that he sent you flowers."

"He never said that."

"No, but I could see it in his eyes."

They were both silent for a moment. Greg reached out for her hand.

"I'm sorry I dragged you into this," he said.

"You didn't drag me. It was necessary."

Greg nodded. "The police had to know about Leonard."

Valerie looked away.

"You still don't believe he attacked Brenda."

"I . . . I don't know, Greg. My feeling, though, is that he didn't. He's weird, yes, but he just doesn't seem the violent type."

Greg sighed. "Maybe you're right." He stood and pulled her up with him, then put his arms around her. They kissed.

"I'd better get back to work," he said.

"Me, too."

Before going home, though, Valerie drove to St. Joseph's hospital. Dr. Jeffries told her that Brenda's condition had not changed. Valerie found that difficult to believe.

Brenda looked much worse than before.

C h a p t e r

15

LEONARD STEERED HIS TRUCK into Valerie's driveway.

This morning, as usual, his mother had scoured the classified section for potential bargains. She'd circled a dozen ads for Leonard, then sent him on his way.

First he'd driven east, making two stops in Aurora, purchasing some old cups and saucers and several pairs of salt and pepper shakers, then passing on every throw rug in a stack of fifty or more. Next he'd gone to Northglenn, where he'd carefully examined a room filled with children's things, buying nothing. His fourth and final stop had been in Arvada, where he'd haggled with an old woman until she'd finally dropped the price on something he knew his mother would appreciate: a blue ceramic table lamp with an extra shade thrown in free.

Now he was supposed to drive directly home. But first he wanted a face-to-face talk with Valerie. A few things needed to be straightened out.

He parked the truck before the garage and climbed out.

A dog barked insistently from behind the high wooden fence that stretched between the garage and the house. Leonard did not much care for dogs. And he was beginning to hate this one in particular for raising such a ruckus.

He rang the doorbell.

No answer.

He rang it again. And then, just to make he could be heard above that annoying barking, he knocked on the door.

Still no answer.

He'd expected Valerie to be here. Hadn't he overheard her at the reception saying that she painted at her house? Well, here it was the middle of the day, and she wasn't home. Where was she? He didn't have time to waste standing on her doorstep waiting for her to return from God knows where. He wanted to talk to her now, to get a few points cleared up.

First of all, there was Valerie's son.

Leonard had been shocked to hear she had a child. The question was, did the boy live with her or with the ex-husband? Leonard wasn't sure what his mother would think about him courting a woman with a son. Maybe it would be okay if the boy didn't actually live here, if he only visited occasionally. He had to know.

Second, and most important, he wanted to know about Greg Barryman. Was he just a casual friend? Or was he courting Valerie, too?

When Leonard had phoned Valerie last night, Greg had been here. He'd heard him in the background. They'd been out, Valerie had said. And so he'd understood perfectly what Valerie had meant when she'd asked him not to call again: don't phone while Greg's here. Obviously, she wanted to see him again or she wouldn't have taken him to lunch, invited him to her reception, and so on. In fact, if it hadn't been for Brenda, *he* would've given Valerie a ride home from the reception, not Greg. And then *he* probably would've gone out with her yesterday, wherever she'd gone.

Never mind. The question now was, did Valerie want to keep Greg from knowing he was seeing her? Or was this to be a rivalry, a contest of wills with Valerie as the prize? He needed to know so that he could proceed in the proper manner. And he certainly needed to know before he brought her home to meet Mother.

And now he'd made a special trip out here to talk to her, and she wasn't home.

He muttered under his breath and banged his fist on the door.

The barking continued from behind the fence. Leonard resisted the urge to get the crowbar from his truck, climb over the fence, and quiet the dog for good. He also considered using the crowbar on the front door, forcing it open, and making himself at home, waiting for Valerie.

Not the crowbar, he thought, the knife.

He climbed into his truck, flipped open the glove compartment, and withdrew from the assorted junk inside a pocket knife with a three-inch blade.

Leonard carried the knife on an inspection tour of the windows.

He wasn't worried about being seen—the house was surrounded by trees, and the nearest residence was hundreds of yards away across a horse pasture. The only open viewing was from the distant end of the driveway, where cars whizzed by on 32nd Avenue.

Leonard patiently made his way around the front of the house. Finally, on the far side he found a window open a few inches. He cut a small slit in the screen with his blade, then used the point to unhook the latch. He removed the screen and set it aside, pushed open the window, and pulled himself through.

He was in a bedroom.

Quickly, he reached out through the open window, raised the screen back in place, latched it, and lowered the window.

Only now did he turn, heart thumping, and take in the room. It was cool in here and dim, almost dark compared with the bright sunlight outside. A large chest of drawers with a mirror stood beside a queen-size bed covered with a rose-and-white spread. There was a walk-in closet at the foot of the bed.

Leonard stood unmoving for a full minute, luxuriating in his surroundings.

Finally, he crossed the room, leaning down to allow his fingertips to trail over the bedspread.

He randomly opened a drawer in the bureau. It was filled with silky, feminine things. Leonard breathed deeply, relishing the faint aroma of a woman, of Valerie. He hesitated, his mouth dry, then reached in and slowly drew out a pair of creamy-white panties. The small, delicate, forbidden garment seemed to him like something rare and priceless. He felt himself becoming aroused.

He swallowed once, then carefully returned the panties to the drawer and slid it closed.

Now he opened the closet and began examining the clothes, sliding hangers from right to left, hesitating when his fingers encountered the feel of silk. He received a jolt, though, when he found several men's shirts.

Greg's?

Leonard refused to believe that. And when he found nothing else suspicious, he assumed the shirts were Valerie's, probably things she wore around the house. He shut the closet door—and then froze.

He'd heard a noise.

Had Valerie returned home? How could he explain himself if she found him in here? He didn't want her to think he was a sneak thief.

Leonard quickly stepped from the bedroom to the hallway, turned a corner and found himself in the living room. He held his breath, listening. The noise he'd heard had ceased.

Probably just the refrigerator, he thought.

Relieved, he crossed the room to the entryway, unlocked the front door, and opened it. He left it open. Now if Valerie drove up, he'd say that he'd knocked, that the door was ajar, and that he'd just stepped inside and called her name.

Feeling at ease now, at home, he moved casually about the living room, admiring a framed print, examining a small sculpture on an end table. He wandered down the hallway to the bathroom. It had a favorable, feminine appearance: pastel towels, soap balls in a dish. He was slightly offended, though, by a pair of pantyhose hanging over the shower door.

Across the hall from the bathroom was a stairway leading to the second floor. Leonard passed it by for now and moved on to the next room.

It put him off completely—a boy's room. Obviously Valerie's son did not just visit on weekends. He lived here. Games, toys, and sporting equipment were stored haphazardly on shelves beside the bed. The walls were covered with a hodgepodge of posters: a man in an orange jersey and blue helmet throwing a football, a turtle-man wearing a bandit's mask, a blurred sports car. . . .

Leonard felt a pang of jealousy. He'd never had this many things when he was growing up, not one-tenth as many. What was so special about *this* boy?

He wished the kid didn't exist. Then there would only be him and Valerie.

He moved down the hall and carefully inspected the room at the end, another bedroom. It smelled stuffy, as if it were rarely used. Perhaps it was for guests. Had Greg ever slept here? Leonard wondered. He hoped not.

He looked out the window, letting his eyes sweep over the backyard. There were lots of trees and bushes and a doghouse beside the garage. The dog was silent now, out of sight.

Leonard ambled into the hallway again and entered the kitchen.

It was larger and brighter than the one at home. He ran his finger along the stove and the top of the refrigerator. Both were satisfactorily clean. He opened a cupboard door and peered in without touching any of the cereal boxes or jars of peanut butter and jelly. At the end of the counter beneath the wall phone he found something of interest: a five-by-seven-inch binder with a vinyl cover embossed with flowers. Valerie's address book.

Leonard opened it with some amusement and randomly flipped

pages. Then he frowned, struck by a thought, and turned back to the B's. There were two entries for Greg Barryman, home and business. Leonard tore out half a page from the back of the book and copied the address. Who knew? They might come in handy.

Now he peered over the waist-high room divider into the family room. Nothing of interest there. Through the window he could see his truck in the driveway.

Parked as if it belonged there, he thought with a smile.

He went upstairs.

He'd never been in an artist's studio before, but he expected something quite different—neat and professional-looking. Instead, the room seemed cluttered with canvases, cupboards, and paint jars. At one end of the room a huge, hideous, half-finished painting stood on an easel. Leonard approached it cautiously, afraid to brush against anything in the room lest he smear himself with paint.

The portrait was complete enough for Leonard to recognize it as a life-sized man, hunched over, one arm extended. But the whole thing reminded him of a fetus, like the one's he'd seen in books—partially formed and grotesque. The face was blank. Leonard clenched his teeth against the taste of bile in his throat.

When he'd first seen Valerie's paintings in the gallery, he'd been disappointed. He preferred realistic drawings, with sharp, clear lines. And since Valerie was so delicate and beautiful, he'd assumed that her paintings would be the same—not blurry, impressionistic images. He'd forced himself to accept her work, though. He figured she could change her style and paint *better* things. And really, at the gallery, where they'd all been neatly framed and nicely arranged, they hadn't been so bad— taken together, that is.

This one, though, this thing in progress . . . it was like some organic monstrosity.

Leonard had the urge to topple the painting from the easel, twist open jars of paint, and empty them on the canvas, obliterating the repulsive image. He resisted, though, and merely shook his head and clucked his tongue. This was *definitely* something he and Valerie would have to discuss.

On the way downstairs he checked his watch. It was getting late. His mother would be expecting him home soon. Still, it was important that he talk to Valerie. He'd give her time to return.

Leonard strolled into the family room and turned on the TV. Then he clicked the remote until he found a familiar channel. He sat on the couch and watched a curly-haired man in a silk suit stalk around the stage, a Bible raised in his hand.

He felt at home.

He waited for Valerie.

16

AFTER VALERIE LEFT THE HOSPITAL, she picked up Matthew at day care and drove home. Several blocks from the house she saw a brown pickup truck back into 32nd Avenue, then head east, away from her. It took her a moment to realize that the truck had come out of her driveway.

"Who's that, Mom?" Matthew had noticed it, too.

"No one we know. Probably just somebody turning around."

It had happened before, since hers was the only driveway for a quarter mile. Now she turned left, steered between the two long rows of trees, and parked in the garage. Dodger greeted them in the backyard.

"I'm going to play outside with him for a while, okay?"

"Sure," she said, unlocking the back door.

The house was cool and comfortably dim compared with the harsh, hot afternoon sunlight. Valerie felt drained, and it wasn't merely because of the heat. The meeting with Greg and Detective Gianelli had taken something out of her. And she was still haunted by the image of Brenda in intensive care.

Valerie dropped her purse on the kitchen table and undressed in the bedroom, changing into shorts and a T-shirt. When she hung her dress in the closet, it seemed as if everything was pushed to one side. She hesitated, then straightened out the hangers. She remembered how she'd dressed in a rush earlier that afternoon. Perhaps that was how her clothes had become disarranged.

In the kitchen she poured a glass of iced tea and carried it to the family room. Then she plopped down on the couch and turned on the TV, intending to watch the early news before even thinking about dinner.

The sound came on before the picture. Valerie thought she was listening to a commercial, until she heard the word "Jesus."

She frowned, watching the picture fade in: a curly-haired man in a suit and vest, waving a Bible. The channel number displayed on the screen was in the 50s, beyond her usual viewing range.

She clicked to a single-digit channel, a local news program. Her frown remained, though, as she tried to recall the last time she'd watched TV.

Sunday night. They'd tuned in a movie, a comedy about a family living in a haunted house. And this morning Matthew had turned on the set while she was fixing breakfast. She'd asked him to turn it off and come to the table, not really noticing what he'd been watching. In fact, he could have been flipping channels at the time and landed anywhere.

She shrugged it off and focused on the local news.

Later she fixed a salad: lettuce, tomatoes, mushrooms, alfalfa sprouts, croutons, and a chopped hard-boiled egg. After dinner, she and Matthew sat on the family room floor and played Go Fish. They were each down to three cards when the phone rang.

"Hi, I'm glad you're home."

It was Leonard.

Valerie felt a stab of fear. She'd been upset by his previous calls, but now she was afraid that he'd been questioned by Detective Gianelli and informed that she and Greg had accused him of Brenda's assault. Was he going to confront her about it? Was he going to *do* something?

"Why are you calling?" she asked, fighting to keep the quaver from her voice.

"Just to talk," Leonard said pleasantly. "How are you?"

Valerie heard no anger or resentment in his tone. Perhaps the police *hadn't* mentioned her and Greg.

"I asked you not to call here again," she said.

"Yes, I know. Really, it would be better if I were there in person, but I'm not sure if I can get out tonight."

"Leonard, I . . . I don't want to talk to you."

"No?"

"We agreed, remember?" She'd tried to sound firm.

Leonard laughed softly. "Sure, that's what we *said*. But that was just for Greg."

"What?"

"He's not there, is he?" Leonard's voice was chilly.

Valerie nearly said no. She suddenly felt alone and vulnerable. "Yes, he is."

"Is he standing right there?"

She wondered if Leonard wanted to speak to him. "He's in the bathroom."

"Good, so is Mother. We can talk for a few minutes."

"Leonard, look, I don't—"

"We've got to meet somewhere soon and get things straightened out."

She paused. "What 'things'?"

"You know. Us. Perhaps later tonight I could come over."

"No." Valerie's throat had become so dry that the word came out like a croak. "And there is no 'us.' "

"Well, you know what I mean."

"No, I don't. I don't have the faintest *notion* of what you mean."

"That's why we have to spend some time together."

Valerie nearly hung up. But she'd done that before and obviously Leonard hadn't gotten the message. "Listen to me," she said evenly, squeezing the receiver so tightly her knuckles ached. "I thought I made it clear that I don't want you calling here anymore. I don't want to be rude, but I have to say this: Don't call back. Ever."

Leonard was silent for a moment. Then, "It's Greg, isn't it?"

"Among other things, yes."

"I know he's there, and if you're saying this for his benefit, I understand."

"It's *not* for his benefit. It's for *your* benefit."

Leonard chuckled. "If you think I'm afraid of him, forget about it."

"That's not what I mean. I . . . ." She drew in a breath, then let it out. "This is our last conversation, Leonard. Good-bye."

"I have to get off, too," he said. "By the way, I like your house. See you soon." He hung up.

Valerie stared at the receiver. Her hand was trembling. She pressed down the lever and started to dial Greg's number.

I like your house?

She suddenly hung up the phone and walked quickly to the front door, knowing it was locked, but wanting to check it anyway.

But it wasn't locked, not completely. That is, the lock built into the knob was twisted shut. But the dead bolt was open. She always kept them both locked. Whenever she left the house by the front door, she'd pull the door closed to engage the doorknob lock, and she'd use her key to lock the dead bolt. The same thing at night before going to bed—except she could engage the dead bolt by twisting a lever on this side of the door.

She twisted it now, locking it.

How long had it been unlocked? The last time they'd used the front door had been Sunday. Hadn't she checked it Sunday night? Perhaps not. Sometimes Greg did that before they went to bed. Maybe they'd both forgotten. Never again.

I like your house?

Valerie shuddered. Has he been here?

She frowned, thinking furiously. Her clothes disarranged in the closet, the TV on an odd channel, the dead bolt open . . .

Had he been *inside* the house?

Panic crashed over her like a wave. She rushed back to the kitchen. Matthew stared at her from the family room.

"Mom, are we going to finish our game or what?"

"No," she said. "I mean, maybe in a little while, okay? I have to make a phone call."

She dialed Greg's number.

"Hi, babe," he said. "I just called you a few minutes ago and it was busy."

"It was Leonard."

"What?"

"Greg, I think he's been here, maybe even in the house. And some of the things he said . . . I'm frightened."

"I'm coming over," he said angrily. "Keep your doors locked until I get there."

Twenty minutes later Valerie let Greg inside. Matthew was glad to see him, but a little surprised—Greg rarely arrived this late.

"We can start our game over," Matthew said, "and you can play, too."

Valerie smoothed the hair on her son's head.

"Greg and I need to talk first," she said. "Why don't you watch TV while we go in the other room, okay?"

Valerie and Greg sat on the couch in the living room. Muted television noise drifted in.

"Tell me what happened," Greg said quietly.

Valerie described in detail her phone conversation with Leonard.

Greg listened intently, his jaw set. But he looked dubious when she explained about the little things amiss in the house.

"Couldn't Matthew have done that?" Greg asked, referring to the odd TV setting.

"Yes, of course, but when you add them all together . . ."

Greg nodded, pursing his lips. "You said both doors were locked, right?"

"Yes."

"What about the windows?"

"I've been leaving them closed during the day to keep out the heat."

"Did you check them when you got home?"

She hadn't, so they checked them now, beginning with her bedroom and ending in the kitchen, finding every window closed and latched. Greg glanced over the room divider at Matthew, engrossed in a cops-and-drug-dealers show.

"He didn't actually say he'd been in the house, did he?" he asked, keeping his voice down.

"No. He just said he liked the house. Maybe he only parked in the driveway."

"Or maybe he wasn't here at all," Greg added. "It could be that the son of a bitch is just trying to scare you."

"I almost wish that's what it was." She shook her head in disgust. "But he *likes* me."

Greg nodded, his face set. "It's time Leonard and I had a little chat," he said.

He brought the Denver white pages to the table, sat down, and flipped open the thick book. There were thirty-four Tullys listed. No "Leonard." No "L."

"I suppose I could call them all," Greg said, "and ask for Lenny-boy."

"Who's Lenny-boy?" Matthew had entered the kitchen unnoticed.

"Just some jerk."

"He's nobody," Valerie said. "How's your program?"

"It's over. Aren't you guys gonna play Go Fish?"

"Sure," Greg said. "Why don't you get everything ready and we'll be there in a minute." Greg waited until Matthew had left the room. "When—*if*—he calls again, tell him you can't talk, but you'll phone him back. Get his number and call me right away."

Valerie nodded. "Except . . ."

"What?"

"He also said, 'See you soon.' "

Greg frowned, then waved his hand. "Probably just a figure of speech. But if anyone knocks, answer the door on the security chain. If it's him, slam the door, call the police, and then call me, okay?"

Valerie nodded again. "Okay. But . . . I hate this."

"I know," he said, rising, going to her, putting his arms around her waist. "But it's just a temporary annoyance. He's confused, is all. Once I talk to him, that'll be the end of it."

"Are you guys coming, or what?" Matthew called from the next room.

"Coming," Valerie said.

Greg kissed her on the tip of the nose. "There is one good thing about this," he said, trying to lighten the mood.

"What?"

"An hour ago I had no idea I'd be getting lucky tonight."

She gave him a playful punch in the stomach. "You must be talking about the card game."

"I most certainly am not."

Later, after Matthew and Greg had won two games each, Valerie tucked her son in bed.

"Good night, baby," she said, kissing his forehead.

"Night, Mom."

Valerie started to move away from the bed, careful not to step on Dodger, who was curled up on the rug.

"Mom?"

She stopped and turned to him. "What, hon?"

"Why did Greg come over tonight?"

"Well . . . just to see us."

"Oh."

"Why do you ask?"

"I don't know. I thought maybe something was wrong."

Valerie felt her stomach tighten. "Like what?"

"I don't know."

She moved to the bed and smoothed the hair on Matthew's head. "Well, nothing's wrong. Everything's just fine, okay?"

"Okay."

"You go to sleep now."

After she'd turned off the light, she stood in the doorway for a few moments, looking at the dark shape of her son in bed. Anger began to burn inside her like a glowing lump of charcoal. Leonard's call had touched not only her and Greg but Matthew as well.

Then anger gave way to a fearful image of Leonard wandering through her house.

She was glad Greg was here tonight.

THEY MADE LOVE in the morning.

Valerie clung to him, her fingers pressed into his back, feeling his muscles contract as he released himself into her. She stroked the nape of his neck. Greg shifted his weight so that he lay partially on her, partially beside her.

"I love you," he whispered in her ear.

"I love you, too."

He raised his head and blew lightly on her chest above her breasts, cooling the perspiration there.

"Mm, that feels good."

"You feel good," he said and kissed her.

They lay quietly for a few minutes, then flinched when the alarm went off. Greg reached over and slapped it silent.

"The day awaits."

"Let it wait," she said and pulled him to her.

"We should start every morning like this," he said.

"You're right."

"If we were married . . ."

"I know."

He smiled and kissed her on the forehead. "You know, it's usually the woman who wants to make a commitment and the man who's reluctant."

She hesitated. "It's just that . . ."

"You're afraid of another eventual breakup," he finished for her. "Another broken marriage for Matthew to adjust to."

She said nothing, her hand moving lightly over his back.

"You know I love you," he said.

"I know."

"And I'd never leave you, no matter what. In fact, you couldn't get rid of me if you tried."

She smiled. She cared more about Greg than anyone in the world, with the possible exception of Matthew. And she seemed to love him more each day. In fact, she truly believed that someday they would be married. But not today. When, she couldn't say. She knew it was partially a matter of summoning the courage to say yes.

"You think you'd enjoy seeing me every morning with messed-up hair?" she asked. "And no makeup?"

"You mean like now?"

"Exactly like now."

"Hey, babe, it turns me on."

He grabbed her playfully and she giggled.

She let him use the shower first, while she started breakfast, making coffee and setting out bowls for cereal and plates for toast.

Since Greg had to make a trip home to change clothes before going to the print shop, Valerie took Matthew to day care. She kissed her son good-bye in the car and watched him until he was safely in the building.

Then she drove across town to St. Joseph's hospital. A nurse told her that Miss Newcomb's condition had not changed. Brenda looked worse, though, Valerie thought, as if she were shrinking inside her own skin. And for the first time, Valerie began to doubt that Brenda would recover.

On the drive home she felt deeply depressed. She tried to focus her mind on the painting in progress. It was difficult. She knew, though, that for her to complete seven large canvases on time it was important to finish this painting by the weekend. And to do so would mean putting in four full days of work. She would have to be strong. She would have to concentrate.

However, when she turned into her driveway, the thought of painting fled her mind like a startled bird.

There was a brown pickup truck parked near the garage.

She'd seen it before—yesterday, backing into the street. She'd thought little of it then. Now, though, she felt certain that the truck belonged to Leonard.

She braked to a halt in the driveway, well back from the truck. There was no movement inside the vehicle. Valerie stared at its rear window, and for a moment she thought there were two people inside. Then she realized she was looking at a pair of headrests. In fact, she couldn't tell whether anyone was in the truck or not.

She sat perfectly still, clutching the steering wheel. What should she do now? If she were in the house, she'd call the police and then Greg. But she wasn't inside. She was out here, and Leonard was between her and safety. Or had he broken into the house?

Then she saw movement through the truck window, a hand reaching up to adjust the rearview mirror. The truck's door swung open.

Valerie didn't wait to see who climbed out. Slamming the Toyota in reverse, she spun the tires, peppering the front wheel wells with gravel. She backed into the street, narrowly missing another car, then sped away, driving to Greg's shop as fast as traffic would allow.

The shop, as usual, was crowded and busy. Valerie caught Greg's eye between the heads of two customers standing at the counter. He excused himself and came around to her.

His smile vanished when he saw the look on her face.

"What's wrong?" His tone was urgent, but low enough to prevent any customer from hearing.

"It's Leonard. He's at the house."

"*What?*"

Before she could say more, he took her by the arm and led her outside.

"Did he try to get inside?" Greg asked, louder now that they were insulated from the people in the shop by the thick glass door.

Valerie shook her head. "His truck was in the driveway when I got back from the day-care center."

"God *damn* him."

"I didn't even get out of the car. I just drove straight here."

"Is he still there?"

"I don't know. He was climbing out of the truck when I left, and I didn't look back. Should we call the police?"

"No," Greg said firmly, "we don't need the police. I'll straighten him out."

"Greg—"

"Just a sec."

He stepped into the shop. Valerie saw him talk for a few moments with Janice, probably telling her to take over. When he came back outside his face was set in hard lines.

"Maybe you should wait here," he said.

"What are you going to do?"

"Tell him we don't want him around. Make sure he understands."

Valerie hesitated. "Okay, but I want to be there."

"I don't think—"

"It's my house, Greg, and it's me he's hassling. Besides," she continued, her voice softening, "I don't want a major confrontation between you and him. I don't want a fight."

"There won't be a fight. Unless he starts something."

"Exactly my point. I'll follow you."

Without waiting for a reply, she climbed in the Toyota and started the engine.

She followed Greg's car north on Wadsworth and west on 32nd Avenue. When they reached the house, though, they found the driveway empty. Greg parked far to the left, near the house, allowing Valerie to steer past him to the garage. Once inside, she flipped the switch, then walked quickly into the sunlight, as the heavy automatic door slid closed. Greg was waiting on the front porch, key in hand.

"Let's look around and make sure everything's all right."

They toured the house, checking the windows and doors. Nothing seemed disturbed. Valerie let Dodger in the kitchen door. He wagged his tail so hard that his rear end swung from side to side. Greg squatted down and rubbed Dodger's ears.

"Maybe you were right," he said, patting Dodger on the head and rising. "Maybe we should call the police. Leonard hasn't actually broken any laws, but at least they could find him and talk to him, warn him to stay away from here."

"Well . . ."

Greg looked at her.

"I hate to say this now," she said, "I mean, after getting both of us upset and all . . . but I'm not absolutely certain it was Leonard who was here."

"You're not?"

She gave him a pained look and sat at the kitchen table. "I didn't actually see his face. It was the truck that made me think it was him. I saw the same one yesterday backing out of the driveway, and when Leonard phoned last night and implied he'd been here and that he'd return . . ." She looked sheepishly at Greg and shrugged her shoulders. "When I saw the truck, I got scared. I just assumed it was him."

"Well, it probably *was* him," Greg said forcefully. "I mean, do we know anybody who owns a brown pickup truck?"

"Well! . . . no."

Greg nodded, pursing his lips. "It was Leonard."

Valerie believed he was right. She hadn't seen the man's face, but somehow she'd known who it was.

"Which means he may be back," Greg said.

"God, Greg, what are we going to do?"

He shook his head. "What *can* we do? We can call the police, but we don't even know for certain that Leonard was here. And *I* can't contact the bastard because I don't know where he lives." He paused. "We'll have to wait for him to call or show up again."

"Oh, great."

"Look, if he phones, you just get his number and call me. I'll talk to him. If he comes over, call the cops and tell them he's harassing you. We can probably get a restraining order against him. Either way it ends there."

Valerie nodded. "I suppose you're right. But I hate this. It's as if he's in control of the situation."

"I know how you feel," he said, reaching for her hand. "But he's not in control, not really. He's just an annoying pest, a fly who'll eventually be swatted."

"I hope you're right."

"Trust me," he said and kissed her. Then he checked his watch. "I'd better get back to work. Janice is probably swamped by now."

She walked him to the door.

"You're coming over tonight, aren't you?"

"Yes," he said. "In fact, maybe I should come here every night until this situation is over."

She smiled. "Suits me."

She locked the door behind him. Then she let Dodger out, making sure the back door was locked.

A prisoner in my own home, she thought.

She poured herself a glass of iced tea and carried it upstairs. The studio felt warm and stuffy, so she cranked open the windows, letting in air that wasn't much cooler. Then she stood before the large canvas, sipping her tea, letting her mind empty into the partially completed painting.

Before long she was immersed in her work, sharing the relaxed tension of the Indian dancer, feeling what he felt, revealing it in his facial expression.

By mid-afternoon Valerie had completed the face, hair, and headdress of the dancer, roughed in his war lance, and detailed the hand holding it. She felt good about her progress. She also felt hungry, and so she was in the kitchen washing a peach under the tap when the phone rang.

"Hi, Valerie, it's John Tenaka."

John was one of the students stretching canvases for her under the guidance of her art teacher, Professor McKinney. He'd been assigned the job of overseer, and he'd promised Valerie the canvases by the end of this week. She hadn't expected to hear from him until then. She feared the worst.

"Hi, John. Is there a problem with the canvases?"

He laughed. "And I thought *I* was a pessimist. No, everything is fine. I'm calling to tell you they're ready."

"That's great," she said, breathing a sigh of relief. The canvases were the only part of the project that had been out of her control—by choice, of course. And although she wouldn't feel completely assured until she'd inspected them, she was confident that Professor McKinney and John Tenaka had done an excellent job.

"When can I pick them up?"

"Anytime," John said. "Just let me know when you're coming up here."

"Can I call you right back?" She got his number, then phoned Greg.

"We can do it tonight, if you like," Greg said. "I'll take the shop's van to your house after work and the three of us will drive to Boulder."

"Great. See you then."

She called John Tenaka, asked him which building he was in, and said they'd meet him there between six-thirty and seven.

"Do you know how to get here?"

"It's been a few years," she said, "but I think I can find it. See you tonight."

She hung up, smiling. Then she took a bite of her peach and wiped juice from her chin with the back of her hand. She tore a paper towel from the roll over the sink and started upstairs. The phone brought her back to the kitchen. She figured it was John calling back to tell her something he'd forgotten.

"Hi," she said.

"Hi. I keep missing you." It was Leonard.

Chapter

8

THE RECEIVER FELT ALIVE in Valerie's hand.

"Every time I drop by your house, it seems you're away," Leonard said. "Are you hiding from me?" His voice was playful.

"I, uh, no." Get a grip, she told herself, remember what Greg said. "Ah, listen, Leonard, I really can't talk to you right now, so—"

"Why not?"

"I . . . there's someone at the door. My neighbor. I'll have to call you back." She started fumbling for a pencil and nearly dropped the receiver, catching it against her body with her arm. "What's your number?"

Leonard paused. "I'm at a pay phone."

"I mean your home number. I'll . . . call you later, when you get home."

Leonard paused again, apparently to think this over. "I guess it would be all right," he said tentatively. Then his voice brightened. "Yes, I think it would be fine if you called me at home."

He gave her the number. She wrote it down. Her handwriting looked heavy and rigid, not her own.

"I'll be home in half an hour," he said.

"Okay."

"But don't wait too long."

"I . . . okay."

"Because Mother and I usually eat an early dinner, and, well, it wouldn't do for me to leave her staring at my empty chair."

Valerie said nothing.

"I'll talk to you later," Leonard said.

Valerie hung up. She took a step back, staring at the phone, wiping her hand as if it were dirty. Her eyes fell to the phone number etched in thick pencil. Then she snatched up the receiver and called Greg.

"Leonard just phoned," she told him. "I got his home number."

"That son of a . . . okay, what is it?"

After she'd read it to him, she said, "He's not home now. He said he was calling from a pay phone."

"Where?"

"I don't know. Why do—"

"Your doors are locked, aren't they?"

Now she understood what Greg had been implying: Leonard could have been calling from somewhere nearby. He might show up at any minute.

"Yes," she said, glancing toward the back door, "they're locked."

"All right, if he does come over, call the police immediately."

"I will." She paused. "Are you going to phone him?"

"You know it. Listen, I've got to get off now, there's—"

"Greg."

"What?"

"When you call him . . . go easy. I mean, I don't want *you* getting in trouble with the police."

"Don't worry, I know just what to say to him. And you did fine getting his number." He said something unintelligible away from the phone before speaking to her again. "Listen, I've really got to get off. I'll talk to you later."

"Okay."

"Are you going to be all right?"

"I'm fine," Valerie said.

After she'd hung up, she rechecked the door locks, then went upstairs and tried to paint. She couldn't concentrate. Every little sound made her jump, made her imagine Leonard creeping up the stairs. She kept glancing at her watch, wondering if Greg had phoned him, wondering what was said.

And then Dodger's barking drifted up to her through the open window.

She tried to ignore it. But when he wouldn't stop, she set down her brush and stepped to the window, listening.

The dog sounded insistent. Valerie could tell that he wasn't simply answering the bark of a distant neighbor's dog. This was more immediate. Something was intruding in the backyard.

Valerie wished she could see down there, but the backyard was on the north side of the house and all the windows upstairs faced west. Apprehensive now, she moved downstairs to the kitchen.

Dodger was still barking angrily, incessantly.

Valerie couldn't see him, but it sounded as if he were near the house, to her right. She stood at the back door, her face pressed against the glass. Now she could just see his rear end. His tail swung slowly from side to side. Apparently, he was concerned with the short stretch of the fence between the house and the garage. His barking hadn't stopped.

Valerie wasn't sure whether to open the back door for a look or just phone the police. She stepped to the windows in the family room, and then the living room, checking the driveway. Empty.

She returned to the kitchen, hesitated, then cautiously opened the back door. She called to Dodger. He continued to bark.

She unlatched the screen and poked her head outside, calling again to the dog. He glanced back at her, then resumed his insistent, almost maniacal barking. Valerie stepped warily onto the back porch—then felt both relief and anger when she saw the cause of the commotion. A squirrel sat on top of the fence, staring down at Dodger, and twitching its bushy tail.

"Dammit, Dodger, come here."

The dog fell silent and jogged toward her, ears drooping, tail wagging.

"Go on, get out of here!" she yelled at the squirrel, angry with herself for getting upset over nothing.

The small animal clucked at her. She looked around for something to throw, snatched up a rubber bone, and flung it as hard as she could. The chew-toy struck the fence and sent the squirrel hopping along the top of the boards to the garage, where it leapt first to the roof and then to the branch of an elm.

Dodger ran after his toy and brought it back to Valerie. He dropped it at her feet and looked up at her expectantly. She smiled and shook her head.

"You're a good boy, Dodger."

She let him in the house and locked the door behind them.

She painted without interruption until it was time to pick up Matthew.

They'd been home for less than an hour when Greg's van pulled into the driveway. Valerie let him in and they kissed.

"Did you phone Leonard?" she asked. The muscles in her shoulders and neck were stiff with tension.

Greg nodded, lips pursed.

"And?"

"I told him who I was, and I said that you and I were a couple, and that we both wanted him to stop calling you. All very civil."

"What did he say?"

Greg sighed. "Well, he was polite as could be. He apologized for any inconvenience he might have caused, and he said it had been a misunderstanding. And then . . ." Greg shrugged. "Then he wished us both good luck."

Valerie felt her tension drain away. "Thank God, it's over."

"I hope so."

She looked at him carefully. "What do you mean?"

"I don't know. It all seemed too easy. I guess I expected an argument from him, resistance, something. But he was immediately and completely contrite. He must have said 'I'm sorry' half a dozen times."

"Are you saying you didn't believe him?"

"Well, he *sounded* sincere." He put his arm around her shoulder. "It'll probably be all right, Val. We'll just have to wait and see."

Matthew banged in through the back door.

"Hi, Greg!"

"Hi, guy." He reached down with his free hand and tousled the boy's hair.

"Are we going to Boulder now?"

"As soon as your mom says so."

Rush hour was over, so the ride north on Highway 36 went quickly.

Greg left the highway and drove slowly along a tree-lined street. They passed before stately old campus buildings, half hidden by pine trees and elms. Young people strolled singly or in bunches along curving walkways. It had been nearly ten years since Valerie had been a student here, and she felt a twinge of nostalgia every time she returned.

Valerie directed Greg to the art building. He steered down the driveway leading around to the loading dock. The back of the building was deserted. They climbed out of the van, and Greg knocked on the steel door beside the dock.

A few moments later the door was opened by a small young man wearing a Hawaiian shirt, baggy shorts, and sandals. His black hair was long in back and shaved close on the sides.

"Hi, John," Valerie said, smiling.

"Hi. Come on in."

Valerie introduced John Tenaka to Greg and then to Matthew.

"How you doing, big guy?"

"Fine," Matthew said. He wrinkled his nose. "It smells funny in here."

"It's not me, honest," John said, making Valerie laugh. "Somebody spilled something this morning."

"Not on my canvases, I hope."

"Not a chance," John said.

The six large canvases were stacked neatly on end, resting on a wooden pallet against the wall and covered with a sheet of clear plastic. Valerie inspected each canvas, front and back, before allowing Greg and John to carry them one at a time to the van. It was a close fit, but they managed to stack them flat, spreading a sheet of plastic between each one.

Valerie had already paid Professor McKinney for the materials, and they'd agreed on a fee for the labor. Now she wrote a check for that amount, payable to McKinney, and handed it to John.

"You did a great job, John," she said. "I really appreciate it. Tell the other students thanks for me."

He held up the check. "This is the kind of thanks they'll *really* understand. But I'll tell them anyway. Also . . ."

"What?"

"I hear you're painting these for an out-of-state showing."

"That's right."

"Well, before you ship them, I wonder if, I mean, I'd really like to see them. I know the other students would, too."

Valerie smiled. "I'm flattered. How about if you all come to my house for a private showing?"

"Hey, that'd be great."

"I'll give you a call in six or seven weeks."

After they'd said good-bye to John, they climbed in the van and drove through town, parking within a block of the Pearl Street mall. Most of the shops were closed, but people were still strolling about, taking in the early evening air. They picked a restaurant on the mall, sat at an outside table, and ate gourmet burgers and beer—Molson for Valerie and Greg, root beer for Matthew.

The sun was down by the time they got home. Greg parked in the driveway near the front door. He swung open the van's doors while Valerie dug out her house key. When she pulled open the front screen, something fell to her feet.

"What's that?" Matthew asked.

"It's . . . a greeting card."

She bent stiffly, her body suddenly tense, and picked it up—a large, square, pale pink envelope. It was blank, front and back. She opened the flap and awkwardly withdrew the card.

On the front was a soft-focus photo of a man and woman walking along a beach at sunset. Inside were the engraved words, "My love for you is forever."

Below that was a single word, carefully centered and written with a ballpoint pen:

Leonard

C   h   a   p   t   e   r

9

AS DUSK GRADUALLY DEEPENED INTO NIGHT, Leonard drove around aimlessly, deciding what to do about Greg Barryman. His anger was mixed with hunger—he'd left most of his dinner on his plate.

Earlier that evening he'd had trouble eating, his mouth dry from anticipation. Even though he'd asked Valerie not to call too early, he was afraid she might phone while they were still at the table, and then he'd have to decide who to put on hold, Valerie or his mother.

As it turned out, though, it didn't ring until he was drying the dinner dishes and putting them away. And it was his mother who answered, because she was next to the phone.

"Yes, he's right here," she said into the receiver, then looked Leonard in the eye. "Who may I say is calling?"

Leonard reached anxiously for the phone even before his mother said, "It's for you, dear."

"Hello?" Leonard said. He clutched the receiver to his face and turned away from his mother, his heart pounding.

But it was Greg Barryman, not Valerie.

Leonard was caught off guard, and it seemed Greg didn't want him to recover, going on and on about how Valerie was his girlfriend and how Leonard's phone calls were upsetting her. Leonard found himself apologizing as a reflex action. The one-sided conversation ended before he had a chance to focus his thoughts and tell Greg the way things *really* were.

Who does he think he is, calling here and trying to threaten me?

Francine sat at the table, watching TV, apparently unconcerned with Leonard's phone call. But her evangelist's sermonizing was tuned to a mumble. The moment Leonard hung up, she asked, "Who's Greg Barryman, dear?"

"He's . . . just someone from the Christian singles group."

Leonard had to think furiously to come up with that lie. He was

115

seething now, and he didn't know how long he could contain his anger. He certainly didn't want to explode in front of his mother.

"What did he want?" Francine asked innocently.

"Just to talk . . . about the group."

"Mm-hm." Her eyes were still on the screen. "I didn't mean to eavesdrop, but I heard you say you were sorry. What was that all about?"

"Oh, well, you see, I was supposed to pick him up tonight. There's a group meeting and I forgot all about it and last week I told him I would pick him up because . . . he needed a ride."

"Needed a ride," Francine repeated, turning slowly to face Leonard, her eyes going through him like needles.

"Yes, his car is in the garage." He looked at the TV screen, the table top, his watch, anywhere but his mother's eyes. "And I'm already late, so I'm going to have to leave now."

He gave her a quick kiss on top of the head, still avoiding her eyes, and started for the back door.

She stopped him in his tracks with, "Leonard."

"What?" He half turned, hanging his head.

"Look at me."

He did, his insides twisted in knots.

"What's going on here?"

"Nothing, Mother. Just the group."

She squinted at him. "Nothing else?"

"No."

She nodded, almost imperceptibly, still looking at him hard.

"You wouldn't be sneaking off to see that young woman of yours, now would you?"

"No, Mother."

"You'd tell me if you were." It wasn't a question.

"Yes."

"When am I going to meet her, anyway?"

"Soon."

Her look softened and she nearly smiled. "Very well, then, come back here and give your mother a proper kiss good-bye."

Leonard sheepishly crossed the kitchen and kissed her on the cheek.

"And you'll come straight home after the group meeting, won't you?"

"Yes, Mother."

When Leonard stepped out the back door he drew in a long breath, nearly a gasp, as if he'd just swum up from the bottom of a deep lake. He sat in his truck, clenching the wheel, staring straight ahead at nothing, thinking about Valerie and about Greg Barryman. He viciously twisted the key in the ignition and gunned the engine. Then he shot a glance toward the rear of the house, knowing his Mother could hear the truck from the kitchen.

He shifted quietly in gear and drove slowly down the alley.

Then he stopped suddenly, slamming on the brakes, realizing he might have made a terrible mistake.

What if Valerie phoned now? And really, there was no reason to think she wouldn't. He'd been disoriented by Greg's call, and he'd left the house without a plan, not knowing where he was going or what he would do.

Leonard shifted in reverse, started back, and stopped. He couldn't go home, not now, not after the lie he'd told his mother.

His thoughts returned to Greg's call. He wondered briefly if Greg had gotten his number from Valerie. If so, he'd probably stolen it from her purse and called without letting Valerie know. Or maybe he'd coerced her into giving it to him. He pictured Greg forcing Valerie to give him the phone number, shouting in her face, making accusations, perhaps even striking her.

Leonard slammed the truck into low, tore down the alley, and screeched into the street, heading for Wheat Ridge.

By the time he reached Valerie's house his anger toward Greg had settled from a boil to a simmer. He'd take care of him. That was certain. But there was no use being stupid about it. Only a fool would rush headlong at his enemy with no plan. The important thing now was to talk to Valerie, to find out exactly what had happened with the phone number.

Then a thought scuttled like a spider into his mind: Was it possible that Valerie had willingly given the number to Greg, even asked him to call?

No, Leonard thought, squashing the notion. Greg is nothing more than a pretender, a rival. I'm sure that's what Valerie will say.

But when he knocked on her door, no one answered. Only the dog barking in the backyard. Leonard was irritated. Was it just a *coincidence* that Valerie was never home whenever he dropped by? He considered going in through the window and waiting for her as he'd done before. Where was she, anyway? Maybe visiting a neighbor. Or Greg. Now *there* was an unpleasant thought that had to be pushed from his mind.

Leonard got into his truck and slammed the door.

He didn't have the patience to wait for Valerie even for five minutes. On the other hand, he wanted her to know that he'd dropped by, that he was still thinking of her. So he'd found a convenience store about a mile away and sorted through the greeting cards until he found just the right one: a couple on a beach with the words "My love for you is forever."

Then he'd driven back to Valerie's house. He'd signed the card and positioned it in the screen door so it would fall at her feet when she opened the door.

And now he drove the streets thinking about Greg, anger burning in his chest like a small, bright flame. He should have set things straight when Greg phoned. But he'd been afraid to argue with him. No, not afraid—unprepared. He'd been caught off guard, that's all. And his mother had been sitting right there. But now he was ready to face him. And he had both of Greg's addresses in his wallet, home and business.

Leonard swung the truck into a hard right turn and thought, Time to act.

The tall apartment building was just off west Sixth Avenue. There was a small foyer enclosed by heavy glass, with steel mailboxes and a telephone intercom. Leonard found the mail slot marked "G. Barryman—484." He lifted the receiver and punched the first two digits. His fingered wavered over the third.

What would he say when Greg answered? They'd probably get into a shouting match over Valerie. Maybe Greg would come down and want to fight.

So what? Leonard thought. I'm not afraid of him. Not really.

But what would it accomplish? He wanted Greg to stay away from Valerie. Perhaps if he gave him something else to think about. A distraction.

Leonard grinned and hung up the phone.

He drove to Greg's shop.

He cruised slowly through the empty, starkly lit parking lot, then drove around the end of the small shopping complex and steered down the alley. The rear of the building was a block-long cinder-block wall, bathed in yellow arc light and punctuated by gray doors.

When Leonard found the door marked "Fast Print," he stopped the truck and climbed out. He was shielded from the houses across the alley by an unbroken line of high wooden privacy fences.

He examined the door. It was steel, formidable. It framed his shadow.

His eyes moved along the top edge, then the sides of the door, then the bottom. He got his crowbar from the rear of the truck, jammed one end under the steel door, and put all his weight on the other end. He barely managed to create a dent.

He kept working at it, though, moving the bar back and forth, side to side, a fraction of an inch at a time.

After twenty minutes he was sweating from exertion. There was now a mangled crescent-shaped opening three inches wide and an inch high at the bottom of the door.

It would do.

He drove to a service station on Colfax and filled the five-gallon gas can in his truck. Back at Greg's shop he attached the nozzle to the can and began pouring gasoline under the door. He was careful not to splash any on his shoes or the outside of the door. The fumes left a metallic taste in his throat.

He poured slowly, patiently, stopping often to see that no gas ran back out from under the door. He didn't know whether the floor inside was tile, carpet, or concrete. Whatever it was, though, it was either soaking up the gas or allowing it to flow in, away from the door.

Leonard stopped pouring before the can was empty. He searched a nearby dumpster for a newspaper, then rolled a few sheets into a long tube, soaked it with the remaining gasoline, and shoved it under the door until only a few inches were showing.

He put away the can, then scanned the alley. Silent and empty.

When he struck the match it sounded like a pistol shot. He touched the flame to the newsprint and watched it blossom. As he jumped in his truck and slammed the door, he heard a faint, satisfying *whumpf.*

The fires of Hell, he thought, and grinned all the way home.

C h a p t e r

ON WEDNESDAY MORNING, after breakfast, Francine scoured the classified ads for bargains while Leonard opened the shop.

He flipped over the CLOSED/OPEN placard on the door and raised all the blinds. Then he dusted, beginning at the front of the shop. He used a rag, not a feather duster. His mother had taught him long ago that a duster simply moves the dust around, whereas a rag removes it. He lifted items one at a time, wiped them carefully, then cleaned the empty space on the shelf before setting them back down.

While he worked, he thought about last night.

It was like remembering a movie. Every detail was sharp in his mind: the feel of the crowbar, the smell of the gasoline, the sound of the gas igniting. But it was as if he'd watched someone else jimmy the door and pour in the gas. He'd never done anything like that before. It simply wasn't his nature. At least, he'd *thought* it wasn't his nature.

Leonard smiled and shook his head. Sometimes he surprised even himself.

He wished he could be there when Greg arrived for work this morning. He'd love to watch his face when he saw the smoldering ruin that used to be his shop. That should keep him occupied for a while and away from Valerie.

The bell jangled loudly over the door.

Two men entered the shop, and Leonard immediately became wary. They barely glanced at the merchandise. Their eyes were on him. That alone would have made him uneasy. But their attitude was even more disturbing, so confident and self-assured, as if they *belonged* here.

"Are you Mr. Tully?"

This from the smaller of the two, the Hispanic. He was shorter than Leonard, but stocky, with dark eyes and smooth features. He wore a light sports coat, dark slacks, an off-white shirt, and a knit tie.

"Y-yes. May I help you find something?" Leonard glanced at the

1 2 0

doorway in back, as if he were seeking help. The murmur of preaching drifted to him.

"I'm Detective Sandoval," the man said, holding up a leather wallet, showing Leonard his badge and plastic-encased photo. "This is my partner, Detective Lott. We'd like to ask you some questions, if we may."

Detective Lott said nothing. He was a big man, over six feet tall, with broad shoulders and a thick, brown mustache that seemed to turn down his mouth in a permanent frown. His linen sport coat was rumbled and his shirt was open at the collar. He, too, held out an open wallet for Leonard's inspection.

"Questions?"

Leonard struggled to look surprised, as if he had no idea why two policemen would want to question him. But he knew exactly why: someone must have seen him last night, some nosy neighbor had looked over the fence and spotted him and his truck, perhaps written down his license number.

"Questions about what?" He noticed that the TV in the kitchen had fallen silent.

Sandoval drew out a pen and a small notebook and asked Leonard, "How well did you know Brenda Newcomb?"

"Brenda . . . ?"

"Newcomb."

"I, ah, well, I know that she owns an art gallery in Cherry Creek and—"

"Did own, Mr. Tully," Sandoval corrected. "She died yesterday at St. Joseph's hospital."

"Died?" Leonard was filled with relief and delight—Brenda could never point the finger at him—followed immediately by terror. Had she already?

"From injuries sustained during an attack last Friday night. That's why the case has been transferred from the assault unit to us."

"Homicide," Detective Lott said, speaking for the first time. His voice was raspy, as if his throat were lined with scar tissue.

"How well did you know her?" Sandoval asked quietly.

Leonard flashed back to the last time he'd seen her, sprawled on the concrete floor of the parking garage, her skirt hiked up. (Put it out of your mind.) "I, ah, not very well. I only just met her last week, Wednesday, I think it was."

"How did you meet?"

Leonard furrowed his brown, as if trying to remember. But he was weighing the situation. These men hadn't come to arrest him. If so, they would have done it already. Which meant Brenda had died without identifying him as her assailant.

He folded his arms and tried not to smile.

"Now, that was interesting," he said. He described his encounter with the purse snatcher and his lunch with Valerie and Brenda.

Sandoval jotted a few notes while Leonard talked. Then he asked, "When did you next see Miss Newcomb?"

"At the art gallery Friday night. The reception."

"Did you speak to her anytime between your lunch Wednesday and the reception Friday?"

"No, sir."

"Why did you go to the reception?" Detective Lott asked him, his voice harsh.

"I was invited."

"By Miss Newcomb?"

"No. By Valerie. She's the artist."

Lott seemed to be glaring at him behind his mustache frown. Leonard looked at Sandoval for help. Sandoval flipped a page in his notebook.

"Did you speak to Miss Newcomb at the reception?"

Leonard licked his lips and shifted his feet.

"Briefly."

"What was said?"

"I don't remember."

"You two got into an argument," Lott said, his voice grating on Leonard's nerves, "and then she threw you out."

"No," Leonard answered quickly, loudly. He felt blood redden his ears. "That's not what happened at all."

Both detectives stared impassively at him and waited, as if they had all the time in the world.

"That's not what happened," Leonard said in a small voice.

Sandoval shook his head, clucked his tongue, and flipped a page in his notebook. When he spoke, it was almost apologetically.

"Mr. Tully, isn't it true that at one point during the reception Miss Newcomb suggested that you were there for a free lunch, then said she didn't want you hanging around, and told you to quote run along unquote?"

Leonard shook his head. "No, and I don't see why I have to answer all these questions. What does any of this have to do with me?"

"Mr. Tully, we're investigating a homicide, and we're asking a lot of people questions, not just you. Any help you could give us would be most appreciated. If you'd prefer to have an attorney present while we talk, that's perfectly all right."

"N-no. Why would I need an attorney?"

"Exactly," Sandoval said with a friendly smile. "Now, please, Mr. Tully," he implored, "we have witnesses to the conversation between you and Miss Newcomb. They've already given statements to Detective Gianelli in the assault unit." Sandoval paused. "I'll ask you again, did Miss Newcomb say those things to you?"

"I . . . she may have. I don't recall."

"Mm-hm." Sandoval made a note in his book. "Mr. Tully, what time did you leave the reception?"

A bead of perspiration trickled down Leonard's rib cage. He pressed his arm to his side and said, "Early."

"Can you be more precise?"

"Around eight."

"Why did you leave?" Lott asked abruptly.

Leonard was getting more and more irritated with Detective Lott. "Because I felt like it," he said.

"Oh, really?" Lott raised his eyebrows, his first change of expression. "I understand the party went on until around ten-thirty and everyone had a great time. Why would you want to leave at eight?"

"I'd seen all the paintings," Leonard said, straining to keep his voice calm, "and I just left, that's all."

"Just left, huh?" One corner of Lott's mustache went up in what Leonard assumed was a smug grin.

"Where did you go when you left the reception?" Sandoval asked him politely.

"I came home."

"Home being here?"

"Yes. My mother and I live in the back."

"I see. And what time did you get home?"

"As I said, I left the reception at eight, so, let's see, I must have gotten here around eight-thirty."

"Did you go out again that night?"

"No."

"So you're saying that between eight-thirty and eleven-thirty on Friday night—"

"When Brenda Newcomb was found unconscious," Lott added.

"—that between those times you were home."

"Yes."

"Was your mother home, too?"

"Well . . . yes."

"Can she verify your presence?"

"I—"

"What's going on out here?" Francine asked, wheeling her chair down the aisle toward them. She stopped at Leonard's side and glared up at the two men. "Leonard, who are these men?"

"They're with the police, Mother."

"The *police?*"

Leonard saw that she acted surprised. Acted.

Sandoval and Lott showed their badges. Sandoval said, "Mrs. Tully, were you home last Friday night?"

"Of course I was home. Where else would I be?"

"All night?"

"Yes, all night."

"Was your son with you?"

"Let's see . . . Friday . . ." She looked up at Leonard. "Didn't you go out Friday night?"

Leonard swallowed. "Yes, Mother."

"What time did he come home, Mrs. Tully?" Sandoval asked.

"Oh, let's see, it was pretty late."

Leonard's knees began to tremble. At that moment he wasn't certain who he feared most, the police or his mother.

"How late?" Lott asked pointedly.

"At least eight-thirty. Perhaps a quarter to nine." She looked up at Leonard. "Isn't that right, son?"

"Y-yes." Leonard wanted to feel relieved. His mother was backing him up. But she'd lied for him, and he knew he'd have Hell to pay.

Francine smiled sweetly at the detectives. "Is there anything else we can help you with?"

Sandoval glanced at Lott, then looked down on Francine. "No, ma'am, that's all we need for now. Thank you for your help." Then he looked at Leonard, gentle concern on his face. "We may need to question you more in the future. If you wouldn't mind."

Leonard shook his head. "No, no of course not."

The men left the store.

"I want to talk to you," Francine said sharply and wheeled her chair toward the back.

Leonard meekly followed. Francine snatched up the remote control from the kitchen table. The sound had already been muted, and now the picture vanished, leaving the two of them alone. Leonard could see fury in his mother's eyes, and it frightened him.

"How dare you tell lies," she said.

"Mother, I—"

"Be quiet!" Her hands were clenched on the arms of her chair. She looked as if she might launch herself to her feet. Leonard had never seen her so angry. At least not since her auto accident. Of course, before that, before her repentance, she used to fly into drunken rages, usually with him as the target of her abuse. But this was different. This was worse.

"You told me quite a story, didn't you, Leonard?" Sarcasm oozed from her voice like lava, burning him. "All about a pleasant dinner date with a nice, young Christian woman, when all along you were sneaking off to some . . . some . . . *art* show. And then—"

"Mother, I—"

"I said be quiet!" she shouted.

Leonard saw a tiny bubble of spittle at the corner of her mouth, and he felt embarrassed for her.

"And then the police come into my shop," she continued, her voice loud, "and you lie to them about when you got home. And if that's not enough, you force me to lie, too, so that I don't have to see my son taken away in chains."

"Mother, I didn't do anything, I swear."

"YOU LIED!"

He winced. "I know," he said in a weak voice. "I didn't mean that. I meant the other thing, with Brenda Newcomb."

Francine didn't speak for a few moments, breathing heavily through her nose, staring holes into him. Finally, she said, "I'm waiting."

"I lied to the police because they seem to think I had something to do with that woman's death and I didn't and I knew they'd leave me alone if I told them I got home before she left the gallery." He drew in a breath. "I was wrong to lie, Mother, completely wrong. But they were wrong, too. They had no right to come here and I just wanted them to leave you and me alone."

"Yes, yes," she said impatiently, "but what about your lie to *me?*"

Leonard sighed. "I was afraid if you knew Valerie was an artist you wouldn't approve of me seeing her. So how could I tell you that I was going to her reception at a gallery?"

Francine made a face and said, "Hmpf."

"I'm sorry I lied to you, Mother. I'll never do it again."

"Hm."

"And Valerie really is a nice person."

"Nice," Francine said with some distaste. She stared hard at her son. "And just what does she paint?"

Leonard was surprised by the question. He wondered if there were a wrong answer. "I-Indians."

Francine nodded, her mouth a thin line. "Well, I suppose *that's* all right."

Leonard began to relax. He smiled and took a step forward, ready to kiss his mother's cheek, kiss and make up. She stopped him, raising her hand palm forward.

"I haven't decided whether to tell the police about your lie to them," she said evenly. "I'm going to pray for guidance. And as for this woman, Valerie, I want to meet her."

"Of course, Mother, but—"

"Soon, Leonard," she said firmly. "Today or tomorrow."

BY MID-MORNING Valerie was engrossed in her painting, detailing the dancer's beads and feathers with painstaking care.

The studio seemed smaller now, with six huge, blank canvases leaning against one wall. They were lined up, waiting, constant reminders of the task ahead.

And so when the phone rang, she was reluctant to stop work. She crossed the room, then paused for a moment in the studio doorway, allowing herself a wide-angle view of the painting. She smiled, satisfied, then hurried downstairs to the kitchen.

"It's me," Greg said, his voice sounding hollow in the phone. "There's been a fire at the shop."

"What?" Valerie was stunned.

"My shop is . . . it's ruined."

Valerie didn't want to believe what she was hearing. "My God, what happened? Was anybody hurt?"

"No, everyone's all right. It happened last night. The fire investigators are there now. They still don't know how it started—at least they haven't told me." He paused. "I don't know yet whether it was arson."

"Arson?"

"Believe it or not, that was my first thought," he said bitterly. "And the first person I thought of was Leonard."

"Oh God, Greg."

"You can see why, can't you? I intimidated him on the phone last night, and sometime later the fire started. Coincidence?"

"But do you really think . . . ?"

Greg sighed heavily. "I don't know. Maybe he's just a convenient scapegoat. In fact, it could've been something electrical. The firemen said the doors were closed and locked, so apparently no one had broken in. And the fire was confined to the back room."

Valerie was thankful for something positive, no matter how slight. "At least it wasn't the whole shop."

"It *was* the whole shop," Greg said, suddenly angry. Then he spoke more quietly, "I'm sorry, I'm . . ."

"It's okay."

She heard him sigh again. It made her heart ache.

"The sprinkler system went on automatically," Greg explained without enthusiasm, "and it kept the fire from spreading to the front. But the sprinklers turned on at the front of the shop as well, and everything got soaked. It looks like all the paper stock is ruined. There's probably water damage to the printing equipment, too, although I haven't had a chance to check everything out. And of course, the whole place reeks of smoke, and the carpet's ruined, and . . . I don't know, it's . . ."

His voice trailed away. Valerie felt his pain. She searched for something to say.

"Won't the insurance cover most of it?"

"Sure, it'll pay for the equipment and the stock and any other damage. But I don't know how long I'm going to be closed—weeks, at least. And most of my customers won't wait. They *can't* wait. They need their printing done now. And once they switch to a new print shop, well . . . I don't know how long it will take to recover from this, Valerie, I . . . don't know."

He fell silent.

"Greg, we'll get through it all right. We will."

He hesitated. "I know."

"It'll take time, that's all."

"I know you're right," he said. "But at this point it's hard to be objective."

"Is there . . . can I do anything for you now?"

"Thanks, but no, not really."

"Can I come to the shop?"

"There's nothing to do there. Even the phone is out of order—I'm calling from the doughnut place. And the smell in here is starting to get to me. I might have to buy a jelly roll."

Valerie laughed softly. "Why don't you come here?"

"I will," he said. "Later. I'm waiting for the insurance agent to show up."

"Okay, then I'll see you whenever you get here."

"Thanks," he said.

"For what?"

"For being there. I love you."

"I love you, too."

After Valerie hung up, she considered driving straight to the shop. Shouldn't she be at Greg's side now? On the other hand, she might just be in the way. The best thing was to wait.

She recalled a line from a college English course: "They also serve who only stand and wait."

Or in my case, stand and paint, she thought wryly, climbing the stairs.

She dipped a brush in turquoise paint and placed a bead on the dancer's moccasin. This phase of the painting required attention to detail rather than emotional involvement. Still, she had difficulty staying focused. All she could think about was Greg and his shop. She knew how much money and effort he'd invested to establish the business and how long it had taken—years. She also understood the pride he had in the work he produced. All destroyed overnight.

She could only guess at what he was going through. She tried to imagine how she'd feel if all of her paintings were destroyed. They could never be replaced. Sure, she could produce other, similar paintings—but they'd never be the same. And the time lost . . .

She forced herself to concentrate on the moccasin.

Time dissolved and the painting progressed.

When Valerie stopped, hours later, it was only because Dodger was barking. She checked her watch, saw that it was after noon, and wondered if Greg had arrived. She listened for the front door, but the house was quiet. Only Dodger barking outside. From his insistent tone, Valerie guessed that he was confronting another squirrel in the backyard.

She considered taking a break now for lunch, then decided she wasn't hungry enough. She'd wait for Greg.

Dodger barked a few minutes more and then stopped.

Valerie resumed painting. However, she found herself listening for outside sounds. She thought she heard a noise downstairs, and shortly thereafter, a creak on the stairs. She turned quickly, seeing nothing but the empty doorway.

She returned to her painting, but her mind drifted. She thought of Brenda, lying alone in intensive care, and she felt the need to see her.

Valerie checked her watch again. It was already one o'clock, and she had no idea when Greg was coming. She could wait for him, and then they could visit the hospital together. Except he might not arrive until much later. If only his phone weren't out of order.

Finally she decided to drive to his shop after leaving him a note here, in case they missed each other, letting him know she'd soon return. She cleaned her brush and went downstairs. Then she froze in the kitchen doorway, her heart in her throat.

Leonard was sitting at the table.

Valerie stared at him, stunned, feeling as if she'd been punched in the stomach.

"What . . ."

"Hi." He gave her a sheepish grin. Then he unfolded his hands, uncrossed his ankles, and stood awkwardly, banging his knee on the table. He winced. "I didn't want to disturb you while you were paint-ing. I went up there and peeked."

"What are you . . . how did you get in here?" Her voice betrayed her mounting fear.

She was trapped in her own house. Leonard blocked the way to both the front and back doors. He was much bigger than she, and no doubt much stronger. It would be impossible to force her way past him.

"I knocked on the front door," he said, as if in apology. "When you didn't answer, I thought you might be upstairs, so I tried the knob. It wasn't locked."

"Get out," she said, trying to sound firm, struggling to hide her fear.

"I just want to talk to you," Leonard said politely. "And give you this."

He picked up a box of candy from the table. It was wrapped in cellophane and tied with a red ribbon. He offered it to her.

"Sweets for the sweet," he said, blushing faintly.

"If you don't leave now, I'll call the police."

Her hand went to the phone.

"Please don't."

Leonard's tone was gentle. But he'd taken a step toward her. He was close to her now, close enough to stop her from using the phone, if that's what he wanted.

Valerie was terrified, unsure of what to do. She didn't want to upset or anger him. She just wanted him to leave.

"Please get out of my house." Her hand tightened on the receiver. "Now."

"I really can't stay long," Leonard said. "And I hope I didn't frighten you. I just want to talk for a few minutes." He smiled shyly and again offered her the candy. "Please," he said. "It's a gift."

Valerie hesitated, fighting panic, thinking furiously, trying to determine the safest course of action. So far Leonard had made no threatening gestures, and she wanted to keep it that way.

Slowly, reluctantly, she let go of the phone and took the candy. She said nothing, praying for Greg to get there.

"You're welcome," Leonard said. He stepped back, pleased, proud. Then he nodded toward the table. "Shall we sit?"

"I . . . no. I think you should leave now."

"Pretty soon. I want to talk first. About us. And Greg."

"Greg?" She pictured him at his ruined shop. When was he coming? She set the candy on the countertop.

"Did you know he phoned me last night?" Leonard's voice held resentment.

"Yes. He told me."

"He took my number from you, didn't he?" Leonard asked, suddenly angry.

Valerie took a step backward. She had to get out of this room, out of the house. But Leonard still stood between her and both outside doors. Then she recalled that the bathroom door had a lock. If she could make it there . . .

"Didn't he?" Leonard repeated.

"He . . . got it from me, yes."

"As I thought. He didn't hurt you, did he?"

Valerie blinked. "What?"

"Because if he did, I'll make him regret it."

Valerie hesitated, and when she spoke she measured her words. "Greg would never hurt me. He loves me. And I love him."

Leonard smiled and waved his hand dismissively. "Well, there's love and then there's love. Give me a chance and I'll show you what true love is."

"*You?*"

Leonard scowled, and Valerie got ready to bolt for the bathroom.

"Yes, me. Why not? I'm prepared to devote myself to you, Valerie. All I ask is a chance."

She shook her head no, almost imperceptibly. Leonard didn't seem to notice.

"The first thing we need is for you to meet Mother." His voice had brightened. "She's dying to see you."

"No, I—"

"We could go right now, if you like. It won't take long."

"No."

"Or this evening."

"N—"

"Tomorrow, then," he snapped, cutting her off. Then he held up his finger, chest high, pointing toward Heaven. "At the latest." He smiled. "I'll call you."

Valerie held perfectly still, afraid to disagree with him, to anger him. Her mouth was so dry she couldn't swallow.

"Okay?" he asked.

She hesitated, then nodded, anything to get him out of here. "Please," she said, trying not to beg. "Just leave now."

"I'm on my way," Leonard said happily. "I'll be in touch."

He gave her a little wave good-bye, then turned and walked through the family room toward the entryway. Valerie held her breath, listening for the front door. She heard instead an engine start in the driveway, gears mesh, a transmission whine.

She hurried to the window and saw Leonard's brown truck back down her driveway toward the distant street.

Quickly, she shut the front door and engaged both locks. She stepped back and stared at the door, as if she doubted its security. Then she rushed to the kitchen, snatched up the phone, and punched in the number for Greg's shop. When she hit the last digit, she remembered that his phone was out of order. She slammed down the receiver.

The doughnut shop, she thought.

She yanked out the phone book and began savagely turning pages, ripping them. Her hands were shaking. Panic had gripped her, and she felt herself losing control.

She balled her hands into fists and squeezed her eyes closed, pressing from each a single warm tear. Her breathing was too quick, too shallow, and she could feel her heart racing in her chest.

Stop it, she told herself. Think. Call the police.

She lifted the receiver, ready to punch 911.

But what could she tell the police? A man had been here, someone she knew. He said he'd called her name before walking in. He'd been polite. No, he hadn't made any threats or sexual advances. He hadn't touched her. *He'd brought candy.* And when she'd asked him to leave, he had.

Her fist went to her mouth. When she pulled it away, there were indentations from her upper incisors, white rimmed in red. A moan rose in her throat.

She grabbed her purse and rushed out the back door.

VALERIE TOOK DODGER WITH HER in the car. Whether it was for his safety or hers, she wasn't sure. She felt weak and frightened, and she hated it. Leonard's casual manner had unnerved her as much as if he'd physically threatened her.

She could predict Greg's reaction when she told him: immediate anger. But perhaps they could level each other out—she'd calm him down and he'd bolster her up. Together they could figure out how best to deal with Leonard.

Valerie didn't know what she expected to see at Greg's shop— perhaps fire trucks blocking the parking lot, the building in smoldering ruins, something. What she didn't expect was normalcy. But there were cars lined up in the lot, people coming and going from the adjoining shops, and not one fireman.

She parked beside Greg's car.

The shop's front door was shut and the "Closed" sign was turned outward. Valerie tried the door, but it was locked. She cupped her hands on the sides of her face and peered through the plate glass window. The interior of the shop was dim, but it appeared no different than before. The counter and copying machine near the front seemed undamaged. Farther back were the familiar outlines of shelves and printing equipment, also apparently unharmed by the fire.

Valerie could see a distant, bright rectangle of light formed by the shop's rear door. As she watched, two figures moved through the opening and one of them closed the door.

She sat in her car and waited.

A short time later a man came out the front entrance carrying a clipboard. Valerie guessed he was the insurance agent. Greg followed him out, closed the door, and locked it. When he saw Valerie, he showed surprise.

"What are you doing here?" he asked, coming toward her car. "I was about to drive to your house."

"I . . ." She shook her head.

"What's wrong? Wait a minute." He went around the car and climbed in the passenger side. Dodger whined with excitement from the backseat. Greg patted his head briefly, staring at Valerie. "You look sick," he said. "Are you all right?"

She shook her head no. "Leonard was just at my house."

"*What!* Did he try to get in?"

"Greg, he *was* in." She told him how she'd found Leonard waiting for her at the kitchen table, politely offering candy. As she spoke she watched Greg's complexion turn white with rage. She'd never seen him like this, and she was afraid of what he might do.

"How did he get in?" His voice was low and strained.

"He . . . said the front door was unlocked."

"Was it?"

"No. I mean, I don't think so. Greg, I don't know. I don't know how else he could've gotten in."

He waved his hand to show that it didn't matter, at least for now. "Did he threaten you in any way? Did he *touch* you?"

She shook her head no. "He was . . . polite."

"Polite. That motherf—. Did you call the police?"

"No I . . . I started to, and then I thought about what I'd have to say. He didn't *do* anything. He—"

"Goddammit, he was in your house!"

She flinched. "Greg . . ."

"I'm sorry," he said, reaching for her hand, then laying his arm on her shoulder, drawing her to him. "I'm sorry, Val." She held him, and he said, "We should go to the police now."

Valerie let Greg drive her car to the Wheat Ridge police building on 29th and Wadsworth. The uniformed officer behind the desk asked Valerie basically the same questions that Greg had: Did Leonard Tully assault you? Did he threaten you? Did he break into your house? Did he refuse to leave the premises when you asked him to?

Valerie had to answer no.

The policeman said there was nothing they could do unless Mr. Tully broke the law. Greg was incensed. He demanded that the police slap Leonard with a restraining order.

"Sir, that is handled through the courts," the policeman said. "Do you know a lawyer?"

"Who doesn't?" Greg said testily.

"Then call him."

There was a bank of pay phones in an alcove at the front of the building. Greg shoved in a quarter, dialed, then was put on hold for a few moments before being connected with Arnold Chesbro. Valerie listened to Greg explain the situation to his attorney and then watched him silently nod his head for what seemed like ten minutes.

Finally, Greg said, "Okay, Arnold, if that's what you think is best. . . . All right, we'll see you tomorrow. Good-bye."

He hung up, looking annoyed.

"What'd he say?"

"We can't do anything until tomorrow at one," he said. "That's the earliest he can see us. We'll have to go to his office and sign affidavits stating our case against Leonard. Arnold will file them with the court along with a motion for a temporary restraining order, which the judge may or may not grant."

"Terrific," she said bitterly.

"Anyway, the judge will set a date for you and me and Leonard to stand before him and state our cases."

"We'll have to appear in court?"

Greg nodded. "Then the judge will make his decision. Arnold said in all likelihood he'll issue a permanent restraining order against Leonard."

"In all likelihood? Then it's possible he won't?"

"It's possible," Greg said.

Valerie heaved a sigh. "So when do we go to court?"

"Arnold said it could take weeks, maybe months, before we actually see a judge."

"Oh, that's just great. And what are we supposed to do in the meantime?"

"We hope the judge issues a temporary restraining order when Arnold files our case. At least that will keep Leonard away from you until the court date. Oh yes, and he strongly advised us—me, actually—to stay away from Leonard, not to talk to him, certainly not to threaten him."

Valerie shook her head slowly. "I didn't think it would be this complicated."

"Me either."

"We don't have any alternatives, though, do we?"

Greg pressed his lips together. "There are always alternatives," he said. He withdrew a slip of paper from his wallet.

"What's that?"

"Leonard's phone number." He opened the phone book. "Maybe we can find his address."

"Didn't Arnold say we should stay away from him?"

Greg flipped pages without answering. Then he stopped and ran his finger down a column. He compared a number with the one on the slip of paper.

"Here it is," he said, "listed under Francine Tully."

"Probably his mother. But didn't Arnold say—"

"Do you have a pen? Write this down." He read her an address on South Broadway, then said, "Let's go."

"Greg, do you think we should?"

"We're just going to drive by, Val."

"But why?"

"Hey, the bastard knows where you live. Let's find out where *he* lives."

She gave him a wry smile and shook her head. "Oh, that makes perfect sense."

Dodger was excited by their return to the car. Valerie wished now—for his sake—that she'd left him in the cool shade of their backyard.

Greg drove south to Sixth Avenue, then east to Broadway and turned right. As they traveled southward the wide boulevard changed from one-way to two-way traffic, and the store fronts became smaller and spaced farther apart. They found the address in a neighborhood of antique stores and thrift shops. It was on the east side of the street, so Greg drove around the block and stopped directly in front, letting the engine idle.

The middle window of the converted bungalow had a hand-lettered sign: This 'N' That.

"Cute," Greg said.

The tiny front yard had been made into a courtyard, paved with flagstones and surrounded by a low wrought-iron fence. Here and there grass pushed up between the stones. All of it lay in the shade of a huge elm that stood to the left of the original concrete walk.

Valerie stared uneasily at the front windows. There were knick-knacks on the inside ledges and colored ornaments dangling behind the glass. She had the feeling someone was in there, watching them.

"Let's get out of here," she said.

Greg shut off the engine.

"What are you doing?"

"This won't take long," he told her and climbed out of the car.

"Greg, don't."

He walked around the front of the car, passed through the opening in the iron fence, and made it all the way up the walk to the front door before Valerie caught him by the arm.

"Greg, please."

"I'm just going to talk to him."

"But your lawyer said—"

"The hell with my lawyer," he said and pushed into the shop.

Valerie hesitated, then followed.

Greg stopped just inside the door, and Valerie stood beside him, surveying the dimly lit interior. One word came to her mind: cluttered. The room was jammed with tables and shelves, all of their available surfaces occupied by secondhand housewares, decorative items, and utensils.

"Jesus," Greg said softly, shaking his head.

"May I help you?"

They were both startled by the disembodied voice. A moment later they saw the head of a woman moving behind a table crowded with lamps. She maneuvered her wheelchair around the table, coming into full view.

She was middle-aged and wore a simple green dress with a white collar. Her graying hair was straight and fell past her shoulders. Valerie saw a slight resemblance to Leonard, mostly in the narrow nose and thin-lipped, smiling mouth. The woman wheeled her chair to within a few feet, looking up at them unabashedly.

"May I help you find something?"

"Ah, no, we—"

"Is Leonard Tully here?" Greg asked, his voice sounding too loud in the small shop.

"Leonard?" She looked from one to the other. Valerie noticed that although her smile had remained in place, her eyes had narrowed. "He's out back doing a chore for me. Is there something *I* can help you with? I'm his mother, Francine."

"We need to speak to him," Greg said.

"About a purchase?"

"Not really."

"What, then?"

"It's personal," Greg said.

"Well." Francine was obviously put out. "If you'll be so *kind* as to wait a minute, I'll go get him."

She turned her chair with a jerking motion, then wheeled it toward the rear of the shop.

C h a p t e r

23

As soon as Francine Tully was out of sight, Valerie pulled on Greg's sleeve.

"Come on," she said, her voice a loud whisper, filled with apprehension, "let's get out of here before something happens."

"Nothing's going to happen," Greg said evenly, not budging.

"We shouldn't even be here. You promised we were just going to drive by."

"We *are* here," he said, as if that explained it.

Valerie shook her head. "You know, Greg, sometimes you really piss me off."

He looked at her, surprised. A smile touched his lips and then was gone.

"I'm not kidding," she said. But she could feel her brief anger dissipating.

"I know," he said. He gave her hand a squeeze. "And I'm sorry. But this is something I have to do."

They heard movement, turned, and there was Leonard coming through the rear doorway.

When he saw them, he halted. Then he came forward tentatively, stopping a full ten feet away. Valerie could see Francine's profile in the distant doorway. Her chair was skewed to the side, as if she were occupied with something in the other room. Her ear was turned toward them.

Leonard's glance slid off Greg and rested on Valerie.

"Hello," he said to her quietly, shyly.

She wanted to be anywhere but here. She nodded hello and looked away.

"You need to get something straight," Greg said without preamble, his tone of voice hard. "Valerie doesn't want you bothering her, and neither do I."

"Bothering?" Leonard's eyebrows went up. He continued to stare at Valerie.

"That's *right,*" Greg said forcefully. "Calling her on the phone, going to her house. We want you to stop. *I* want you to stop."

"You?" Leonard slowly raised his eyes to Greg and looked at him with disdain. "You can't tell me what to do."

"Listen, you son of—"

"Greg," Valerie cautioned, grabbing his arm as he stepped forward, pulling him back.

Greg made a fist and pointed his index finger at Leonard.

"You stay the hell away from her," he said, seething. "I mean it."

Leonard's face was flushed, whether from embarrassment or anger Valerie couldn't tell. He gave her a puzzled look and said, "Valerie?"

Greg started to say something else, and she stepped in front of him, coming closer to Leonard.

"Leonard, this whole thing has just gotten out of hand." Her voice sounded distant, not her own. "I mean, I'm grateful for what you did, getting my purse back and all, and I appreciate the flowers and the candy . . . but that's the end of it. You're a nice man, and I'm sure there are plenty of girls who'd love to have your attentions. But you see, Greg and I, well, we're together. And you and I . . . there's nothing there, Leonard, there can't be. So let's just leave it at that. I mean, I'm glad we met, but now it's time to say good-bye." She felt foolish, as if she were a child reciting a speech. Now she forced herself to hold Leonard's gaze. "Do you understand?"

Leonard looked hurt. "Yes. Perfectly."

Valerie's shoulders drooped, her tension melting.

"Good-bye, then."

She turned to leave, taking Greg's arm firmly, letting him know that she didn't want him to say another word until they were outside. They'd taken two steps toward the door when Leonard said, "Wait."

They stopped and faced him.

"Please," he said gently, "could I ask you a favor?"

"No, you—"

Valerie nudged Greg with her elbow. "What is it?" she asked.

"Could I . . . would you let me introduce you to my mother?"

"What?"

"I've told her about you, and she'd really like to meet you. Please."

His arms were at his sides, his palms turned forward, pleading. "It will only take a moment."

Valerie sighed. Anything to put an end to this madness. "Okay, but then we—"

"Good." Leonard hurried away from them.

"What the hell is going *on?*" Greg wanted to know.

"I don't know. Let's just humor him, and then we'll be out of here."

"Jesus."

Leonard returned, pushing Francine before him. They were both smiling broadly.

"Mother, I'd like you to meet Valerie Rowe."

"How do you do," Francine said brightly, acting as if this were the first time she'd ever laid eyes on Valerie.

Valerie shook her hand, felt the strong grip.

"Leonard's told me so much about you," Francine said.

"He has?"

"Yes. And I must say, you're even prettier than he described."

"Mother." Leonard was embarrassed.

Greg sighed in disgust.

"And you are?" Francine looked up at Greg, her smile hardening.

"Greg Barryman," he said flatly. "Pleased to meet you."

Francine nodded, not offering her hand. She said to Valerie, "I understand that you're an artist."

"Yes."

"What brings you to our little shop?"

"Well . . ."

"We were just passing by," Greg said. "And now we really must be going. Right, Valerie?"

"Ah, yes, it was nice meeting you."

"Can't you stay awhile?" Francine said. "I have lemonade."

"Thank you, no."

"Next time, then."

Valerie nodded. "Good-bye." She took Greg's arm.

"Good-bye, Valerie," Leonard said to her back.

Leonard and Francine watched them move down the walk, climb into their car, and drive away.

"She seems very nice," Francine said.

"Yes, she is." Leonard managed to speak calmly, although he was shaking with rage at Greg Barryman. The man had threatened him in his own home, dragging Valerie here to witness it, putting her up to that pathetic little speech about how she appreciated the flowers but now it's time to say good-bye.

I'll decide when it's time, Leonard thought.

But he couldn't help feeling a hint of resentment toward Valerie. She'd acted as if she were on Greg's side. Of course, he'd probably forced her to behave that way. At least she'd treated his mother with kindness. Still, she could've had a little more regard for *his* feelings.

"Why don't you ask her here for dinner?" Francine said. "Sometime soon."

"I will." But he could see now that it would take time and effort to free her from Greg.

"How about tomorrow?" his mother asked.

"I . . . don't know."

"Why not?"

"It's just that . . . she's busy with her painting and—"

"She has to eat, doesn't she?"

"Mother, what I mean is she may not be able to come here soon, that's all."

"Well, when she does come, just make sure she comes alone. Not with that Greg fellow."

"Okay."

"Who *is* he, anyway?"

"He's . . . her cousin."

"Well, I can't say that I like him very much."

"Neither do I," Leonard said.

Francine paused. "I couldn't help overhearing when you were talking to them alone. He sounded angry."

"Angry?"

"Yes. I couldn't hear exactly what he was telling you, but I could see that he was upset."

"Oh, that. His print shop burned down."

"Oh my. Well, no wonder he was upset."

Greg drove north on Broadway.

"Jesus, the old lady is as weird as he is."

Valerie sat sideways, facing Greg, her left hand over the rear of the seat, scratching Dodger's ears.

"We shouldn't have gone there," she said.

"Why not? All in all, I think it went well."

Valerie shook her head. She patted Dodger's head one last time, then turned forward, staring through the windshield.

"What about the restraining order?" she said.

"What about it?"

"Do we still need it?"

"Yes."

"Don't you think Leonard got the message?"

"I do, but let's make sure. I don't want to have to screw around with him again."

Valerie agreed reluctantly. She did not relish the thought of standing before a judge and explaining how the nice young man's attentions were giving her the creeps. Remembering Leonard's last visit made her think of Brenda—she'd been ready to go to the hospital when he'd showed up.

Now she asked to go there.

Greg parked in the street a block from the hospital—in the shade in deference to Dodger.

"We'll be back soon, boy," he said.

They returned sooner than they had expected, after the doctor in intensive care sadly explained that Brenda Newcomb had passed away the previous day. Valerie was devastated. She sat in the car and cried. Greg held her, trying to comfort her.

"If there's a Heaven," he said quietly, "she's there now."

Valerie desperately wanted to believe that. Although she'd never considered herself a religious person and she rarely gave thought to an afterlife, now she wanted to believe. She wanted to think of Brenda as still in existence . . . somewhere.

She wiped away her tears. "Let's just go," she said sadly.

They picked up Matthew at the day-care center and drove to the print shop. Greg followed them home in his car. The phone was ringing as they walked in the back door. Valerie answered.

"Hello, Valerie? This is Sharon from the gallery. I've called you several times since yesterday. . . ."

"I've been in and out of the house," Valerie said.

"I don't know if you've heard about Brenda. . . ."

"Yes," Valerie said, feeling her eyes burn again with tears. "We've just come from the hospital."

"It's . . . it's so terrible."

"I know."

"Although it may be better this way," Sharon said. "Her doctor told me they were certain there'd been brain damage, so even if she'd regained consciousness . . ." Her voice was cut off by a sob. After a moment she said, "I'm . . . I'm sorry."

"Sharon, is there anything I can do?"

"No, but thanks. I called to let you know that Brenda's brother has made arrangements for a memorial service Friday." She told Valerie the time and place. "Brenda wished to be cremated, so there will be no burial. As to the gallery, well, I believe her brother will inherit it. If so, there's some question whether he'll keep it or sell it. For now we're temporarily closed. I can't run things by myself. And your paintings . . . I mean, if you want to take them out, we'd understand and—"

"Just keep them for now," Valerie said.

"I was hoping you'd say that. If we open again soon, it would be much easier with your works still hanging."

They exchanged condolences and good-byes. Valerie hung up, and the phone immediately rang.

"Hello?" She thought it might be Sharon calling back.

"Hi, Valerie, it's me."

A shock went through her.

"I'm so glad you stopped by to meet my mother," Leonard said. "She—"

"What are you *doing?*" Valerie said, her voice shrill. "Why are you calling here?"

"What's wrong?" Greg stood in the kitchen doorway.

"Just leave me alone!" Valerie shouted and slammed down the receiver. She held it down and pressed her forehead to the back of her hand, squeezing her eyes shut.

"Valerie, what is it?"

The phone rang again, and Valerie moaned.

"Is that *him?*" Greg was incredulous. He moved to her side and pried the receiver from her hand.

"Hello," he said angrily. He paused, listening to silence. "If that's you, Leonard, goddammit, I'll—" The dial tone cut him off. He hung up and muttered, "Fucking bastard."

"Greg, what are we going to do?" Valerie touched his arm. It was rigid.

"I'll kill that son of a bitch," he said tightly.

His words frightened her, even though he didn't mean them. She was certain of that. Completely certain.

VALERIE WAS IN NO MOOD TO COOK, and neither of them felt like going out to eat, so Greg fixed a pasta salad and warm garlic bread. The activities in the kitchen seemed to help Greg calm down from Leonard's phone call. Valerie, though, remained tense.

They sat on the patio in the cool shade that preceded dusk. The air smelled faintly of roses and sage.

Valerie picked at her food, her stomach as tight as a fist. She struggled with her emotions—anxiety at Greg's reaction to Leonard's call, sadness and pain over the loss of Brenda, anger and fear toward Leonard's persistence. And she began to wonder if Leonard had been responsible for Brenda's death and for the fire at Greg's shop.

The possibility filled her with horror. If Leonard *had* done those things, what might he do next?

"I'm done, Mom."

Valerie smiled faintly at her son. "Okay, hon."

Matthew climbed down from his chair. "Hey, Greg, do you wanna throw the Frisbee?"

"When we're finished eating." He glanced at Valerie's plate. It had barely been touched.

"Go ahead," she said.

Greg reached for her hand. "Are you okay?"

"Fine." She managed a smile.

"I'll help you with the dishes."

"No, you cooked, I'll wash. Go on."

Later, they played Monopoly on the floor in the family room. Valerie's mind was not on the game, but by Matthew's bedtime she controlled nearly half the board, including all four railroads and the high-rent properties.

"Can't we play a little longer?" Matthew pleaded.

"I think your mom's the winner," Greg said. "We'd better quit while we've still got our self-respect."

Matthew gave Greg a puzzled look. "What does that mean?"

"It means you're off to bed," Valerie said, tousling his hair.

After she'd tucked Matthew under the covers and kissed him good-night, she found Greg sorting out the last of the property cards and the play money.

"Would you like a glass of wine?" she said.

"Sounds good."

She poured two glasses from the jug in the refrigerator. They sat on the couch in the living room, her head on his shoulder, while the stereo played Mozart. She tried to focus on the good things in her life: she was with the man she loved; her son, sleeping peacefully a few rooms away, was healthy and bright; her career as an artist was flourishing.

But she was apprehensive, fearful of an outside force, something beyond her control. It was as if her life were a well-conceived, intricate image in stained glass—and someone was hiding nearby, brick in hand.

Later, in bed, they made love. It was soft and gentle and quiet, and when it was over Valerie clung to Greg, falling asleep in his arms.

Leonard dressed quietly in the dark, then sat on the edge of the bed and tied his shoelaces. He moved from his room like a shadow, crossed the hallway, and stood in his mother's doorway. After a moment he could hear her snoring.

He walked silently down the hall to the back door, then eased it open, making no sound. Outside, the midnight air felt cool on his face. The small paved backyard was bathed in yellow by the arc light half-way down the alley. His truck lay in the shadow cast by the neighbor's fence.

Leonard shifted into neutral, released the hand brake, and let the truck roll into the gentle slope of the alley. He coasted nearly to the street before he started the engine.

He switched on the lights and drove to Valerie's house.

He'd been fuming all afternoon, ever since her visit. Oh, he'd been pleased that she'd come by to meet his mother—but bringing Greg with her, that had been uncalled for.

He'd had a difficult time hiding his anger from his mother, and it wasn't until dinnertime that he'd finally calmed down. He'd replayed the little scene in the shop at least a dozen times, listening to Greg's words, listening to Valerie, watching their faces in his mind, highlighting an expression, shifting an inflection, until finally he'd gotten it right: Valerie appreciated what he was doing—giving her flowers and candy, courting her; Greg alone wanted him to stop. Valerie was afraid of Greg, afraid to speak her mind in front of him.

That's why Leonard had phoned her this afternoon. But inexplicably, she'd hung up on him. When he'd called back, though, he understood why—Greg had been there, interfering as usual. Well, he certainly wouldn't be there now, not this late.

All I need, Leonard thought, is a face-to-face talk with her. A long one this time. Alone. With no interruptions.

Twenty minutes later he slowed the truck, then turned off 32nd Avenue into Valerie's driveway. He stopped a short way in, killing the lights and the engine.

He climbed out and stood in the gravel drive. The night was quiet and dark. A car went by on the street behind him and quickly faded into silence. The house was nearly hidden from him by the trees. Leonard could see the distant garage and a car parked before it. He wondered briefly why Valerie would leave her car outside at night.

He walked toward the house, staying on the grass beside the driveway to muffle his footsteps.

He stopped at the corner of the house and stared at the car. It wasn't Valerie's. He knew her car—she'd driven off in it the first day they'd met. And he'd seen it through the garage window earlier today, just before he'd broken into the house to deliver the candy.

This car looked familiar, though. And then he realized it was Greg's. He'd seen it on the night of the gallery reception, when he'd stood in the shadows and watched them leave together.

Leonard glared at the dark house and thought, He's in there now, in bed with her.

Blood roared in his head, and his stomach burned as if he'd swallowed battery acid. He strode back to his truck and reached into the bed.

The crowbar felt cold and heavy.

He saw clearly what he would do next: pry open the front door, walk directly to Valerie's bedroom, and switch on the light. He'd take a moment to relish the looks on their faces. Then he'd order Greg out of the house—and if he resisted, well, there was always the crowbar.

Leonard walked back toward the house. The night air chilled his forehead, and he realized he was perspiring.

He wondered how Valerie would react when he threw Greg out. Would she be grateful? Or would she feel sorry for Greg?

Leonard stood at the front door, the crowbar hanging loosely at his side. He began to wonder if Valerie might resent him for breaking in. It was possible. He stood there for a long time, thinking it over. Finally, reluctantly, he muttered under his breath and turned his back on the house.

Then he paused, glaring at Greg's car.

I ought to smash out his windows, he thought. Or slash his tires. Or . . .

He frowned, thinking. Then he walked quickly and quietly to his truck. He laid the crowbar in the bed and got his knife from the glove compartment.

He clicked open the blade and went to Greg's car.

Leonard lay on his back beside the car, his head toward the rear, and wriggled his way underneath. The gravel bit into his shoulders and buttocks. He knew what to look for, that is, what to *feel* for, since it was pitch dark under the car. His hand moved like a pale spider over the inside of the left rear wheel until it rested on a narrow, tough, flexible hose. He cut partway through the hose. A few drops of brake fluid fell on his hand.

He knew that the next time Greg used the brakes some of the fluid would be forced through the cut. And the next time. And then again, until the fluid was gone. Or until there wasn't enough left to matter. Leonard could only pray that when the brake pedal went down for the last time, it would happen at an opportune moment.

He crawled out from under the car and moved quietly to his truck, then wiped his hands with a rag and brushed off his clothes. He drove home. He hoped his mother was still asleep.

In the morning, Valerie sliced strawberries, poured cereal and milk, and made toast and coffee, while Greg called his insurance agent, who said he was still waiting to hear from the arson investigators. Then he phoned a service representative, requesting an inspection of the printing equipment that morning. Lastly, he called the telephone company about restoring service to his business line.

Valerie was pleased to see how Greg's mood had changed since the previous morning, from depression to practicality.

"A phone repairman will meet me at the shop in an hour," Greg said, sitting, sipping his coffee. "Once the line is fixed, I'll have Janice come in and help me contact our regular customers. We'll have to explain the situation and hope that most of them will stick with us.

Also, I need to get a few contractors there for repair estimates. Then," he said, reaching for her hand, "I'll take you to an early lunch. How does that sound?"

"Great."

"Because at one o'clock, we go see Arnold."

Valerie nodded. She was apprehensive about starting legal action against Leonard. She'd never dreamed things would go this far. Greg must have seen something in her face, because he put his hand on hers.

"It'll be all right," he said, giving her a smile.

"I know."

"Where would you like to have lunch?"

"I don't care."

"Simms Landing?"

"That would be nice."

"What about me?" Matthew asked.

"What *about* you?" Valerie smiled and gave him a gentle poke in the ribs.

"Hey!"

"What are you and the other kids going to do today?"

Matthew shrugged. "Same old junk. Swimming or T-ball and probably lunch at some park and then we'll have to read or something and then probably some other game." He shrugged again.

"Boy, sounds like a rough day," Greg said.

"I'd rather be with *you* guys."

"I know, hon," Valerie said. "But this weekend we'll do something fun together, okay?"

Matthew brightened. "Really? Like what?"

"Well . . ."

"How about a trip to the mountains?" Greg offered. "Say, Glenwood Springs."

"Hey, neat."

"We could drive up Saturday, maybe ride horses and—"

"Cool!"

"—and spend the night up there."

"I like 'driving up and spending the night'—but horses?"

"Come on, Mom."

"Yeah, Mom," Greg said with a grin. "Come on."

She sighed, smiling. "Outvoted again."

"All *right!*"

Later, after Greg had left with Matthew, and Valerie had washed the breakfast dishes and walked Dodger, she climbed the stairs to her studio. At first she struggled with the painting, but soon she became immersed in it. By ten-thirty, when the ringing phone called her downstairs, she'd completed the beads and feathers of the dancer's costume.

"How's it going?" Greg asked.

"I was about to ask you the same thing."

"Better than expected. The service man says the printing equipment just needs to be disassembled, cleaned, oiled, and put back together. He can do it all right here. Probably take him two days, tops."

"Hey, that's great news."

"The only problem is he wants to wait until the contractor is finished ripping up the carpet and putting in new dry wall and painting and whatever else needs to be done, and that could take some time. I'm trying to change his mind right now."

"Does that mean our lunch date is off?"

"Hell no," he said happily. "I just need to go home and change clothes. Everything here still smells like smoke."

"You're calling from the shop?"

"Oh yeah, I forgot to tell you, the phones are fixed. Anyway, I'll pick you up in an hour."

"I'll be ready."

She went upstairs to clean her brushes and stopped just inside the doorway, letting her eyes take in the entire painting. It was nearly completed. The only things left to do were some details in the dancer's headdress and a few highlights here and there.

Her face broke into a wide smile, and she realized that she felt better than she had in days. She might even finish the painting this afternoon, depending on how long she and Greg took for lunch. Or tomorrow morning at the latest. Either way, ahead of schedule.

She hummed to herself and cleaned her brushes, happy that Greg would be there soon.

25

AT NOON VALERIE PHONED GREG at home.

It was not like him to be late, and he was half an hour overdue. She told herself she wasn't worried so much as curious about what was keeping him. She let the phone ring a dozen times before she hung up and called the shop. Janice told her that Greg wasn't there. "He left at eleven. I thought he was meeting you for lunch."

"So did I," Valerie said, forcing a small laugh. "I guess he got sidetracked en route."

"Well, if he shows up here first, I'll tell him you called."

"Thanks."

Valerie phoned Greg's apartment at twelve-fifteen and again at twelve-thirty. No answer. She called the shop.

"He hasn't been in." Janice sounded concerned. "Do you think something's happened?"

"No," Valerie said abruptly, squeezing the receiver. "I'm sure everything's all right. He may have been delayed at his apartment and the phone isn't working or . . . I don't know. Have him call me the minute he comes in, though, will you?"

She phoned Greg's apartment every ten minutes for the next half hour. A cold lump of fear began to form in her chest. She told herself that everything was all right, that Greg simply had been delayed. But in her heart she knew that something was terribly wrong. Had Leonard . . . ?

At 1:05 she called Greg's attorney.

"No, Greg isn't here," he said. "I've been expecting you both. Is there a problem?"

"I . . . don't know. I'm trying to find him."

"Perhaps he's on his way here."

"No. He was supposed to pick me up."

"Well, if he takes much longer . . . the trouble is, my schedule is filled until early next week. I may not be able to see you until then."

Valerie hung up and phoned the shop again. Greg had not returned. She told Janice that she was going to his apartment.

Before she left the house, she wrote Greg a note asking him to phone the shop, then wait for her return, in case—she hoped—he arrived while she was gone.

As she drove to his apartment building she pictured Greg lying on his living room floor, not moving. . . .

She parked on the street and hurried up the walk. Standing impatiently in the small vestibule, she lifted the receiver, jammed her thumb on the button beside Greg's name, and waited for him to answer, dreadfully certain that he wouldn't. She tried the button a few more times, and then she pushed the one beside "Manager—A. Schroeder."

"Yes?" A man's voice.

"Mr. Schroeder, this is Valerie Rowe." She'd met him only once, several months ago. "I'm a friend of Greg Barryman."

"Yes?"

"Could you come to the front, please. I'm . . . I'm afraid something may have happened to Greg."

He paused and then said, "Just a moment."

Through the interior glass door Valerie saw a man step into the hallway and approach her. He was in his mid-fifties, tall, thin, and pale, wearing a yellow sport shirt, gray slacks, and white jogging shoes. A pair of half-glasses perched on the end of his nose. He pulled open the door and peered at Valerie over the tops of his glasses.

"What's this about Greg?" His voice was a mixture of concern and suspicion.

"He was supposed to pick me up nearly two hours ago," Valerie said. "It's possible that he's in his apartment and unable to use the phone."

Schroeder hesitated, then nodded and held the door for her. "Let's go up there," he said.

They rode the elevator to the fourth floor and walked along a carpeted hallway to 484. Schroeder knocked several times before he used his master key to open the door. He preceded Valerie through the doorway, calling Greg's name.

Valerie walked past him to the bedroom, then the bathroom and the den. She pulled open the sliding glass door and looked out on the balcony.

"He's not here," Schroeder said, stating the obvious.

Valerie used the phone to call her house, praying that Greg would answer. She got the next best thing: a busy signal. She hung up and smiled at Schroeder.

"It's busy. He must be there." She kept her hand on the receiver, intending to wait a few minutes and call back. Impatient, though, she dialed the shop. Janice answered.

"Thank God you called," Janice said, and Valerie's heart sank. "I've been trying to reach you. In fact, I just got through phoning your house." She hesitated. "Greg's been in a traffic accident."

God, *no*, Valerie thought. "What happened? How bad was it?"

"I don't know for sure," Janice said, "but they took him to Lutheran in an ambulance. The hospital called a little while ago."

Valerie felt numb, as if she, too, had been in an accident. "Did they tell you if he was seriously hurt?"

"Not over the phone."

Valerie fought despair. Maybe it's not as bad as it sounds, she told herself. "I'm going there now. I'll call you after I've seen him."

Half an hour later, Valerie still had not seen Greg. She'd made it to the hospital in less than ten minutes and learned that he was in the postoperative room. Since then she'd made several trips from the waiting area to the nursing station, and each time she'd been told that Dr. Halverson, the doctor who'd operated on Greg, would be out shortly to talk to her.

Finally she was approached by a man in green surgical attire and black athletic shoes. From a distance he looked very young, too young to be a surgeon.

"Are you the woman who's been asking about Mr. Barryman?"

"Yes."

"I'm Dr. Halverson," he said, extending his hand. Now that he stood close to Valerie, she could see that he was at least her age. His handshake was warm.

"Doctor, is he . . . going to be all right?"

"He's sustained severe injuries," he said, "but I'm confident he'll recover. It may take time, though."

He went on to describe Greg's condition in detail—head trauma, broken left arm and left leg, cracked ribs. . . . Valerie felt the strength drain from her body.

"He was unconscious when he was brought in," Halverson said. "He may come to when the anesthetic wears off."

"He *may?*"

"We're hopeful that he will."

Valerie slumped in a chair.

"We're doing everything we can for him," Halverson said.

"Can I see him?"

"Not yet. Perhaps this evening. Although tomorrow would be better."

She nodded dumbly. "Can you tell me about his accident?"

"Apparently he ran a red light on Wadsworth, and his car was hit broadside by a moving van. The driver of the truck was injured too, though not seriously—a broken wrist and head lacerations." Halverson checked his watch. "I'm afraid I have to go."

Valerie stood and shook his hand. "I appreciate your time, Doctor. And, well, thanks for all you've done."

He nodded and left her standing alone.

Valerie walked numbly to the drinking fountain. Her lips felt parched, and the water was so cold it hurt. She took small swallows, trying to soothe her queasy stomach. Then she found her way downstairs and outside into the harsh sunlight.

She experienced a moment of déjà vu—and then she understood why. Last Saturday after she'd first visited Brenda in the hospital the sun had seemed too bright. And a few days later Brenda had died.

"No," Valerie said aloud, causing an elderly couple passing by to turn and stare.

Valerie walked stiffly to the parking lot. She'd forgotten where she'd parked, and now she wandered up and down the aisles, searching, feeling frustration and anger build within her until she was ready to either scream or smash her fist into the nearest windshield.

At last she found her car and drove home, her vision blurred by tears.

She let Dodger in the back door. He was excited to see her and he wanted to play, but he seemed to sense her mood and quickly calmed down. He followed her to the living room and lay at her feet. Valerie sat and stared out the window, feeling helpless, powerless. She knew she had to do something, anything, before she sank too far into depression.

She checked her watch. Too early to pick up Matthew. Too early to visit the hospital again. Maybe she should have stayed. No, what good would it have done? She'd go back later. For now, perhaps she could mark time by working on the painting, maybe even finish it. Although she doubted that she could concentrate, thinking about Greg.

She rose stiffly, walked to the kitchen, and phoned Janice, telling her what she knew of Greg's condition.

"I'm going back this evening. Maybe they'll let me see him."

"Will you keep us informed?" Janice asked.

"Yes, of course."

"Good. And, Valerie."

"Yes?"

"I know he's going to be all right."

"Yes," Valerie said. Although she couldn't help thinking that she'd felt the same way about Brenda. "I'll talk to you later," she said and hung up.

Later, she picked up Matthew at day care. She explained as gently as she could what had happened to Greg, then drove to the hospital.

The doctor had placed Greg in intensive care, where he lay unconscious. Children weren't allowed to visit, which was all right with Valerie—she was afraid of how Greg might appear to Matthew. She left her son in the waiting room, then went to see Greg. He looked worse than she'd imagined. His left leg was raised in traction and his lower left arm was encased in plaster. Both eyes were blackened and his face was swollen and pale. His forehead was swathed in bandages. An IV needle was stuck in his right arm and taped there, oxygen tubes trailed from his nostrils, and wires ran from his head and chest to a monitor over the bed.

He was so still and colorless that for a brief, terrifying moment Valerie thought he was dead. Then she saw the moving lines on the monitor, the slight rise and fall of his chest. She stood beside the bed and touched his hand. It was cold.

"You're going to be okay," she said softly, feeling tears track down her cheeks. "You're going to be okay."

When she finally walked out to find Matthew, her legs and back were stiff from standing.

"Can I see Greg?" he asked, eyes wide.

"No, honey, not now."

"Why not?"

"He's sleeping and he needs his rest. We'll come back tomorrow, okay?"

When they got home Valerie fixed toasted-cheese sandwiches for dinner. She was ravenous, and realized that she hadn't eaten since morning. While she was washing the dishes, the phone rang. She prayed that it wasn't the hospital calling. There would be no reason, unless something bad . . . She pushed the thought from her mind, dried her hands on a dish towel, and lifted the receiver.

"Hello?" Her voice was tentative.

"Hi, it's me."

Leonard.

Valerie hung up at once. A few moments later it rang again. She backed away, then sat at the table, her eyes never leaving the jangling plastic box. Matthew came in from the backyard. He looked from the ringing telephone to his mother.

"What's the matter, Mom?"

"Nothing, honey," she said dully. "Why don't you go back outside and play with Dodger."

The phone continued to ring.

"Do you want me to answer it?"

"No!"

Matthew stepped back as if he'd been slapped. Valerie rose and went to him.

"I'm sorry," she said and gave him a hug. "I'll answer the phone. You just go back outside, okay?"

"Okay," he said uncertainly. He watched her over his shoulder as he went out the door.

The phone was still ringing.

Valerie gritted her teeth, then lifted the receiver.

"Hello, Valerie?"

She spoke with controlled fury: "What do you want?"

"I phoned Greg's shop to see how the repairs were going, and I heard about his accident." Leonard's tone was conversational. "What a shame."

"Just leave us *alone*."

"We never seem to get anything settled over the phone," he said seriously. "We need to spend some time together, especially now that Greg's out of the picture."

"Just leave me the fuck alone!" she yelled.

"And your language. That's something else we'll need to discuss."

Valerie slammed down the receiver. She waited a few seconds, then lifted it quickly to her ear. When she heard a dial tone, she stretched the cord across the counter top, opened a drawer, and jammed the receiver between long boxes of aluminum foil and plastic wrap.

She brought Matthew and Dodger inside, locked both doors, and secured all the windows.

Later, before she went to bed, she rechecked the locks.

26

ON FRIDAY MORNING Leonard awoke with a plan.

He'd lain awake most of the night, staring at the dark ceiling, trying to figure how to take advantage of his present good fortune—namely, having Greg out of the way. He couldn't have hoped for better results from cutting the brake line. And he knew that now was his best chance to be alone with Valerie. He wanted to make the most of it.

But even with Greg gone there were problems. Valerie's cooperation, for one. She might resist him. And there was no telling how long Greg would be hospitalized. With any luck, for a long time. And really, all he needed was a day or two alone with Valerie. He'd prove to her that his intentions were honorable. He'd treat her special and show her how good he could be for her.

Of course, there was the problem of Valerie's son. True, he was only a minor inconvenience. But he had to be dealt with. On the other hand, if handled properly, the boy could be an asset.

The biggest problem, though, was closer to home. *At* home, in fact. His mother.

Leonard knew what to do with Valerie and the boy, but his mother was something else. Oh, eventually he'd tell her what he'd done—that is, what he was about to do. She'd be angry with him, angry for doing it and angry for lying to her about it. But he knew she'd get over it, especially when she saw the splendid result.

So at the breakfast table he told her about his dream—the one he'd invented last night.

"The cabin was struck by lightning," he said, sipping his juice, trying to look worried.

"Hm." Francine opened the newspaper on the table, turned to the back, then began to slowly run her finger down a column of classified ads.

"It was so real," Leonard said, "I could hear the thunderbolt and feel the heat of the flash."

"It was only a dream, Leonard." She circled an ad with her pencil.

"The roof caught fire and—"

"It was only a dream," she said pointedly, looking up at him for the first time.

"Sometimes dreams come true."

"Yes, well." She returned to her advertisements.

"Sometimes they're a sign, a revelation. Sometimes . . . God talks to you in your dreams. You've said so yourself."

Slowly Francine raised her eyes to him.

"What are you trying to say?" she asked.

"I think the dream was a message. I think something has happened to the cabin."

Francine continued to stare at him, her lips pursed.

"I think . . . I should go up there and have a look. Today. This morning."

"I need you here, Leonard."

"But we can't neglect the cabin."

"Weren't you just at the cabin last Saturday?"

"Yes."

"And wasn't everything all right?"

"Yes, but—"

"Well, then."

"The dream, Mother."

She held his gaze, as if testing his resolve. Then she blinked and looked away, mumbling something.

"Excuse me?"

"Nothing," she said, then, "Have you ever had a dream like this before?"

"Never." His voice was firm.

She sighed.

"If everything's all right up there, I can be back before noon."

She said nothing.

"Of course, if there *is* damage, I'll have to stay and fix as much as I can before it gets dark."

Francine made a face as if she'd just swallowed foul-tasting medicine. "Yes, well, all right."

*   *   *

After breakfast Valerie phoned the day-care center and told Mr. Dawkins that she was keeping Matthew home today. Leonard's call last night had upset her terribly, and she couldn't stand the thought of being home alone.

More than ever she wanted a restraining order against Leonard. She phoned Greg's attorney. She was told that he'd be out of his office all day, so she set up an appointment for the earliest available time, Tuesday morning at ten. Valerie hated having to wait until then, but there was no choice.

She and Matthew walked Dodger and fed him, then they changed clothes and drove to the hospital.

Greg had been drifting in and out of consciousness. Although he looked much the same as he had yesterday—traction, casts, bandages, IV tubes—Valerie could see signs of improvement. The swelling in his face had gone down, and his color had begun to return. Also, his eyes appeared less blackened than before. His chest rose and fell more strongly.

Or maybe she was simply forcing herself to see what she wanted to see.

She stood beside his bed for a long time, holding his limp hand. Then she choked back a sob and went out to the waiting room.

"Can I see Greg now?" Matthew wanted to know.

"I don't know, honey. He's still sleeping."

"Still?"

"Yes." Even if the hospital allowed it, she wasn't sure she'd take Matthew into intensive care. How would he react to seeing Greg bandaged and swollen, encased in plaster and attached to tubes? What nightmares might that sight bring?

"Can't I just peek in?" Matthew asked.

"Not now," she said quietly. "Maybe when he's feeling better."

"When will he?"

"I don't know, honey. Soon, I hope." She put her hand on his shoulder. "Let's go home."

The moment Valerie unlocked the front door she remembered that Brenda's memorial service was today. She checked her watch. The services started in thirty minutes. She phoned Sue Lawson, the mother of Matthew's friend Jerry, and asked her if she'd watch Matthew for an hour or so.

"He can stay all day, if he likes," Sue said. "Jerry's sitting around the house bored to death."

Valerie told Matthew that he was going to stay at Jerry's house while she . . . visited a friend. She didn't want to explain about the memorial service, about Brenda dying—not so soon after seeing Greg in the hospital.

The service was held near downtown Denver in a Protestant church, an old gray stone building with tall, narrow, stained-glass windows and a steeple topped with a cross.

Fifty or so mourners were clumped together in the first few pews on either side of the central aisle. Valerie found a place to herself in the middle of the nave. She saw a few familiar people, including Sharon, who was seated in front.

After the service Valerie stood outside, exchanging condolences with people she knew. Sharon told her that Brenda's brother wanted to talk to her next week about her paintings.

"He's decided to keep the gallery," Sharon said. "I know Brenda would be pleased."

"I'm sure she would."

As Valerie drove home, she thought about how much she already missed Brenda. And she thought about her paintings, particularly the one in progress. For the first time since she'd learned of Greg's accident she felt like working. So when she arrived home, she phoned Sue Lawson and asked if she wouldn't mind keeping Matthew until three. Then she changed clothes and climbed the stairs.

She could not stop thinking about Greg. But she found she could still paint. She began adding feathers and beads to the dancer's headdress and brushing in highlights along his back and legs. She stopped several times, stepping away from the canvas, taking it all in.

Around two o'clock she stood back, arms folded, regarding the painting. The corners of her mouth turned up in a smile. It was finished.

She felt proud, as if she'd just completed a monumental task. But also she was the least bit sad—the hours of intimate, pleasurable involvement with this work had ended.

Valerie cleaned her brushes and put away her paints. Then she showered, slipped into a dress, ate a quick snack, and picked up Matthew at the Lawsons'. They drove to the hospital.

Dr. Halverson met them in the hallway with good news.

"Greg fully regained consciousness around noon," he told her. "His vital signs have stabilized, and I've moved him out of intensive care."

"Thank God," Valerie said, relief washing over her. "May we see him?"

"Of course. He may be groggy, though."

Five minutes later Valerie and Matthew were standing at Greg's bedside. Valerie thought he looked better than this morning, and certainly better than yesterday. The swelling in his face was nearly gone, and his breathing was strong and regular.

Valerie stood by the bed, Matthew at her side.

"Is he sleeping?" he whispered.

"I think so, hon."

She held Greg's hand. It was limp, but warm and dry. She bent down and kissed his cool cheek.

His eyes fluttered open.

"Hi, Greg," Matthew blurted.

Valerie smiled and felt Greg feebly squeeze her hand.

"Hi, honey," she said softly, warm tears filling her eyes.

Greg moved his mouth, as if trying to speak.

"It's all right," she said, "you don't have to talk. Matthew and I are here and we love you and you're going to be just fine."

Greg continued to mouth words, so Valerie put her ear close to his face.

". . . Val . . . love you . . ."

"I love you, too," she said, but his eyes had already closed and his hand had gone limp. His chest rose and fell slowly, rhythmically.

On the drive home Valerie had to keep wiping tears from her eyes. Matthew wanted to know why she was sad. She told him she was crying because she was happy. When he said that didn't make sense, she explained that sometimes adults acted funny.

He gave her an odd look and said, "No kidding," which made her laugh.

She parked in the garage, and when she opened the side door, Dodger attacked them with a slobbery tongue.

"Hey!" Matthew said, playfully pushing Dodger away.

"Why don't you play with him for a while, and I'll take care of a few things in the house. Then we'll go someplace to eat."

"Okay, o-*kay,* Dodger. Wait out here and let me go get the Frisbee, will ya?"

Valerie unlocked the back door, and Matthew dashed past her to his room. A moment later she heard him thumping around, apparently searching for the Frisbee.

"Hey, don't tear your room apart!" she shouted, smiling.

She set her purse and keys on the countertop and went up to the studio. For a while she stood in the doorway, examining her work from across the room. She felt extremely pleased, and she wanted to bask in the moment, because she knew that tomorrow she'd have to get started on the next painting.

She crossed the room, intending to lift the canvas from the easel, an awkward task. Then she heard Matthew coming up the stairs.

"You're just in time to help me," she said, turning.

But it wasn't Matthew.

It was Leonard.

27

LEONARD STOOD IN THE DOORWAY with one hand on the jamb. He wore a blue denim shirt with the long sleeves rolled up, khaki pants, and work boots.

"Hi," he said, a shy smile on his face.

Valerie was too stunned to speak.

Leonard raised his hands chest high, as if in surrender. "Please don't be frightened." But there was a knife clenched in his left hand.

Valerie stared at the knife, afraid now even to breathe. Leonard seemed to notice it for the first time. He blushed with embarrassment.

"Oh, sorry." He folded the blade into the grip and put it in his pocket.

"Get out of here." Valerie's voice was strained. "Get out of my house."

"Of course," Leonard said. "That's why I'm here." Then he grinned impishly at the confused look on her face. "What I mean is, we're all leaving. Come on."

He motioned for her to follow. Then without waiting, he turned and walked downstairs, leaving her alone in the studio.

Valerie stood immobile for a full minute, dazed by Leonard's sudden and brief appearance, by his summoning her down the stairs. Her first thought was to stay in the room, to slam the door and barricade it. Perhaps she could squeeze through the window (although she knew the opening was too narrow) and drop to the ground (but the fall was dangerously long) and run to the nearest house, except . . .

Except Matthew was downstairs.

Was he still in his room, she wondered. Was he hiding? Or was he outside playing with Dodger? There was only one way to find out.

Valerie clenched her fists and walked down the stairs, certain that Leonard was waiting for her.

She stopped on the bottom stair and peeked around the corner into the empty hallway. To her immediate right was the doorway to the kitchen. She couldn't quite see the telephone hanging on the wall. Farther down the hallway was the door to Matthew's room. It was open, offering a view of only one corner—the closet door, the end of his toy box, his baseball mitt on the floor. . . .

She stepped off the last riser and called out softly, "Matthew?"

No answer.

She called his name again, louder this time.

Still no answer.

He must be outside, she thought.

She had no idea where Leonard was. He could be in one of the bedrooms, in the kitchen, in the backyard with Matthew, anywhere. Should she run out the back door or the front door or try for the phone? She reckoned that she had time to do only one thing, so it had better be right.

She believed that if she dialed 911 there would be a trace on her number the moment they answered, even if she didn't get the chance to speak. But would they automatically send the police if she were suddenly cut off? She didn't know. She'd scream for help and hope for the best.

She lunged for the kitchen doorway, just as Leonard stepped out of Matthew's room.

"Ah-ah-ah," he said, playfully scolding her.

She snatched up the receiver.

"You'd better come look at your son before you call the police."

Valerie hesitated, glancing at Leonard. He stood with his arms folded loosely across his chest, his eyebrows raised, a smile touching one corner of his mouth.

"Because once you make the call . . . well." He clucked his tongue. "I won't be responsible for what happens to the boy. And the police can't get here fast enough to save him."

He turned and walked casually into Matthew's room.

Valerie gripped the receiver so hard it hurt her hand.

He's in there with Matthew, she thought with sickening clarity. If the police come, what will he do? Panic? He has a knife.

Leonard poked his head around the door jamb. "Coming?" he said brightly, and then withdrew.

Valerie stared at the empty doorway. Then she squeezed her eyes closed, thinking, This isn't happening. Slowly, she hung up the phone. She walked down the hallway to her son's room.

Valerie nearly cried out when she saw Matthew lying on the bed. He still had on his T-shirt, jeans, and tennis shoes, but his wrists were tied behind him and his ankles were bound together with a thick white cord. A strip of duct tape stretched across his mouth. His eyes were filled with terror.

Leonard stood at the foot of the bed. Near him lay several lengths of cord and a roll of tape. He shrugged helplessly, as if someone else had bound and gagged the boy and he'd been unable to prevent it. The thumping sounds Valerie had heard earlier had not been Matthew searching for his Frisbee.

Suddenly, she threw herself at Leonard, overcome by rage.

"Goddamn you!" she cried, clawing at his eyes.

But he was too quick for her, and he grabbed her wrists before she could touch him. "Please," he said, his voice calm.

She struggled, kicking at his shins, and managed to free one hand. She swung at his face. He ducked, and her fist struck the top of his head, a glancing blow that pained her knuckles.

"Please, don't," Leonard said loudly, wincing, pushing her away.

Valerie stumbled into the wall. Matthew's baseball bat was leaning in the corner, and she snatched it up.

Leonard backed away, withdrawing the knife from his pocket. Quickly, he sat on the bed, opened the blade, and touched it lightly to Matthew's right cheek, just below his eye.

"Valerie, please," he begged her, "I don't want anyone to get hurt."

She raised the bat with both hands, trembling with rage. "Get away from my son or I'll kill you." But her eyes were fixed on the knife point.

"Think of the boy." A plea.

The knife twitched on Matthew's cheek. Valerie winced, tightening her grip on the bat. If she swung it, he'd cut Matthew. If she ran out and called the police, he'd cut Matthew.

"Please put down the bat."

"Get away from him."

"Please," was all he said.

Valerie hesitated, feeling her rage failing, deserting her. Matthew's safety was all that mattered. The bat felt useless in her hands. "Goddammit, what do you *want?*"

"I want you to put down the bat."

Her next act was an unnatural one, contrary to her deepest instincts, like forcing herself to put her hand in an open flame. She only wished she could do something as easy as that to free Matthew.

She threw down the bat. It clattered against Matthew's toy box.

Leonard exhaled, relieved. "Good," he said.

"Now get away from my son."

Leonard stood. "Not until I tie you up."

"No." Valerie backed away.

"Valerie," he said, parent to child, "it's time to stop playing games."

She backed into the doorway, glanced down the hall, and gauged the distance to the telephone. Why hadn't she used it when she'd had the chance? How could she have been so stupid?

"Listen," Leonard said irritably, "if you even try to use the phone, I'll hurt him, that's all there is to it. I don't *want* to, but I will." He leaned down and touched the point of the knife to Matthew's chest. The boy tried to shrink away from it. "Now get over here and sit down." Then his voice softened. "Please. Trust me. It'll be all right." He tried a smile. "You two will be together."

Valerie could see no way out. Leonard was too big for her to fight. And she couldn't run away—she *wouldn't*—not with Matthew there.

She swallowed with difficulty, hating and fearing what she was being forced to do. Slowly, she moved to the bed and sat. She touched Matthew's cheek, feeling the alien harshness of the tape.

"It'll be all right, baby." She started to remove the tape.

"No," Leonard said firmly. "Not yet. Not until I tie you." He picked up a length of cord. "Please put your hands behind your back."

Valerie hesitated.

"Come *on*."

She put her hands behind her, and he quickly bound her wrists. She flinched as the cord bit into her skin.

"Sorry," he said.

He came around the bed and knelt before her, then tied her ankles together. It was the first time in her life that she'd been so utterly restrained. And now her initial shock and anger seemed to be drowned in a deepening dread. She wondered if submitting to Leonard had been her most terrible mistake.

"What . . . what are you going to do?"

"We're taking a ride. Where are your keys?"

"Keys?"

"Come on, come on, I have to move your car."

"They're . . . in the kitchen. On the countertop."

"Don't worry," he said, "we're going someplace nice. You'll see." He picked up the roll of tape, and when he tore off a strip it sounded like a cry of agony.

"Please don't."

"I have to."

She jerked her head away from him.

"It's only temporary," he said apologetically. "I promise."

She would not face him.

"It won't hurt, honest. See, Matthew is taped and he's not complaining." He chuckled. "Sorry, bad joke. Look, Valerie, it's just for a little while. Please don't make this any harder for me than it already is."

"Harder for *you!*" she shouted, turning toward him.

And he pressed the tape quickly across her mouth.

She shook her head from side to side, as if she could throw off the tape.

"I really am sorry it has to be this way," Leonard said. There was a pained look on his face. He leaned down and put his arms around her.

Valerie tried to cry out through the tape, but her voice was reduced to a muffled groan. She thrashed from side to side, trying to break free from Leonard's grasp.

He let go and stood back, shaking his head in exasperation.

"I'm not going to *do* anything," he said. "I'm not like that." He waited for the wild fear to leave her face. "Look, I just want to sit you down on the floor so I can tie you to the bed frame. I have to leave the house for a while, and I don't want you crawling into the kitchen or the living room. Okay?"

He waited. She barely nodded her head.

He put his arms around her and eased her down to the floor. That close, she could smell him—a mixture of sour sweat and sweet cologne. And something else . . . sawdust?

She sat with her back to the bed. He looped a length of cord between her wrists and around the bed frame.

"There," he said, standing, smiling. "I won't be gone long." He hurried from the room, his words hanging in the air like poison gas.

Valerie heard him walk down the hallway and through the kitchen. A moment later the front door opened and closed. The house was silent.

Valerie immediately began twisting her wrists and pulling against the bed frame, trying to free herself. When she heard Matthew whimpering, she stopped and sat back against the bed, turning her head toward him. He was facing Valerie's side of the bed. He looked pitifully afraid, near panic, and his glance darted wildly about the room, touching everything but Valerie. She ached to free him from his bonds and hold him close.

She tried to say his name through the tape, but it came out as a loud mumble. Nevertheless, she made the sound again and again, until Matthew looked at her. She held his eyes with hers.

Some of the panic eased from his face. His eyes brimmed with tears and he made a mewling sound. Valerie tried to give him a consoling look, but she felt ridiculous with her mouth taped and her arms pinned behind her. She suppressed her own panic and nodded at Matthew, trying to tell him that she was with him, that things were bad now, but only temporarily.

His eyes implored her. She continued to nod. Finally, almost imperceptibly, he nodded back.

Again she struggled to free her hands, viciously twisting her wrists, feeling the bite of the cord. She feared her skin would tear. And then she hoped for it, thinking that if her hands and wrists were slick with blood, she could slip free from her bonds.

Minutes passed, and still she struggled. Then she heard the front door open.

A moment later Leonard stood in the bedroom doorway, a pleased look on his face.

"Ready?" he said.

C h a p t e r

LEONARD RUBBED HIS HANDS WITH GLEE.

Valerie shrunk away from him, pressing her back to the side of the bed.

"Looks like we're all set," Leonard said. "You first."

He moved toward the bed, reaching for Matthew. The boy emitted a muffled yell and twisted away from him.

"Let's not be difficult."

Leonard grabbed Matthew by the shoulders and dragged him across the bed. Then he tried to lift him like a baby, with his arms beneath Matthew's knees and back. But Matthew twisted and kicked and squirmed so violently that Leonard had to let go. He grabbed the boy again and hoisted him over his shoulder. Matthew jerked and flopped like a netted fish.

Leonard had trouble hanging on to him. Valerie pounded her heels on the floor, trying to get Leonard's attention, trying to make him stop.

Leonard staggered toward the doorway, as Matthew continued to thrash about. Valerie could see her son's face contorted with terror. She yanked on her bonds with all her might, fighting desperately to get to Leonard and her son, moving the bed a foot across the floor.

Suddenly Leonard turned, stepped to the bed, and dropped Matthew like a sack of laundry.

He stood back, his face red from exertion.

"I'll just have to roll you up in a blanket," he said irritably.

Matthew squirmed to the far edge of the bed. Valerie could see only his backside. She heard his muffled cries. Leonard tossed the pillow to the floor and began pulling the blanket from beneath Matthew.

Valerie banged her heels on the floor, thumped her back against the bed, and tried to cry out "no" through the tape.

Leonard looked down at her, annoyed. "*You're* not going to start, are you?"

Valerie held his eyes and said something beneath the tape. He glared at her, his mouth pressed in a tight, crooked line.

She said it again, staring at him.

Then he sighed heavily, leaned down, and gently pulled the tape from the side of her mouth, letting it hang from her left cheek.

"What is it?"

Valerie gulped air and licked her lips.

"Please," she said, "do you have to do this? Can't you just leave and—"

"We're all leaving together." He checked his watch. "And there's no time to waste. If you give me any trouble I'll roll you up in a blanket, too."

"No," she said, fighting hysterics. "He could suffocate."

Leonard shrugged his shoulders. "I doubt it." He reached down to press the tape over her mouth.

Valerie jerked her head away from him. "No, wait, please. Let me talk to him first. I'll get him to hold still."

Leonard hesitated.

"Please."

"Oh, all right."

Leonard reached across the bed and grabbed Matthew by the shoulders. He pulled the boy toward Valerie, then turned him so his head lay near hers.

"Take his gag off. Please. Just so we can talk."

Leonard shifted his weight from one foot to the other.

"One minute," he said. "And then we're leaving, one way or the other."

He gently pried the tape from Matthew's mouth.

Before it was even off, Matthew began crying out to his mother, nearly screaming in her face.

"Boy," Leonard said, shaking his head and stepping back.

"It's all right, Matthew, it's all right," Valerie said, her voice a soothing drone.

Matthew began to quiet down, speaking between sobs.

"My hands hurt. . . . Who is that man? . . . Why is he hurting us? . . . I don't want to do this anymore. . . ."

"He won't hurt you," Valerie said, then looked at Leonard and said it again: "He won't hurt you."

Leonard rolled his eyes and sighed heavily.

"He's just going to take us somewhere," Valerie said, terrified by her own words.

"Where?"

"I . . . I don't know, honey."

"Someplace nice," Leonard put in.

"You just have to hold still and not fight him and he won't hurt you."

"I don't want to go with him."

"We have to, Matthew. It'll be all right. I'll be with you. We'll be together." She felt like a fool and a traitor, abetting Leonard.

Matthew said nothing, searching her eyes.

"We'll be together," she said, "but you have to be brave."

He licked his lips.

"Okay?"

"Okay, Mom," he said quietly.

"Now he's going to carry you out to his truck and leave you for a minute while he comes and gets me. But I'll be right with you, okay?"

Matthew nodded, his cheek pressed to the bed.

"So just be brave and don't try to fight and it'll be all right."

"Time to go," Leonard said.

He pressed the tape over their mouths, then scooped Matthew off the bed and carried him from the room. The boy went without a fuss, staring silently at Valerie over Leonard's shoulder. She felt as if her heart was being torn from her body.

She struggled against her bonds, realizing that escape was hopeless—at least for now. She sat quietly and waited for Leonard.

He returned a minute later.

"So far so good," he said and gave her a quick smile. Then he untied the cord holding her to the bed frame, lifted her off the floor, grunting as he did so. He carried her before him, turning sideways to aim her feetfirst through the doorway.

He walked unsteadily through the house to the open front door, then stopped, turned his back to the doorway, and leaned his head out so that he could look down the driveway without showing himself. Apparently satisfied that the way was clear, he carried Valerie to his truck.

Dodger was barking wildly from behind the backyard fence.

Leonard hoisted Valerie up and over the side and laid her heavily on the floor of the truck bed, keeping one arm under her shoulders so that she wouldn't bump her head.

Valerie lay on her side facing Matthew. The blanket spread beneath them offered little cushion from the steel bed. She could hear Dodger continuing to bark.

"Lift up," Leonard told them. He placed a rolled blanket to pillow their heads.

Then he wrestled with something on the ground beside the truck. Suddenly, a heavy canvas tarp dropped over Valerie and Matthew. She heard Leonard lashing it to one side of the truck, and then the canvas was lifted as he fastened it to the other side. It stretched above them, blocking out the sunlight and muffling Dodger's barking. Valerie felt as if she were in a coffin.

She heard Leonard move away from the truck and enter the house. Soon Dodger's barking became intense, vicious. Then the dog yelped once and fell silent, which sent a sickening jolt through Valerie.

A minute later the truck rocked as Leonard climbed in and slammed the door. The engine coughed to life. Valerie felt the truck jerk—first forward, then backward, then forward again, turning around in the driveway. They motored slowly away from the house, crunching gravel beneath the tires, stopping at the end of the driveway.

Valerie could hear a few cars breeze by on 32nd Avenue. Then the truck lurched forward onto the smooth asphalt surface. The gears shifted and the tires hummed as the truck gathered speed.

Valerie had no idea where Leonard was taking them or what he intended to do. But she believed their situation could only get worse.

I've got to do something now, she thought, while we're in traffic, while there are people around.

She wrestled with her bonds. But her wrists had become so sore that she soon gave up, knowing that further struggle was useless. If she weren't gagged, she could conspire with Matthew, have him turn back to back with her and attempt to untie each other.

She peered through the dim light at her son's face. His eyes were closed and his expression was slack. She felt a new surge of panic, believing for a terrifying moment that he'd suffocated. But he'd merely fallen asleep—or was trying to—escaping from their predicament, at least temporarily.

Valerie felt herself being tugged to the left side of the truck, as Leonard turned right and accelerated. She guessed that they were on Kipling Boulevard now, heading south. She tried to picture the surroundings and visualize exactly where they were.

Shouldn't she be counting the seconds? Then later she could tell the police how far they'd gone and—

No, she thought, fighting her paralyzing fear. I've got to do something *now*.

She stared up at the tarp stretched above them. She knew if it weren't for that, she could simply sit up and show every passing motorist the woman bound and gagged in the rear of the truck. She wondered how securely Leonard had lashed the tarp. She rolled onto her stomach, pressing her face to the blanket, and brought her knees under her. Then she arched her back, forcing it up against the tarp.

The canvas gave, bowing up a foot or so, but did not pull loose from the sides of the truck.

Valerie could hear vehicles all around them, and she tried to imagine what the canvas must look like to someone outside the truck. A hump in the middle. She crouched down, then pressed up and down, up and down, trying to catch the attention of some unseen rescuer.

Her knees and back ached from the effort.

A waste of energy, she thought. If anyone even notices, they'll just think the canvas is flapping in the breeze. I need someone to see *us*.

She lay on her side, easing the pressure on her knees. Then she squirmed like a snake, moving feet first to the rear of the truck's bed. Her last hope was that the back hatch wasn't secure. If she could kick it open, anyone following would see her and Matthew inside.

She lay on her back, brought her knees up, and kicked out with all her might, banging her feet on the steel hatch. It felt as solid as a rock wall, sending a wave of pain through her shoes all the way up her legs. She took a deep breath, gritted her teeth, and kicked out again. And again.

The hatch didn't budge. The only thing Valerie managed to do was make a racket banging on the metal.

Maybe that's enough, she thought. Maybe someone in a nearby car will hear me.

She kicked the hatch again.

Without warning, the truck lurched to a near stop. Valerie slid uncontrollably to the front of the bed, banging her head against the cab. Matthew was pressed against the cab as well, his eyes wide, his cries muffled by the tape across his mouth.

The truck accelerated rapidly, sliding Valerie and Matthew backward along the bed. Then the brakes were slammed again, and they were thrown painfully against the cab.

Someone had heard her efforts, all right. Leonard. And he'd just told her to stop.

Valerie lay still, tensed, waiting to be tossed around like a doll in a shoe box. But nothing happened. The truck continued smoothly ahead, tires humming happily on the asphalt.

Valerie looked at Matthew. His eyes were squeezed shut, as if he were willing himself away from there. Valerie squirmed sideways until her body was pressed against his. She tried to comfort him. And herself. There was nothing else to do.

The ride seemed to last for hours. But it could have been minutes or days—Valerie had lost all sense of time and direction.

Eventually, the truck slowed and began to jerk and bounce. Valerie realized they'd left the pavement. Her terror was renewed, for she believed they must be near their destination. And wherever they were going was far from civilization. She began to count the seconds and the minutes, fighting the urge to urinate.

Another hour passed before the truck stopped and the engine died.

Valerie could hear nothing but the ringing in her ears. She thought it possible that she and Matthew were about to die. The truck jounced as Leonard climbed out and slammed the door. She heard him groan with pleasure, and imagined him stretching his limbs from the long drive. He began fumbling with the canvas lashing.

A few moments later the tarp was thrown aside. Valerie squinted up at Leonard, who was backlit by a royal-blue sky.

"We're here," he said, smiling.

29

LEONARD CLIMBED INTO THE TRUCK BED and helped Valerie and Matthew sit up. Then he gently peeled the tape from their mouths. Valerie recoiled from his touch.

"Now that wasn't so bad, was it?" he said.

Valerie saw that they were in a clearing encircled by aspen and pine trees. There was a cabin nearby. Wooded hills rose in the distance. Leonard watched her taking it all in.

"Like it?"

"What?"

"My place," he said with pride. "Do you like it?"

Valerie held his gaze for a heartbeat . . . and understood that Leonard was not going to kill them. At least not now. She turned to Matthew.

"Are you all right, honey?"

"I don't feel good."

"Tell me what's wrong."

"The rope hurts my hands and my legs. And my side hurts, too. And I have to go pee real bad."

Valerie could empathize with each of his complaints.

"My son has to go to the bathroom," she said. "Will you please untie him."

"Of course." Leonard looked offended. "You're not hostages, you know."

He untied their ankles, dropped the rear hatch of the truck, and helped them out. Valerie's legs were stiff and sore.

"This way," Leonard said.

They followed him past the cabin, their shoes crunching on the flat, gravelly ground. Valerie noticed that the cabin's windows were covered with new heavy wooden shutters, and secured with padlocks. She feared what lay inside. She considered running. But how fast could she move with her hands tied behind her?

Leonard led them to a weathered outhouse at the edge of the clearing. He unlatched the door and pulled it open. Inside was a wooden bench with an oval hole cut in the seat. A roll of toilet paper hung on one wall. Valerie expected the place to stink, but there was only a faint, musty odor.

Leonard untied Matthew's hands and nudged him inside. Then he did the same to Valerie.

When she told him they were finished, Leonard had Matthew come out first. Valerie was forced to wait until he called her. When she opened the door she saw that he'd retied Matthew's hands behind him. Leonard's hand rested on the boy's shoulder.

"I don't want you running away," he explained.

Even so, Valerie considered making a break for it. She figured that with Matthew in tow Leonard couldn't catch her. She could escape into the woods. But then what? She had no idea where they were or which way to run. Besides, she couldn't leave Matthew behind. As long as Leonard held her son, he also held her, no matter if she was physically free.

She stepped out of the enclosure and allowed Leonard to bind her hands.

"Are we in the mountains, Mom?"

"Bright boy," Leonard said. He led them to the cabin.

"Where are we?" Valerie asked. "Why have you brought us here?"

Leonard didn't answer, but merely unlocked the heavy padlock that secured the door. He pushed the door inward and motioned them inside. When they didn't move, he took them each by the arm, smiling.

"Come on, it's clean."

Valerie and Matthew stepped into the cabin—a single square room with a wood-burning stove, a table and chairs, and a pair of cots against the far wall, illuminated only by the indirect sunlight from the open door. Leonard untied Valerie's hands and told her to sit on one of the cots.

"What . . . are you going to do to us?" Valerie asked, facing Leonard, fighting to maintain her dignity.

"If you sit down," he said pleasantly, "I'll untie your son."

Valerie sat. After Leonard had removed Matthew's bonds, he lit the tall, glass hurricane lamp.

"There's a spring nearby," he said, moving to the door. "I'll fill a canteen for you and be back in a few minutes."

He stepped out and closed the door, shutting out the sunlight. Valerie heard the padlock snap in place. The room was lit now only by the weak yellow light from the hurricane lamp.

Valerie hurried to the door, pressing her ear to the rough wood. Leonard's footsteps receded into silence.

He was gone, and she was desperate to get her and Matthew out of there before he returned. She grasped the U-shaped metal handle and yanked—but the door held fast. She noticed screw holes and indentations in the wood, as if something had recently been removed.

Probably an inside lock, Valerie thought.

She found a peephole drilled high in the door, and by standing on her toes she could just see out: distant trees, scrubby vegetation, the rear of Leonard's truck.

She quickly checked the cabin's three windows, searching for a way out. Each window had four glass panes set in a hinged wooden frame. She tugged on one frame, but it was stuck fast. Not that an open window would have allowed them to escape—beyond the glass was a heavy mesh screen, and beyond that a sturdy wooden shutter, padlocked on the outside.

"I want to go home."

"I know, honey," Valerie said, searching now for a weapon.

A few hours ago, in her son's room, she'd threatened to kill Leonard with a baseball bat. She'd spoken without thinking, out of her head with fear and rage. But now she had time to consider it.

Even if she had the means, could she kill Leonard? Perhaps she wouldn't have to. Perhaps she could just disable him and they could escape, maybe even in his truck.

Valerie found a box of firewood beside the Franklin stove. She dug through it, finally selecting a piece of split wood three inches thick and a foot and a half long. Then she stood by the door jamb with her back pressed to the wall. Matthew stood beside her, away from the door. They waited for Leonard.

When his footsteps sounded outside, Valerie raised the club over her shoulder, holding it with both hands, as if she were standing at home plate, ready to smash a line drive.

She heard Leonard insert a key in the padlock. The door remained closed. Silence. What was he doing? Why didn't he come in? Valerie shifted her weight to her back foot, the club held high.

"I . . . don't . . . *see* . . . you," Leonard said in a singsongy voice, as if they were all children playing hide-and-seek. His words were partially muffled by the thick door. "Come out, come out, wherever you are."

Valerie guessed that he was looking in through the peephole. She held her breath, waiting.

After a few moments Leonard said, "Okay, game's over." His voice had lost its playfulness. "Sit on the cots were I can see you. Now."

Valerie didn't move.

Leonard muttered something unintelligible. The he said bitterly, "Okay, fine, have it your way. But don't blame me when you get thirsty tonight."

Valerie heard him withdraw the key.

"I'm going now. There's food on the shelves."

"Wait," Valerie said, lowering her club and stepping around to face the door.

"There are matches, too, so you can have a fire tonight when it gets cold. And try not to burn the place down."

Valerie felt her throat constrict. "You can't just leave us here."

"See you tomorrow," Leonard said.

"Wait!"

His footsteps moved away. Valerie dropped the hunk of firewood and pounded on the door with her fists.

"Come back!" she shouted.

She raised up on her toes to look through the peephole. The engine started, and she saw the truck roll away.

"You can't just leave us!"

The sound of the truck faded in the distance.

Valerie stared hopelessly at the door. Then she noticed Matthew crouched beside the wood stove, looking at her as if she were a madwoman. She reached out for him.

"Come here, honey."

Matthew rushed to her side and wrapped his arms around her. He buried his face in her abdomen, as if he were attempting to return to the womb. Valerie caressed him, feeling him shiver with fear.

"It's all right, baby. We're all right. We're safe here."

And in truth they probably were safe, she thought, at least for the night. Assuming Leonard didn't return.

She laid Matthew on one of the cots. He rested his head on the thin, coverless pillow, and she stroked his hair until his shaking subsided.

Then she stood and lifted the hurricane lamp from the table. She carried it around the cabin, pushing its light into every corner, search-ing for a crack, a rotted board, some weak spot for her to concentrate her efforts on, some place for her to break out. But the walls and floor were solidly built with heavy wood. And the door was as thick as the walls. It was much too heavy for her to try to shoulder open—even if it were hinged to swing outward, which it was not.

Only the windows remained as possible exits. But they were fitted with steel mesh screens and stout wooden shutters.

The latter were so new that Valerie could smell freshly cut wood, making her recall the scent of sawdust in Leonard's hair.

He must have installed the shutters today, putting the finishing touches on their prison. At least he doesn't plan to murder us, she thought. Prayed. But how long does he intend to keep us here? What does he plan to do with us? Her mind began to conjure up vile images. No, she thought, shaking her head. There *must* be a way out of here.

She stood again before the door.

I could set it on fire, she thought desperately, and burn our way out.

She guessed, though, that the cabin would become engulfed in flames, and they'd die horribly before they could escape.

She carried the lamp to the foot of Matthew's cot, as shadows danced about her. In the corner of the room was a crude arrangement of shelves and drawers. She set the lamp on the top shelf and began sorting through the meager inventory: a dozen or so cans of food, tin plates, cups, spoons, a can opener, a box of matches . . . but no knives or forks. And no water, she thought with dismay.

"I'm thirsty."

Matthew was sitting up. Valerie smiled at him.

"Are you hungry, too?"

"I don't know."

She sorted through their supplies and selected a can of sliced peaches. They drank the juice, ate all the fruit, and munched crackers from a box.

"Are we going to stay here tonight?"

"Yes, hon."

"What about Dodger? Won't he get hungry?"

Valerie recalled how Leonard had left them in the truck and gone back into their house, how Dodger had yelped and then fallen silent. She feared the worst.

"I . . . think he'll be okay."

"When will that man let us go home?"

"Soon, honey. Soon, I'm sure. Shall we play a game?" Anything to get their minds off where they were.

"Okay," he said. "The zoo game?"

She smiled crookedly. "Sure."

"I live in a zoo and start with 'a.' "

"Antelope," Valerie said. "I live in a zoo. . . ."

Later, as the cabin grew chilly, Valerie built a fire in the stove with wads of newspaper, kindling, and a log. The stove emitted a surprising amount of heat. She tucked Matthew under the blanket, extinguished the lamp, and lay on the other cot.

For the first time since Leonard had entered her studio she allowed herself to think of Greg, lying helpless in the hospital. She wished that he were well, that he were coming for them. How long would it be before someone missed them? Who'd miss them first—Janice, Sharon, one of the neighbors . . . ? Would anyone *do* anything?

Eventually, she fell asleep. She dreamed uneasily of Leonard's return.

C h a p t e r

30

WHEN LEONARD ARRIVED HOME THAT EVENING, he could barely hide his elation.

"So," Francine said, waiting for him to explain why he'd been gone all day.

Leonard sat at the kitchen table, shaking his head and trying to look somber. "Not good," he said, filled with excitement. "There, ah, was a lot of damage. The lightning caused a fire."

"Fire?" Color drained from Francine's face.

Leonard realized he might have gone too far with his lie. They both knew the cabin was old and that a blaze could bring it to the ground.

"The building is still intact," he said quickly. "There was just some damage to the roof and one of the walls. Nothing I can't fix."

Francine looked relieved. "How long will it take?"

"Several days at least. Possibly more."

"So the damage is major," she said, frowning.

"Mm, yes."

"Then perhaps we should have a professional look at it, a, what do you call them, a contractor."

"No."

Francine's frown deepened. Leonard tried on a weak smile.

"What I mean is," he said, "it would be too expensive to hire some-one. Besides, I can do the work."

Francine seemed to grudgingly accept this, perhaps because she had little choice but to trust her son.

"All right," she said finally. She wheeled her chair into her bedroom, emerging a few minutes later with a wad of ones and fives. She handed them to Leonard. "I know you have your own money, but this will help you buy lumber and such."

Leonard took it, racked with guilt for deceiving her.

"And when you're finished, I want you to take me up there for a look, do you understand?"

"Yes, Mother."

Much later, Leonard lay awake in bed, reliving the day's events.

That morning he'd decided it was time to act. Strike while the iron is hot, he'd thought, while Greg is conveniently out of the way. He'd been afraid to think too far ahead, to speculate about possible consequences. He feared he might lose his nerve. So he'd taken lumber to the cabin and built shutters for the windows. Not that he thought the heavy mesh screens weren't sufficient to keep Valerie in. But if she or the boy yelled for help while he was away, well, there was always the chance some hikers might pass within earshot. The shutters would muffle their screams.

Then he'd driven back to the city, entered Valerie's house through a window, and waited for her and Matthew to come home.

He'd been calm and sure of himself, right up until he had them bound and gagged and was carrying them out. Then he'd been so nervous he could hardly walk. What if a witness—a neighbor, the mailman, one of Matthew's playmates—had suddenly showed up? What would he have been forced to do? Silence them. (Put it out of your mind.) And worse, whatever he'd done would have been witnessed by Valerie and Matthew. What would he have been forced to do about that?

(Put it out of your mind.)

The important thing was, *she was his!* He smiled in the dark. It was incredible what a person could accomplish once he set his mind to it. Oh, there was still work to do, but the hardest part was over. Now it was only a matter of time before Valerie understood him, before she saw how good he could be for her. Before he won her heart.

Then doubt crossed his mind like a shadow over water.

Perhaps taking her to the cabin had been excessive. Perhaps he should have continued to court her here in the city, taken his time about it.

Well, what was done was done. There was nothing now but to see things through to the end. And he was certain that everything would work out just fine.

Valerie woke up Saturday morning cold and stiff.

The fire in the stove had gone out sometime during the night, and the room was dark, save for pale light seeping in under the door. Valerie sat up in the cot. Her hair felt matted to the side of her head. She ran her fingers through it, thinking of a shower. She still wore her dress, which was twisted and sharply wrinkled. She stood and tugged at the fabric, pulling it around, then hugged herself, shivering from the cold.

Matthew lay curled up beneath his thin blanket. Valerie spread her blanket over him, then she slipped on her shoes, relit the hurricane lamp, and built a fire in the stove. Yellow flames soon danced behind the black metal grille.

"Mom, I'm cold."

Matthew was sitting up on his cot, fists pressed to his chest, arms tight to his sides. Valerie moved two chairs before the stove. They sat, each wrapped in a blanket, holding out their palms to the warmth of the fire.

Matthew seemed to be taking their situation in stride—perhaps even better than she—as if they were on some sort of camping trip. But Valerie could feel him clinging to her, holding on for all he was worth, sensing her every mood. And so it was important that she act calm—even though her insides were twisted by fear and anxiety.

Gradually, the chill left her body. She stood on her toes at the door and pressed her eye to the peephole. The clearing still lay in shadow, but she could see bright morning sunlight on distant trees.

She wondered when Leonard would come back.

What if he doesn't? Ironically, that thought frightened her nearly as much as his return. If he left them, they could die of thirst before anyone found them.

She licked her dry lips and thought, No, he didn't go to all this trouble just to abandon us. She thought of Greg, lying in the hospital, and she knew that sooner or later he'd worry about them and call the police. I know he will, she thought. He *must*.

Then she heard the truck.

It stopped somewhere nearby, out of sight of the peephole. The engine died and the door slammed shut. Valerie snatched up a heavy piece of firewood and stood beside the door, ready to deliver a blow to Leonard's head the moment he entered the cabin. But she felt weaker than she had yesterday when she'd taken this position. And less sure of herself.

She heard a noise from the window across the room.

Suddenly, the shutter swung open and sunlight poured through the window, silhouetting Leonard's head and shoulders.

"Good morning," he said, his voice muffled by the glass.

Valerie lowered the firewood club, feeling foolish. Leonard opened the other shutters, and the cabin was flooded with light. His footsteps sounded outside the door. A key grated in the padlock.

"Please move where I can see you," he said.

Valerie knew what Leonard's response would be if she disobeyed—he'd leave them locked inside with no water. She took Matthew by the hand, and stepped around the cots, facing the door. She still gripped the hunk of firewood.

The door swung open and Leonard stood in the doorway, a grocery sack under one arm, a canteen dangling from his hand.

Valerie pushed Matthew behind her and held her club with both hands.

"Well," Leonard said, smiling pleasantly. He put everything on the table—sack, canteen, padlock. Then he rubbed his hands together. "Anyone ready for breakfast? I brought milk and orange juice."

"You stay away from us," Valerie said. She was still deathly afraid of Leonard, but she was somewhat confused by his cheerful behavior.

"I thought your son might be hungry." He nodded at the club in her hand. "You certainly don't need that."

Valerie wanted desperately to believe that his good humor and offer of food were signs of rationality. The thought bolstered her.

"Why are you keeping us here?"

"We'll talk about it over breakfast. Please put down your, ah, dangerous weapon." He smiled.

Valerie hesitated, then lowered the club. But she did not drop it.

Leonard shook his head, still smiling. "Look, I'm not going to hurt you. I promise." He drew an X on his chest. "Cross my heart and hope to die."

"Let us go."

Leonard sighed with exasperation. "Well, if that's going to be your attitude, I'll have to leave you locked in here all day." He reached for the canteen and grocery sack.

"No, wait," Valerie said, taking a step forward, thinking of Matthew. "Please."

Leonard looked from her eyes to her hand. Valerie hesitated, then tossed the useless piece of firewood at his feet. Leonard put it in the box by the stove. "Better if we get rid of these blunt instruments," he joked, and set the box outside the door. Then he pushed the door closed and dragged the table in front of it, barricading them in.

"Why are you keeping us here?" Valerie demanded, still apprehensive, but somehow less afraid.

"You're my guests," Leonard said.

"That doesn't explain anything."

"Let's eat first, and then we'll talk."

"*Goddamn* you," she blurted, "what do you *want* from us?"

Leonard's eyelids drooped and the corners of his mouth sagged. His entire face seemed to settle, like wet cement.

"Don't raise your voice to me," he said quietly, coldly.

Valerie saw madness in his eyes, and she felt a chill of fear. Any doubts she might have had about Leonard's rationality were gone. He was not sane. He was their keeper. He controlled their water, food, heat, and light. And he'd already threatened them with a knife. From now on she'd have to be very careful about what she said, how she behaved. She had to think not only of her own welfare but of Matthew's.

"And don't blaspheme the Lord's name," Leonard said. His tone was as flat and hard as a steel blade. He stared at her without blinking. "Do you understand?"

Valerie nodded, feeling Matthew pressed against her side.

Leonard stared at her a moment longer. Then his face brightened. "Well, then," he said lightly, "how about some breakfast?"

At Valerie's request, Leonard took them outside—one at a time—and let them use the outhouse and then wash as best they could with water he poured from an extra canteen in his truck. He confessed to having forgotten toothpaste and toothbrushes. Valerie rinsed her mouth with water and spit it on the ground.

Back in the cabin, Leonard closed the door and shoved the table against it. Now he could move freely about the room without worrying that Valerie or Matthew would make a dash for freedom.

He laid out the table with mugs, spoons, tin plates, and paper napkins, arranging the three place settings with care and precision, the pink tip of his tongue tucked in one corner of his mouth.

"There," he said, straightening up from the table, turning to Valerie and Matthew. They watched him warily from the cot. "Well, come on." He motioned them to their chairs.

Leonard sat facing the door, with Valerie to his left, Matthew to his right. He poured juice into mugs, then fixed them each a bowl of cereal and milk. They ate without talking, Leonard making small smacking noises of approval. Valerie was glad to see that Matthew ate hungrily. But she was revolted, as well. She felt as if they were in some mad stage play, an obscene imitation of a family breakfast. Anger grew within her, threatening to overwhelm her fear.

She pushed aside her bowl and asked as calmly as possible, "How long do you intend to keep us here?"

Leonard dabbed at his mouth with a paper napkin. "As long as it takes."

Valerie suppressed the urge to yell in his face. She had a sudden comical image of herself snatching up her spoon and stabbing it impotently at Leonard's chest.

"What do you mean?" she asked, forcing calmness into her voice. "As long as *what* takes?"

"For us to get to know each other." Leonard shrugged his shoulders. "For you to like me."

Valerie blinked.

"And I'm sure you will, once we're better acquainted. Perhaps we should begin."

He stood, scraping the chair on the floor.

"First I'll tie your hands," he said.

C h a p t e r

31

WHEN GREG OPENED HIS EYES Saturday morning the first thing he saw was a nurse's uniform. The woman stood beside his bed, looking at the monitor on the wall behind him. Then she glanced down and saw that he was awake. She smiled.

"Good morning."

" . . . 'morn . . ." Greg's voice was raspy and his mouth was dry. He cleared his throat. "Good morning," he managed.

"How do you feel?"

"Headache. And I'm thirsty."

She poured him a glass of water then raised his head and helped him drink. Now he noticed someone else in the room—a tall, somber, thin man in a dark suit. The man would have looked like a mortician if not for his bright blue eyes and floral tie. Arnold Chesbro, attorney at law.

"Look up here," the nurse said. She shined a penlight in Greg's right eye, then his left, watching the reaction of his pupils. Then she held his hands in hers and said, "Squeeze." Her fingers were strong and soft. "Good," she said. "Do you know what day this is?"

"I . . . how long since the accident?"

"Two days."

"Two . . . ?"

"Right."

"Saturday?"

"Right again. What month is it?"

"August."

"Who's the president?"

Greg gave her a weak smile. "Is this a pop quiz?"

"Yes."

Greg named him.

"You get an A. I'll tell Dr. Halverson you're awake."

After she'd left, Arnold moved to the bedside, smiling.

"Hello, Greg. How are you feeling?"

"Not so good." He awkwardly shifted his upper body, hampered by the casts and the traction. His head and leg hurt and his arm itched. "Thanks for coming." He managed a smile. "Don't you work on Saturday anymore?"

Arnold nodded. "That's another reason I'm here. I wanted to talk to you before the Lakewood police do."

Greg blinked. "The police?"

"They've been wanting to question you for the past few days. But ever since your accident you've—"

Greg squeezed his eyelids closed. "The worst moment of my life." He opened his eyes and looked at Arnold. "The brake pedal . . . flat to the floor. Then the grille of a truck . . . coming right at me." He swallowed. "The driver, is he . . . is that why the police . . ."

"The driver is fine. It's not that. It's about the fire at your shop."

"What about it?"

"It was deliberately set."

"Jesus. The police are certain?"

Chesbro nodded. "The arson investigators found traces of gasoline and damage to the rear door. It appears as if someone poured gas under there and then lit it."

Greg stared into the distance, his head aching—whether from anger or from his recent injuries he couldn't tell. "That son of a bitch," he said under his breath.

"Do you have any idea who—"

"Of course I do," Greg said weakly. "Leonard Tully."

"I see. Well, I'm sure the police will want to know about him. But they'll also want to talk about you."

Greg's head was throbbing, making it difficult for him to follow Arnold's implication. His left arm itched furiously, but when he reached to scratch it he encountered unyielding plaster.

"What are you saying, Arnold?"

"It's only routine police work, Greg, but they'll want to know where you were on Tuesday night when the fire started."

"I was . . . with Valerie. What difference—"

"Good, then you have an alibi."

"Alibi?" Greg said loudly, raising his head. He winced from the pain and lay back down.

"Take it easy, there's nothing to worry about. In cases like this the first person they always question is the owner of the building that was torched. Now, this Leonard Tully, is he the same Leonard Tully you phoned me about with regard—"

"Yes, for God's sake, there's only one."

Arnold nodded. "After you spoke to me on Wednesday, did you have any contact with him?"

"Contact?" Greg's head was pounding, making Arnold's voice seem distant. "We . . . Valerie and I went to see him."

"You talked to him? Against my advice?" When Greg didn't answer, Arnold asked, "Did you threaten him in any way?"

"Threaten . . . no . . . just told him to stay away from Val." He squeezed his eyes shut, trying to escape from the pain and from Arnold's questions—the two had merged.

"Are you certain that's all? Because if you did, the police will want to know about it, and in that case I should probably be here when they—"

"No," Greg said. He thought he'd spoken loudly, forcefully, but his voice sounded faint to his ears. His eyes were still closed tightly, and white spots danced before them. "Ask . . . Val," he said, "when she . . . gets here."

"Is she coming this morning?"

"I'm . . . sure."

Valerie was terrified of what Leonard would do once her hands were tied. But she was also scared of what he might do if she fought him. He might harm Matthew. And so she let him tie her hands behind her back. She told Matthew it would be okay.

"We're going for a walk in the woods," Leonard said. He moved the table and opened the door.

Valerie hesitated, then came forward, with Matthew clinging to her side.

"Not him," Leonard said. "Just you and I."

"But why?" Valerie didn't want to be separated from Matthew—for her own sake as well as his.

"Because I *said* so." Leonard had spoken loudly, but now he looked contrite. He sighed and said, "Look, I just want to talk to you alone." He arched his brows, as if he were trying to appear harmless, trying to put her mind at ease.

Valerie was not reassured. She didn't want to go into the woods with him, and she didn't want to leave Matthew behind. But she knew she had little choice.

"I'm going to leave for a little while," she explained to Matthew. "But I'll be back pretty soon, okay?"

"Where are you going, Mom?"

Matthew looked so frightened that Valerie had trouble manufacturing a smile.

"Just for a walk, honey."

"Can't I go with you?"

"No," Leonard said sharply.

"No, baby." Valerie's tone was gentle. "You have to stay here. It'll be all right. I won't be gone long." She bent down. "Give me a kiss."

Matthew threw his arms around her neck and kissed her cheek. He hung on tightly, as if he feared she'd never return.

"It's okay, honey," she said, and he let go. She moved sideways past Leonard, keeping her eyes on Matthew. "See you in a little while."

Leonard came out behind her and pulled the door closed. "Man oh man," he said, exasperated, his patience at an end. He snapped the heavy padlock in place. "He acts like a baby."

"Can't you see he's a frightened little boy?"

Leonard snorted. "Well, *I* never acted like that when I was his age."

He took her arm and led her around to the side of the cabin. She could see Matthew through the window standing in the center of the room, facing the door, as if he expected her to return at any moment.

"Excuse me," Leonard said, swinging the shutter.

Matthew turned. "Mom?"

Leonard closed the heavy wooden shutter and locked it with a padlock. Valerie could hear Matthew calling to her from inside, his voice muffled.

"Do you have to do that?"

"Yes," Leonard said, leading her around the cabin.

"But he can't get out the window. And he wouldn't feel so frightened if he could see outside."

Matthew was waiting at the rear window. He shouted through the glass, "Mom, I don't want to be in here!"

Leonard closed the shutter and locked it, then led Valerie to the last window.

"Why are you doing this?" she pleaded.

Matthew screamed, "MOM!"

"*That's* why," Leonard said and slammed the shutter in Matthew's face.

The boy continued to cry out, his voice barely audible through the heavy wood.

Valerie was in agony. "God damn you," she said under her breath.

Leonard pursed his lips. "There's no need to curse."

Then he took her arm, pulling her away from the cabin. He retrieved a canteen from his truck and walked her across the scrubby, gravel-strewn clearing. They entered the woods.

Leonard led her in the general direction of the prostitute's grave.

32

"JUST SMELL THAT AIR." Leonard was obviously in fine spirits. He strode ahead of Valerie, leading her along a narrow, sun-dappled route through the trees. "And the trees. It's so beautiful up here. God's country."

Valerie saw no beauty in the leafy aspens, blue-green fir trees, and sparse, tiny, brilliantly colored wildflowers. There were only three things she was aware of: the cord around her wrists, Leonard's back, and Matthew, locked in the cabin.

Valerie was afraid to speculate why Leonard was taking her into the woods. She didn't believe it was to rape her—or kill her. He could have done either before. But she had to fight a feeling of panic, a feeling that she was a lamb being led without protest to slaughter.

She stared at the middle of Leonard's back a few yards before her. Maybe she should turn and run. But how far would she get before he caught her? Besides, there was Matthew. . . .

Eventually Leonard slowed his pace. He put out his arm for her to join him, to stroll side by side.

"So," he said, as if they'd just been introduced on a blind date, "tell me about yourself."

Valerie looked up at him and blinked, her fear giving way to confusion. "What?"

"You know," he said. "I want to hear those hundreds of little things that couples know about each other. Like, what's your favorite food? What books do you like? Who would you be if you could be anyone in the world? You know. All of that stuff."

"Are you serious?" Valerie couldn't believe what she was hearing.

"Of course I'm serious," he said, laughing. It was the first time Valerie had heard him laugh. The sound was strained, higher pitched than his voice, nearly a giggle.

Valerie gave him a pained look. "This is"—she stopped herself from saying, *insane*—"ridiculous," she finished.

"It is not," he said, still with a laugh in his voice. "Come on, it's what people do."

"What people *do?*" Valerie heard her own anger. She feared she could no longer contain it. "You mean kidnapping?"

Leonard halted so abruptly that Valerie took two steps before she stopped and turned to face him.

"I did not kidnap you," Leonard said evenly.

"No? Then what would you call it?"

"Kidnapping," he said, ignoring her question, "is when you hold someone for ransom. This has nothing to do with *kidnapping.*"

"Then what is it, Leonard?" She'd raised her voice, but it sounded hollow, lost among the trees. A bird gave out a single, sharp cry. A warning.

Leonard looked contrite. "I just thought . . ."

"Thought *what?*"

He looked at her, grinning sheepishly, then looked away. "I thought it would be the best way for us to get to know each other."

Valerie watched him, saying nothing. She suddenly felt much older than he, as if she were dealing with an adolescent. For the first time she believed she understood him—at least a part of him. Perhaps this was something she could use.

"You see," Leonard said, glancing at her, then at the ground, "I thought that if I could get you alone, you know, if we could be together away from all those distractions in the city, well, we—"

"Distractions?"

"You know, your painting, other people, and so on. If there weren't any distractions we'd be free to talk and get to know each other."

Valerie nodded. "I understand," she said, trying to adopt a parental tone of voice. "But there are other ways for us to do that, other places."

"No," he said, looking at her. "No, I don't think so."

She gave him a wry smile. "But don't you think this is a bit extreme?" She half turned to display her bound hands.

He cocked his head. "I guess."

"Then why don't you just take us back to Denver and we'll forget it ever happened."

"No."

Valerie opened her mouth, then closed it, deciding not to argue, choosing another tack. "Why did you pick me, Leonard? I mean, I'm a lot older than you and—"

"Not so much."

"—and I'm sure there are plenty of women closer to your age who—"

"No," he said. "There's no one else. Just you."

"But why me?"

He shrugged as if the answer were obvious. "Because I love you. I've loved you since the moment we first met."

Valerie was repulsed. But she wasn't surprised. She knew that Leonard's earlier actions—sending flowers, phoning her, bringing her candy—had been signs of his infatuation. Still, actually hearing him use the word "love" disgusted her.

"Don't ask me to explain it," he said, "because I can't. I guess I was ready for someone, and there you were."

Valerie said nothing.

"I know, I know," Leonard said. "You don't love me. Not yet, anyway. That's only natural. But in time I think you will."

She stared at him levelly. "How much time?"

"I don't know. A couple of days."

She shook her head. "Leonard, it takes more than two days for most people to fall in love."

"A few weeks, then," he said, his voice tight. "A few months."

"You can't keep us here that long."

"And why not?"

"Leonard, for God's sake, don't you think my friends will start wondering where Matthew and I have gone? They'll look for us. The police will—"

"No one will find you here."

Valerie wondered if he might be right. "But you can't keep us here *forever*," she said, trying to make it sound like a fact, not a plea.

"No." He frowned. "I . . . I know that."

"So eventually," she said, feeling as if she'd regained control, "you'll have to take us back. I mean, we'll all go back to Denver, right? Eventually."

"Well . . . sure."

"Then why not now?"

"Because the whole *point* is for us to get to know each other and we haven't even begun."

"But—"

"Besides, I can't take you back until I'm sure about you."

Valerie frowned at him. "What do you mean?"

"I need to be sure about how you feel. About what you'll tell people."

"What I'll tell them? You mean about how you're holding Matthew and me prisoner?"

"You see? That's what I mean."

"But what *can* I tell them?"

Leonard pushed up his bottom lip. "Well . . . I thought you could say that we'd all taken a trip together, a camping trip. That's why I moved your car."

Valerie nodded quickly. "Sure, okay. We can all go back today and—"

"No. Not until I'm sure about you."

Valerie was losing her patience. "But how can you *ever* be sure?"

"I'll know," he snapped.

"But how long will—"

"*I'll know!*" Leonard shouted, making her draw back. "I'll know, that's all." He stared at her, red-faced, daring her to argue. She remained silent. He took a calming breath and let it out. "Come on, let's walk," he said, as if they'd just made up after a lovers' quarrel. "And talk. Like an ordinary couple."

They walked side by side through the woods, neither of them speaking. After twenty minutes Valerie was perspiring. The sun was hot where it fell on them through the trees. Leonard stopped before a large, flat rock and unslung the canteen, offering her a drink. He had to hold it for her. Water ran down her chin.

"Sorry," he said.

"Wouldn't it be easier if you untied my hands?"

He shrugged. "You might try to run. And if you got away, well, you could get lost up here."

Valerie realized he was probably right. In fact, she doubted if she could find her own way back to the cabin.

Leonard sat on the rock, palms down, knees up.

"Let's rest here awhile," he said.

Valerie hesitated, then sat a few feet from him.

"Do you feel like talking?" he asked, as if they were old friends.

"Not especially."

"I really do want to know about you."

Valerie said nothing.

"Okay, then, I'll go first. Let's see, where to begin. Well, I was born right here in Colorado. . . ."

Leonard said that his father had been a great war hero who had been killed in Vietnam, that he and his mother had carried on alone, that lots of men had courted her because she was so beautiful. . . . Valerie tuned him out, nodding her head as if she were listening. She concentrated on working the cord loose from her wrists. If she could get free and grab a rock or a stick, surprise him, knock him unconscious . . .

Leonard rambled on and on, totally absorbed in himself. He stood and paced before her, as if he were teaching a class, describing his school days in detail, how he'd been surrounded by imbeciles, not allowed to join in their stupid games.

Leonard 101, Valerie thought wryly, twisting her wrists, trying not to let the movement show. She thought about Matthew. She wondered if he felt as hungry as she did. At least he has more than water from a canteen, she thought, straining against the cord.

It held fast. Eventually, she gave up.

"Let's walk some more," Leonard said.

He helped her off the rock and led her deeper into the woods. He continued to talk, his voice a drone.

But when he spoke of his mother and her religion, Valerie took notice.

"Does your mother know you have me here?" she asked abruptly, interrupting him in mid-sentence.

Leonard broke stride, nearly tripping. "My mother? Well, no, not yet. I'll tell her, though. Eventually."

"What's she going to think about this?"

Leonard stopped and faced her. He licked his lips and swallowed, bobbing his Adam's apple.

"Why do you care what my mother thinks?" he asked.

Valerie felt she'd found a weakness. If she could make Leonard feel guilty enough, guilty in the eyes of his mother, perhaps he'd let them go. "I'm just wondering how your mother will feel about your kidnapping us and taking—"

"It is not kidnapping."

"Whatever you want to call it."

"You have no right to question what my mother thinks," Leonard said angrily. He glared at her, jaws clenched.

"Come on, Leonard, you know she'd disapprove of—"

"Shut up!" he shouted, shaking his fist in her face.

Valerie was suddenly sorry she'd prodded him.

"She's not like you," he said loudly. "Not at *all* like you. She'd understand everything. *Everything.* She'd understand all about this and cutting the brake line and—"

"The brake line?"

"—and Brenda and—"

"Brenda?" Valerie stared at Leonard in horror.

Leonard set his jaw. "No," he said in a low voice, looking away. "That's not what I meant."

"You . . . ?" Valerie whispered.

"I said NO!" He grabbed her arm and gave her a shove. "We're going back."

He pushed her angrily through the trees. She stumbled along, trying to walk fast enough to stay ahead of him.

Leonard didn't stop until they'd reached the cabin. Valerie was exhausted. Leonard unlocked the door, then roughly untied her hands and pushed her inside. He kicked the box of firewood in behind her, then slammed the door and jammed the lock in place.

Matthew was so thankful to see his mother that he flung himself at her. Valerie held him tightly. Outside, Leonard gunned the truck's engine and roared away.

Valerie was still horrified by Leonard's words. He had practically confessed to killing Brenda and putting Greg in the hospital. What did he plan for her and Matthew?

She let go of her son and began desperately scouring the cabin's floor, walls, shutters, and door, even the ceiling, searching for a weakness, for a way out.

She found nothing.

Chapter
33

GREG WOKE UP SUNDAY MORNING with a headache and dull pains in his left arm and leg. Still, he felt much better than he had the day before.

He'd been questioned on Saturday by the Lakewood police about the fire at his shop. It had been difficult to concentrate—his head still throbbed—but he'd explained that he'd been with Valerie on the night of the fire, and he'd told them all he knew about Leonard Tully.

Later, he'd been visited by Janice and Mitch from the shop.

Valerie and Matthew, though, had not come.

He'd phoned Valerie's house late Saturday afternoon, getting no answer. He'd meant to phone again in the early evening—if they didn't visit—but at some point he'd fallen asleep and slept until morning.

Now he glanced at the clock on the wall: 7:20. They'd be up by now, he knew. He dialed Valerie's number.

No answer.

Maybe they're walking Dodger.

The nurse entered the room, briefly examined him, asked him how he felt about breakfast, then left. A few minutes later Dr. Halverson came in. He examined Greg's arm and leg, shined a penlight in his eyes, and checked his blood pressure and pulse.

"You're coming along fine," he said. "We'll have you out of here before you know it."

After he left, Greg phoned Valerie's house again. No answer. It was eight-forty.

Maybe they're on the way here, he thought. Hoped.

But he was beginning to sense that something was wrong. He phoned the house every half hour until noon. Then he called Janice at home.

"How are you doing?"

"Better, thanks," he said. "Could you do me a favor? Drive to Valerie's and see if she's home. If she's not, check out the house and then call me, okay?"

"Well, yes, but . . . is something the matter?"

"I don't know, Janice. I hope not."

Three quarters of an hour later the phone rang, and Greg snatched it off the cradle with his right hand, jerking too quickly, sending a flash of pain through his left arm.

"No one's home," Janice told him.

"Where are you calling from?"

"A gas station. When I got to the house I rang the bell and knocked on the door. No one answered. Dodger didn't bark, so I don't think he was inside or in the backyard. I walked around the front and side, trying to look in the windows. Most of the curtains were pulled and I couldn't see much. I even peeked through the back fence, but no one was in the yard, not even Dodger. Then I stood under the studio windows and called Valerie's name. Nothing."

"Something's not right," Greg muttered, more to himself than to Janice, wishing he'd told her where to find the spare key.

"I went back to the driveway and looked in through the garage door window. Her car's gone."

"You're certain?"

"The garage was empty. Where do you think they are?"

"I don't know. But I'm going to call the police."

Greg phoned the Wheat Ridge police and described the situation, realizing that his words did not exactly inspire urgency: his girlfriend, her son, and their dog weren't home; her car was not in the garage; he hadn't seen her since Friday; it was possible, though, that she might have visited him yesterday or last night when he'd been asleep; he was worried.

The policeman nudged Greg into admitting that there could be any number of innocent explanations. However, he said that a patrol car would be dispatched to check out the house. Greg implored him to search inside, telling him where to find the spare key, hidden near the garage.

Valerie awoke Sunday morning with a foul taste in her mouth. She felt itchy and longed for a bath. Mostly, of course, she was desperate to get herself and Matthew out of the cabin.

In frustration—and desperation—she threw herself against the door, trying vainly to break it down. She managed only to hurt her shoulder.

She again considered setting fire to the door, thinking it through this time. She could douse it with oil from the hurricane lamp—there was plenty in its large glass bowl—and touch it off with a match. Then she'd wrap herself in a blanket and burst through when the door became weakened by fire.

But what if she couldn't burst through soon enough? The fire would spread. . . .

No, she'd have to find another way out.

She *had* to. Because now she dreaded that Leonard wasn't just a kidnapper. He might be a murderer.

If what he'd blurted out yesterday was a confession, she realized, he'll have to kill her. And Matthew.

But as the day wore on—with no sign of Leonard—her hopes began to rise. Maybe he wasn't coming back. Of course, that could mean a slow death for her and Matthew after their food and water ran out. But perhaps that was preferable to facing whatever Leonard had in store for them.

She rested her hand on Matthew's shoulder.

He was still seated at the table. They'd shared a can of pear halves for breakfast, then bread, water, and part of a can of beans for lunch. Now Matthew was maneuvering a pair of spoons as if they were toy cars, racing them around a track formed by two mugs, a box of crackers, and the hurricane lamp.

The sound of an engine.

Valerie's head jerked up. She heard the vehicle approach and stop. Somehow, it hadn't sounded like Leonard's truck. Or was she simply deceiving herself, altering her perception of reality? Hoping for a miracle—a rescuer—she stood on tiptoe at the door and pressed her eye to the peephole. Her heart sank.

The familiar brown pickup was parked nearby.

Valerie jumped when she heard a shutter swing open. Leonard peered in, his face partially obscured by the heavy mesh and the streaked glass pane.

"Good morning." His tone was neutral. "Or I guess I mean 'good afternoon.' "

He moved around the cabin, opening the other shutters.

Barricade the door, Valerie thought in panic. Keep him out, keep him away from Matthew.

But she knew the effort would be futile. If Leonard wanted in, he could get in. If he couldn't force open the door by himself, he could ram it with the truck.

Valerie drew Matthew away from the table. Leonard unlocked the door and stepped in, setting down the heavy padlock and a paper bag. He looked apologetic. Valerie watched him warily.

"Sorry I'm so late," he said. "Sunday, you know. I had to take Mother to church. You both probably want to use the outhouse. I'm sorry, but I'll have to tie your hands." He removed lengths of cord from the bag.

Valerie hesitated. Had Leonard forgotten about yesterday? Or perhaps he *hadn't* confessed to Brenda's death. Whatever the case, he wasn't acting like a man about to commit murder. Valerie let him tie her hands and then Matthew's—before them, not behind.

After they were finished at the outhouse, Leonard brought them back inside the cabin. He left the door open.

"Sit here, please," he told Matthew, pulling a chair from the table. Matthew looked at Valerie.

She asked Leonard, "What are you going to do?"

"Please." His tone was pleasant.

Valerie hesitated, then told Matthew it was okay.

"And you sit on the cot," Leonard said, removing a long cord from the sack. "We need to talk. Alone."

As soon as Matthew sat down, Leonard began tying him to the chair. The boy struggled, crying out.

"What are you doing?" Valerie said, coming forward.

Leonard ignored her, pinning Matthew's arms to his sides and wrapping the rope around his chest and the back of the chair. He removed a roll of tape from the sack and tore off a strip.

"Don't!" Valerie cried.

"I'm not going to *hurt* him."

Leonard held Matthew's head still and pressed the tape over his mouth. Valerie grabbed at Leonard, hands together. He pushed her firmly away. Then he tipped Matthew's chair on its back legs and dragged the boy from the cabin. Valerie followed.

"What are you *doing?*"

Leonard righted Matthew's chair a few yards from the cabin, then turned to Valerie.

"Back inside," he said.

"What—"

"I said get in there." His tone was hard.

Valerie hesitated, looking at Matthew. He was wriggling against his bonds, but otherwise seemed to be all right. Leonard came toward her. She backed into the cabin.

"Sit down on the cot."

Valerie saw no alternative. She sat.

Leonard pushed the door closed. "Alone at last," he said.

Chapter

34

VALERIE WATCHED HIM CAREFULLY, her body tense. He seemed different from yesterday. Not as shy. More determined. She was afraid of what might happen next.

Leonard leaned a hip against the table's edge and folded his arms across his chest. He stared at Valerie, his head cocked to one side. After a moment he spoke.

"Yesterday I said something that I believe you . . . misinterpreted. Do you know what I'm talking about?"

Valerie could guess. "No," she said.

"Brenda." He spat the name. "I'll be truthful, I didn't like her very much. In fact, I didn't like her at all. But I didn't kill her. And it's important that you believe that. That you *know* that."

"I—"

"See, the problem is," Leonard said before she could lie, "you actually believe I'm capable of something like that." His eyes narrowed. "Don't you?"

Valerie said nothing.

Leonard nodded, his lips pursed. Then he asked conversationally, "Do you know what I could do to him?"

"What . . ." She shook her head, not fully understanding his meaning.

"Your son," he said. "Do you know what I could do to him?"

"I . . . don't know what you mean."

Leonard spread his hands and smiled broadly. "Anything I want." Then he put one hand in the crook of his elbow, touched a finger to his bottom lip, and looked up at the ceiling. "Let's see, I could cut him, of course, or lay him under a tire and run over him with the truck."

". . . No."

He looked down at Valerie. She stared back, holding her breath. His eyes rose again to the ceiling.

"Or I could remove the bench from the outhouse and drop him headfirst into the pit. That would be nasty. Or I could drag him into the woods, tie him to a tree, and just leave him there to starve." He lowered his gaze until it rested on her face. "Couldn't I?"

She shook her head, terrified. "Why are you saying these things. What do you wa—"

"Couldn't I!" he shouted, coming off the table, stepping forward until he towered over her. "COULDN'T I!"

She shrank from him. Twenty minutes ago he'd seemed friendly. Now he looked ready to kill.

". . . Yes," she said, barely moving her lips.

"Yes," he repeated, almost in triumph. He stepped back, straightening his shoulders. "And you couldn't stop me." He waved his hand. "No one could. I could do anything to him. *Anything.*"

She tried to swallow, afraid to speak.

"But you know what?" he said, arching his eyebrows. "I won't. And you know why?"

He waited for her to answer. She shook her head no.

"Because I'm not a violent person." One corner of his mouth curled up. "You see what I'm saying? I couldn't have hurt Brenda, because I'm not a violent person. If I were I'd probably do one of those things I just described. I mean, why not? Who could stop me? Who'd ever know?" He spread his hands, palms up. "But I'm not violent and I'm not going to do any of those things. Or some others I could think of. Do you see what I mean?"

Valerie hesitated.

"Well?"

"Yes," she said quietly.

Leonard smiled. "So you agree, I'm not violent."

Valerie held his eyes for a moment, then looked away and mumbled, "No."

"What was that?"

"I said *no,* you're not violent."

Leonard nodded, smug. "Well, okay, then."

Valerie hoped this insane exercise was over. All she wanted now was for Leonard to free Matthew from the chair.

"You still don't trust me, though, do you? You still think I'm a bad person."

"Didn't I just agree that—"

"I don't mean violent," Leonard said. "I mean bad. Evil. Don't you?"

Valerie looked at him, then looked away.

"You kidnap—" She stopped herself. "You're holding us against our will."

"But I haven't hurt you, have I?"

Valerie said nothing.

"Haven't I been nice to you? Haven't I provided for you? Food, water, shelter . . . I'll bring you whatever you—"

"Just let us *go*," she cried.

He came toward her. "Do you know," he said, raising his voice, "what a lot of men would do—what *most* men would do—if they were in my position? Alone in a cabin with a beautiful woman?"

He reached for her neck.

She raised her hands, and he slapped them away.

"Put your hands in your lap!" he shouted. "Do it!"

She tried to get away from him, but he pushed her back onto the cot. Then he removed the knife from his pocket, showing it to her, not bothering to open the blade.

"Do you want me to go play with your son?"

Valerie's eyes flicked from Leonard to the door. She pictured Matthew outside, completely helpless, bound to a chair.

Leonard watched her face, saw her reaction. "No? Then sit up and keep your hands in your lap."

Valerie held her hands before her, ready to ward him off.

Leonard heaved a sigh. "Have it your own way," he said, turning, moving toward the door.

"Wait."

Leonard stopped, but kept his back to her.

"All right," she said. She sat up on the edge of the cot, her fists clenched in her lap.

Leonard looked over his shoulder and smiled. "Good." He returned the knife to his pocket, then stood before her at arm's length.

Her head was level with his stomach. She looked away.

"I'm not like other men," he said harshly. "Do you know what they'd do, Valerie? Do you know what another man would do?"

He reached for her neck, stopping an inch away, balling his fist under her chin as if he were gathering the top of her dress in his grip.

"The first thing"—he flexed his biceps and yanked his arm away from her—"he'd *rip* off your dress."

Leonard stared down at her. He nervously wet his lips, as if he were imagining her naked from the waist up.

"Just rip it right off," he said. "And you'd be sitting there with your bare breasts . . . you'd just be sitting there."

Slowly Leonard raised his hands, cupping them, moving them toward her.

"And then he'd hold them," Leonard said. "He'd take them in his hands." He held his hands a few centimeters from her, not quite touching her. "He'd rub them," he said, swallowing hard, moving his hands, rotating them side to side, nearly brushing the fabric of her dress. "Squeeze them. Feel how smooth and firm they were. Play with them. Do anything he wanted. And he'd keep doing it. . . ."

Valerie could hear him breathing hard now. She gritted her teeth, looking away, loathing and fearing the moment when his fantasy would spill over into reality, when he'd finally lay his hands on her.

". . . and your nipples, he'd play with them, and . . . and they'd be hard. He'd pinch them. . . ."

Valerie sat perfectly still, not watching Leonard's hands, sensing them moving before her, almost touching her.

"And he'd keep doing it," he said, his voice higher pitched than before, "and doing it and doing it. And you might not want it to feel good, but after a while it would. And he'd keep doing it until he could tell that you liked it, really *liked* it."

Leonard lowered his right hand, apparently wiping perspiration on the front of his pants. His left hand still hovered millimeters over Valerie's right breast. Both hands were in motion. It was a moment before Leonard spoke again.

"And when he was ready, . . . when *you* were ready, then he'd make you do things." His voice had become thick, and he continued to rub his pants. "He'd make you . . . and you'd *want* to . . . he'd make you take his, take him out of his pants." Leonard swallowed, making an animal sound low in his throat. "You'd . . . you'd have to hold it in your hand . . . and *feel* it and . . . and then he'd . . . he'd make you—" Leonard swallowed with difficulty, his fingers fumbling with his zipper. His eyes had lost their focus. "He'd make you . . . put it in your mouth, Valerie." His hips moved forward. "And . . . and it would be *in* there and . . ."

Suddenly, Leonard stepped back, breathing rapidly, and pressed his fist to his mouth. His eyes were wide in horror, as if he'd just awakened from a nightmare and found that he'd actually committed rape. Then he lowered his arm and shoved his hands in his pockets. He licked his lips, his tongue flicking like a lizard's. There was a sheen of perspiration on his pale forehead.

"That's—" He cleared his throat. "That's what he, what *they* would do." Now he crossed his arms and tucked his hands in his armpits. He stared at the floor. "If they were in my position." He cleared his throat again and looked at Valerie. "Wouldn't they?"

Valerie sat rigidly, filled with hate and nausea, feeling as if she'd been violated.

"Well, wouldn't they?" His eyebrows were raised and his mouth was parted, to show his innocence.

"I . . . don't know."

"Sure they would," he said and cleared his throat a final time. "*They* would. But *I* won't. Don't you see? I'm not that kind of man." He shrugged his shoulders and smiled weakly. "I'm not." He spread his arms, pleading for her to agree, banging the back of his hand on a chair. He winced and rubbed his hand.

"Will you . . . untie Matthew now?" Valerie asked quietly.

"What?" He frowned at her, as if he hadn't understood, then said, "Oh, him."

He turned his back on her and went outside, leaving the door open. Valerie could see Matthew wriggling in the chair, trying to free himself. She fought back tears, telling herself to hang on. Eventually, Leonard would let them go. Or someone would rescue them. Somehow, she and Matthew would get out of here. Somehow. They had to.

Before something happened.

Chapter

35

MATTHEW RAN THROUGH THE DOORWAY, his face wet with tears. He threw himself at Valerie. Obviously, the situation had become intolerable for him. Valerie held him close, and his small body shook with sobs. She smoothed his hair with her bound hands and whispered to him, telling him everything was all right now.

Leonard brought the chair inside and shoved it under the table. He looked irritated. He glowered at Matthew. The boy continued to sob into Valerie's dress.

"What's *his* problem?"

"For God's sake," Valerie said, nearly crying, her hands on the back of Matthew's head, "he's an eight-year-old boy and he's scared to death."

"Well, *I* never hurt him."

"Never *hurt* him?" Valerie's voice was loud in the small room. "You tied him to a chair, taped his mouth, and—"

"That was necessary."

"Necessary?" Valerie shouted, feeling her self-control slipping away. "Necessary for *what?*"

"So that you and I could have a little privacy. All I want is—hey, can't you shut him up?—all I want is for us to talk and get to know each other and—will you *please* shut him up?—and I didn't want him interrupting us. Like he's doing *now.*"

Matthew's sobs had become shrill. Leonard glared at him, his face red. He stepped forward, fists clenched at his sides. "Will . . . you . . . SHUT . . . UP!"

Matthew wailed in terror, clutching Valerie's dress.

Leonard shook his fist at Matthew, his index finger extended like a weapon. *"That's* what I'm talking about."

"Please," Valerie pleaded, turning her back to Leonard, wrapping Matthew in her arms, shielding him with her body. "Please, you're just making things worse."

"Oh, *I'm* making things worse!" Leonard shouted above Matthew's cries. "What about *him? He's* the one screaming his ugly little head off!" He grabbed Valerie's shoulder, trying to move her away from Matthew.

"No!" She yanked away from him, then half pushed, half carried Matthew to the corner of the room, where he hunkered down like a small, frightened animal. Valerie folded herself around him. "Damn you," she said over her shoulder, tears streaming down her face. "Why don't you just leave us alone?"

Leonard watched them, his mouth a thin white line. Muscles wormed at the points of his jaw.

"If I had my way," he said hoarsely, "he wouldn't even *be* here."

"Then let him go," Valerie begged.

"It's too late for that." Leonard removed the knife from his pocket and clicked open the blade, then came forward, the knife held before him.

"You shut him up this minute." Leonard's voice was low and mean. "Or I will."

Valerie hunched over Matthew, looping her arms over him, wrists together, her back toward Leonard. She tasted her own tears as she stroked Matthew's face with her fingertips. The boy could not stop his cries of terror. Valerie waited for a blow from Leonard's fist or the sharp pain of his knife.

Neither came.

She continued to stroke Matthew's face, holding him close and whispering, "Calm down, honey, it's all right."

Finally, his wails turned to sobs. And eventually his sobbing subsided. Valerie wiped the tears from his face. She looked over her shoulder, and was surprised to see that Leonard was no longer standing behind her.

He sat in a chair, facing them, one arm resting on the table. He'd put away the knife. He regarded them thoughtfully.

"I'm sorry," he said. "I really didn't mean to frighten him."

Valerie didn't even try to guess what was going through Leonard's mind. She felt both anger and fear, and she was unsure which emotion to follow, not wanting to show either. She helped Matthew to his feet, then had him lie down on one of the cots. After she pulled off his shoes, she covered him with a blanket, awkwardly, her hands together.

"There, baby," she said. "You rest."

"I was wrong to tie him to the chair." Leonard sounded genuinely sorry, apparently unmindful that moments ago he had threatened Matthew's life.

Valerie sat beside Matthew on the cot and stroked his hair with her hands. The cord bit uncomfortably into her wrists, but she kept stroking him, humming softly. Eventually, his eyes closed and his face relaxed. She sat there for a long time, totally attentive to her son.

"Is he asleep?" Leonard asked in loud whisper, making Valerie start. He'd been sitting so quietly that she'd almost believed he'd left the cabin.

She kept her eyes on Matthew and nodded yes.

"Then we should leave."

Valerie looked at him. "What?"

Matthew stirred beneath her hand.

"You and I still have a lot to talk about," Leonard said softly. "We should go outside where we won't disturb him."

Valerie bit back a sob of frustration.

"Why can't . . . why don't you just let us go?"

Leonard smiled easily. "We can talk about that, too."

Matthew turned on his side, pulling his knees up, pressing the back of his hand to his chin and mouth. Valerie straightened the blanket over him.

Leonard stood and pushed his chair quietly and precisely beneath the table. He held out his hand to Valerie.

"Shall we?"

Valerie knew that resistance was futile. At the very least it would rouse Matthew, perhaps send him into another hysterical fit, his cries going through her like knives. At the worst there was Leonard's knife. Better for her and Leonard to leave Matthew in peace.

She leaned down and kissed her son softly on the cheek. Then she stood and walked out the door with Leonard behind her. He locked the padlock, while she waited in the hot afternoon sun, watching him carefully. His attitude, even the way he carried himself, was completely different from a short time ago. He seemed relaxed, even caring. Vulnerable.

He faced her, a light smile on his lips.

"Are you ready?" he asked, as if they were dear friends, off on a Sunday walk.

She forced a smile in return. "Yes, but . . ."

He looked concerned. "What is it?"

"My wrists are really sore." She held them out to him. "Can't you untie me?"

"I . . . don't know."

"I promise I won't run. You know I won't try to get away, not while you have Matthew locked up." She had other ideas.

Leonard chewed the inside of his cheek, thinking.

"We've got to learn to trust each other," Valerie said. And if I get behind you with a rock, she thought, I'll bash in your fucking head.

"Well . . . okay."

Leonard untied her, and she rubbed her wrists.

"Thank you," she said, smiling. Then she nodded toward the trees. "Lead on."

Instead, he took her gently by the arm and steered her into the trees, staying slightly behind her. They walked for twenty minutes, neither of them speaking. The only sound was the trilling of elusive birds. Valerie scanned the ground for a good-sized rock or heavy branch. There were many.

"I did all the talking yesterday," Leonard said at last. "Now it's your turn."

"What would you like to know?" Valerie wished she could get behind him, just for a moment.

"Everything." Leonard's voice was cheery. "Where you were born, where you grew up, everything."

"Okay, let's see, I was born in Washington. . . ." She began to recount her childhood, hoping to put Leonard at ease, off guard. So far, he had not let go of her arm. As she talked, she searched the ground for a suitable weapon, hoping that eventually he'd forget himself and turn his back on her. She talked on and on about her early school days and her love of art and how her parents had encouraged her.

Leonard interrupted her: "Are they the ones who told you to paint that way?"

"Excuse me?"

"Your style. It's . . . messy. Not precise."

"What do—"

Suddenly Leonard jerked hard on her arm.

"Shut up," he hissed.

"Wha—"

"Shh!" He clamped his hand over her mouth and looked past her, his body tense, alert. Valerie listened, but heard nothing. Leonard pulled her toward a large pine tree and shoved her roughly to the ground. He lay beside her, holding her left arm behind her back and pressing his hand over her mouth.

"Don't make a sound," he whispered harshly. "Someone's coming."

C h a p t e r

36

VALERIE'S HEAD WAS FILLED with the scent of dry pine needles and the faint soapy odor of Leonard's hand. Leonard embraced her from behind, his right leg thrown over her knees. Small rocks bit into her hip. She could see nothing but a small patch of ground and a portion of the tree trunk. She felt Leonard's warm breath in her hair.

Then there were voices.

"I say we're lost." A woman.

"We're not lost." A man. "We're right *here*."

Laughter.

From at least three people, Valerie guessed, possibly four. Two men and two women. She could hear them moving through the trees, crunching pine needles and snapping twigs. They seemed to be coming closer, although Valerie knew that judging distance by sound could be deceiving, especially in the mountains. The hikers might be fifty feet away or two hundred yards. She pictured them in their boots, walking shorts, and colorful backpacks—out for a Sunday hike, or maybe a weekend camping trip . . .

. . . While she lay pinned to the ground by a psychopath.

"Admit it, we're off the trail." A woman's voice, different from the first one.

"Well, maybe."

"Oh, now he says 'maybe.' "

Laughter.

"Okay, okay, let's have another look at the map."

Valerie heard a thumping sound, as if a backpack had been dropped to the ground. And not too far away. She still could not see anyone.

But she decided it was now or never.

She reached up quickly with her free hand, grabbed Leonard's wrist, and yanked, trying to pull his hand from her mouth. If she could only scream, just once . . .

"The stream is right here, this blue line."

"Well, even *I* knew that."

Leonard's hand didn't budge. Valerie tried to yell anyway, but it came out as a feeble groan.

"All I'm saying is, we were on the trail until there. When we crossed the stream, we lost the trail."

"Do you mean we've got to go back?"

"Do you have a better idea?"

"But that's at least a mile."

"More like two."

Valerie was kicking and thrashing about and shoving the ground with her free arm, trying to buck Leonard off her back. He increased the pressure on her other arm, twisting it painfully behind her back.

"That's not so far. We—wait a minute. Did you hear that?"

Leonard rolled on top of Valerie, his hand still clamped over her mouth, the full weight of his body pressing down on her.

"Hear what?"

"I don't know. Over that way."

Valerie tried to kick, but it was useless. She felt the air being squeezed from her lungs.

"Maybe an animal."

"A bear?"

"Don't be silly. There aren't any bears around here."

"Tell me that when one bites you on the ass."

Laughter.

Valerie bit Leonard's palm, sinking her teeth into the roll of flesh just below the base of his middle finger. If he didn't let go, maybe she could make him cry out.

But he only grunted with pain. He pressed his hand more firmly to her face and twisted her arm until she thought it would break.

She could taste blood. And so she bit harder. Leonard held her even tighter, keeping his hand in place. And still she bit. Then he pinched her nostrils closed with his thumb and index finger.

And suddenly Valerie couldn't breath. She tried desperately to free herself.

"There. Did you hear it?"

"So what? It's probably just a squirrel."

Valerie's lungs felt as if they'd burst, and her heart beat madly.

"Come on, let's get going. It's at least an hour back to the stream."

"If we can *find* the stream."

Laughter, barely audible through the roaring in Valerie's ears. She felt as if she were dying. Her vision blurred, and then went black.

Slowly, Valerie came to.

She blinked her eyes, looking up at a patch of blue sky framed by pine branches. Something cold and smooth was pressed lightly across her lips, like a finger, requesting silence. She knew immediately what it was—the blade of Leonard's knife. Its point barely touched the side of her nose.

"They're gone," he said quietly. He was sitting beside her on the ground, casually holding the knife in his left hand. "But just the same, I don't want you to cry out. Do you understand?"

She nodded her head as much as the knife blade would allow.

Leonard stood, folded his knife, and brushed off the seat of his pants. Valerie got to her feet, feeling dizzy. She saw that Leonard's right hand was wrapped in a handkerchief. The white cloth was stained with blood.

The sight of it filled her with fear. Leonard would punish her for that. She'd seen him angry before, and now that he had a genuine reason to be mad, she expected the worst.

"Let's go," he said. There was sadness in his voice.

He pushed her gently ahead of him, walking closely behind her, directing her through the trees. Valerie had lost her bearings, but she felt that he was taking her deeper into the woods. And she could think of only one reason why—he was going to kill her. She considered trying to run, or perhaps turn and fight. But she was so weak that she wobbled as she walked.

She wondered how he'd kill her. Would he smash her head with a rock? Or use the knife?

Her stomach was queasy, and her forehead felt cold and clammy. Her neck muscles were tight, waiting for the blow. She kept walking, stumbling forward, while pine branches snatched at her arms.

And suddenly they emerged from the trees.

Valerie was so startled by the sight of the cabin in the clearing that she stopped abruptly. Leonard bumped into her from behind.

"Sorry," he said.

He followed her to the cabin, undid the padlock, then stood aside for her to enter.

Matthew rushed across the room and clung to her.

"Mom! I was scared. When I woke up I was all alone."

"It's all right now, baby." She held him close, waiting now for Leonard's tirade and for whatever punishment he had planned.

But he merely stood in the doorway, as if he were a guest who wasn't certain whether it was time to leave. He stared absently at his injured hand. He flexed his fingers and grimaced.

Valerie could see that he was lost in thought. Apparently, any anger he'd held for her had dissipated. For the first time since the kidnapping he looked lost and confused, unsure of what to do next. As if he needed . . . a friend.

"I'm . . . sorry about your hand," she said, trying to sound as if she meant it.

Leonard looked up, embarrassed. Then he shook his head and dropped his hand to his side.

"Never mind," he mumbled, eyes downcast.

"May I see it?" If she could distract him, maybe Matthew could dash out the door. . . . "If you have some disinfectant I could—"

"There's nothing like that up here." He wouldn't meet her eyes.

"Then let me clean it with water."

"No, it's all right. I . . . it was my fault. All of it was my fault." He reached for the door. "I . . . have to go now."

Valerie watched him carefully, her hand resting on Matthew's shoulder. Leonard was acting differently than ever before. He seemed sad, depressed. She wondered if he was ever coming back.

"Where are you going?"

Leonard frowned, still averting his gaze. "Home. I . . . have to think."

He stepped outside, shut the door, and locked it.

Valerie heard the engine cough awake and the truck rattle away. She moved to the side window and watched the truck follow a pair of ruts in the ground and disappear into the trees. The sounds faded to silence.

37

VALERIE STOOD AT THE WINDOW a moment longer before she realized what she was doing—looking out the window.

Leonard had left without closing and locking the shutters.

Valerie peered through the streaked glass and heavy mesh screen, searching for his truck in the distant trees. Would he remember leaving the shutters open and immediately return to the cabin? Or had he forgotten completely?

Valerie recalled how he'd looked and acted just before he'd left. Confused, preoccupied. Maybe he wasn't coming back—at least until tomorrow.

"Mom, when are—"

"Shh, honey, be quiet for a minute."

Valerie pressed her ear to the glass, straining for the sound of Leonard's truck. She could detect the faint twittering of a bird, the chirp of a cricket, nothing more.

He said he was going home, Valerie thought. He might not remember the shutters until then. If he did, would he drive all the way back here today?

She pulled the window sash, trying to swing it open. But it held fast. Then she tried the other two windows, but they were stuck too.

"What are you doing, Mom?"

"Trying to get us out of here. Bring me that spoon."

Matthew gave her a spoon from the table. Valerie jammed the handle between the frame and the sash and tried to pry open the window. She succeeded only in bending the spoon. Then she noticed a tiny metal disk embedded in the wood—and another, not six inches away. And another.

The window wasn't stuck, she realized. Leonard had nailed it shut.

Quickly, she inspected the other windows. They'd also been fastened shut with nails.

"What I need is a crowbar," Valerie muttered.

She checked the box of firewood. There was little left, nothing large enough to use as a battering ram. So she dragged a chair to the nearest window, held it by the top of the backrest and the front edge of the seat, and told Matthew to move away.

She hesitated, though, before lifting the chair.

Leonard might come right back, she thought. What if he drove up while she was breaking out the window? How would he react to that?

Fuck him.

Valerie lifted the chair above her shoulders and drove one of its legs into the window, shattering the glass. Matthew cried out in surprise, as silver shards fell to the floor. Valerie jabbed the chair at the window again and again, breaking out all four panes. With each blow the chair rebounded off the heavy steel mesh screen.

She banged the chair leg against the screen a few more times, before her arm and shoulder muscles burned from the weight of the chair. She set it aside, her shoes crunching on broken glass. Then she examined the screen.

The wooden cross-member within the frame still held jagged fragments of glass, and broken pieces lay between the empty frame and the heavy screen. The screen itself was undamaged, except for a few shallow dimples from the chair leg.

Valerie again lifted the chair and began banging it into the screen with all her might. She stopped after a few minutes, breathing heavily, examining her work.

She'd managed to break out the interior pieces of the wood frame, leaving an empty square large enough for her and Matthew to crawl through. If it weren't for the screen. The steel mesh was more dimpled than before, but it showed no sign of breaking. Valerie leaned in for a closer look at the edges. They were flush with the sides of the window. She imagined the screen was fixed to the outside of the cabin with heavy nails, perhaps even screws or bolts. If she kept pounding away with the chair, she wondered which would give out first, the screen or her strength.

Then she remembered the hikers.

She checked her watch. It was after four. How long had it been since she and Leonard had heard them in the woods? At least an hour. Probably more. How far could the hikers have gone? Perhaps they were still within range of her voice.

Valerie cupped her hands to the sides of her mouth and shouted, "HELP! HELP US!"

She stopped, listening, praying to hear a faint cry of "Where are you?" or "We're coming."

But there was nothing, not even a bird or a cricket.

"HELP US! HELP!"

She didn't know how far her voice would carry or if there was anyone out there to hear—but for the moment it was all she could think of to do. Matthew watched her with wide eyes and open mouth.

"Come over here, honey."

Valerie put the chair beneath the window, and Matthew stood on the seat, his head level with hers. They both shouted at the top of their voices, stopping only to catch their breath—and to listen for an answer.

Leonard drove home. He steered automatically, unconsciously, his mind filled with thoughts of Valerie, his hand throbbing with pain.

For the first time since he'd met her he felt unsure of himself, unsure of her. He'd been so *certain* that she was the one woman in all the world for him. And he'd been just as certain that he could court her and win her over.

Taking her to the cabin, though, had been a mistake, that was obvious now. But how could he have known unless he'd tried? Sure, he'd expected her to be frightened and even angry—at least until he'd proved to her that his intentions were honorable. But her behavior had become totally unpredictable. She was acting like a cornered animal. She'd *bitten* him.

He held up his wounded hand, still wrapped in the bloodstained handkerchief. Hadn't he heard that you could get rabies from the bite of a human?

He ground his teeth, shutting out the pain, remembering when she'd sunk her teeth into his flesh, like some wild creature. He'd shut off her air, pinching her nose until she'd passed out. At the time he'd briefly considered keeping his hand in place until she suffocated. He'd even had a mental image of digging her grave near the prostitute.

Two graves, actually. One for the boy.

The boy, Leonard thought, had been a problem from the beginning. He should have gotten rid of him before he brought Valerie to the cabin. *Then* things might have worked out.

But it was too late for that, he knew. And maybe it was too late to win over Valerie. The question was, what was he to do with them?

Leonard steered the truck down the alley and parked behind his house. As quietly as possible he opened the back door and slipped inside, hoping to get to the bathroom before his mother heard him, before she saw his hand wrapped in a bloody handkerchief.

He moved quietly along the hallway toward the bathroom door. Ahead lay the kitchen, from which emanated the loud voice of a TV evangelist. He pictured his mother sitting at the table, enraptured by the screen.

Quickly, Leonard stepped into the bathroom, closed the door, and locked it. He unwrapped the handkerchief, gently peeled it from his hand, and dropped it in the wastebasket. His palm was sticky with blood.

He ran warm water from the tap, then held his hand in the stream, washing away the dried and drying blood. He winced from the sting of the water and from the sight of his palm. There were two opposing, crescent-shaped wounds in his hand. The flesh was purple and puckered. Valerie's teeth marks were well defined.

He swore under his breath.

"Leonard?"

He flinched, startled. Francine was right outside the bathroom door, not three feet from him.

"When did you get home?" she asked.

"Just"—he had to clear his throat to speak—"just now."

"Are you all right? You sound funny."

"I'm fine. I just . . . have to wash up."

"Oh," Francine said.

Leonard listened for a moment. Silence. Apparently, his mother had wheeled herself quietly back to the kitchen. He swung open the mirrored door over the medicine cabinet and took down a bottle of hydrogen peroxide. He unscrewed the cap, held his right hand palm up over the sink, and poured.

"Leonard?"

He grunted with pain, squeezing his eyes shut.

"Leonard, are you sure you're all right?"

He spoke between clenched teeth. ". . . Yes."

"Excuse me?"

He breathed deeply a few times. "I said yes, I'm fine."

"Did you finish the repairs at the cabin?"

"Not quite."

"When will you?"

"Tomorrow."

"Because you've been neglecting your work around here, you know."

"Yes, Mother."

She was silent for a moment. Then he heard her wheeling her chair away.

He poured more disinfectant over his palm. It burned, but not nearly as much as before. He found a jar of salve in the cabinet and spread it over the wound, wondering if this was the proper treatment for a bite. Then he wrapped his hand with a gauze bandage.

He examined his work. It was a crude job, but it would have to do.

Now he'd go out to the kitchen and fix dinner. When his mother saw the bandage, he's say that he'd cut his hand on a piece of glass. She'd believe him, no problem.

The problem was Valerie and her son.

He couldn't let them go. Not now, anyway. Valerie would run straight to the police, and the next thing he knew he'd be in prison. And he'd heard what convicts did to new young prisoners.

The thought made him shudder.

He could kill them, of course, and bury their bodies.

But was it really too soon to give up on Valerie? Maybe if he kept her there for a few more days, perhaps a week, she'd start to see that he wasn't such a bad guy. In fact, he was a pretty *nice* guy when you got right down to it. And really, had he treated her so badly? No, not at all.

He certainly hadn't *bitten* her.

Leonard leaned close to the mirror. In the reflection of his pupils he could see the tiny man, the tiny Leonard.

Could he ever trust Valerie not to go to the police? Could he afford to ever set her free?

The tiny Leonard stared back, mute.

He'd have to sleep on it.

Chapter

38

EARLY MONDAY MORNING Greg phoned the Denver police department and asked for Detective Gianelli.

"Have the Wheat Ridge police called you yet?"

"No," Gianelli said. "Were they supposed to?"

"Yes, dammit, I told them you'd explain about Leonard."

"Take it easy. Tell me what's going on."

"Something's happened to Valerie," Greg said, forcing himself to calm down. "I'm certain of it."

He told Gianelli how yesterday afternoon, after not hearing from Valerie and Matthew all day, he'd called the Wheat Ridge police, expressed his concern, and told them where Valerie's extra door key was hidden. Two patrolmen had entered Valerie's house and found no sign of Valerie, Matthew, or the car. Also, they'd found no signs of violence.

Greg had learned this over the phone from a Sergeant Willis, who'd been emphatic about the last point. Willis had asked Greg if there was a chance Valerie had simply taken Matthew somewhere for the weekend. Greg had to admit it was a possibility, although unlikely. Then, as briefly as possible, he'd told Willis about Leonard Tully and about the involvement of the Denver police, particularly Detective Gianelli. Willis had advised Greg not to worry too much and said he'd contact Gianelli.

"I haven't heard a peep," Gianelli said.

"You've got to do something. I don't think they understand the danger she and Matthew might be in. And it's probably my fault—I must've sounded like a lunatic trying to tell them about Leonard."

"All right, I'll give them a call."

"Jesus Christ, don't just call," Greg said loudly, "go arrest Leonard. He's done something to them, I *know* it."

"All right, calm down. I know you're upset. I'm concerned too, but we can't just arrest the man based on only your suspicions. I'll go talk

225

to him. But first I'll take a look through Ms. Rowe's house. Maybe there's something the Wheat Ridge cops missed. I'll call you if I find anything."

Greg hung up. He felt like a prisoner, bound to his bed. If he had been able, he would have gone directly to Leonard's house and inflicted whatever pain was necessary to make him talk.

But all he could do was lie there and pray that Valerie and Matthew were alive and well.

Early Monday morning Valerie woke up shivering.

The stove was cold and the last of the firewood had been burned. Chill air wafted in from the shattered screened window.

Valerie rose and laid her blanket over Matthew, careful not to wake him. She sat at the table and warmed her hands over the small, hot flame of the hurricane lamp. Her muscles ached—not just from the cold, but from her efforts to escape the night before.

Yesterday afternoon she and Matthew had shouted for help until their throats were raw and their voices hoarse. They'd stopped only when she'd felt certain the hikers she'd heard earlier in the day weren't coming. She and Matthew could have continued shouting until their voices gave out completely, but what would be the use? The cabin was remote, away from frequented trails. The hikers had been lost, their presence an exception. No one else was out there to hear their cries.

So Valerie had worked all night trying to break out the heavy mesh screen.

She'd banged it again and again with the chair, each blow sending shock waves through her arms. She'd swung the chair until she could no longer raise it to the window. For dinner she'd opened a can of beans, and afterward she'd gone back to work on the screen. But not for long— her shoulders and arms trembled with fatigue. She'd dragged one of the cots closer to the stove, put in the last of the firewood, and huddled against Matthew, trying to keep him warm. Eventually, they'd slept.

"Mom, I'm cold."

Now Matthew was sitting up on the cot. The blankets were wrapped around him Indian style.

"I know, hon."

Valerie sat beside him, hugging him.

"Why don't you warm your hands by the lamp and I'll fix us something to eat."

They ate the last of the crackers and a can of cold tomato soup. Then Valerie resumed work on the screen. She had no idea when Leonard would return. She felt certain, though, that he'd never again forget to lock the shutters.

She raised the chair above her head and slammed it with all her might into the heavy screen. And again.

And again.

She pounded at the screen until she could barely swing the chair.

And finally, something began to give.

She'd felt it in the last few blows. The chair hadn't rebounded as sharply from the screen as before. The blows felt mushy, as if the screen were beginning to weaken. Valerie examined it closely, searching for signs of a break. But it looked as solid as ever, undamaged, merely dimpled from the leg of the chair.

Valerie smashed the chair into the screen a few more times.

Something was definitely giving way. She could feel it, and her hopes soared. She set the chair down to take another look at the screen.

The chair wobbled.

Then she realized that it wasn't the screen that was failing, it was the chair.

"Goddammit!" she cried out, raising the chair over her head. She drove it with all her might into the screen, snapping off the weakened leg. Then she threw the chair aside and slumped on the cot, her face in her hands, fighting back tears.

Matthew touched her shoulder, then sat beside her and laid his head on her arm.

"It's all right, Mom. You can get us out of here. I know you can."

Valerie held him close, feeling more love for him at that moment than she ever had.

Early Monday morning Leonard awoke with his hand throbbing.

He locked the bathroom door and unwrapped the bandage. The sight of his palm made him sick to his stomach. His hand was swollen, and the wound was oozy and raw. Valerie's teeth marks were still well-defined in his flesh.

He ran warm water on his hand, wincing in pain. Then he clenched his jaw and poured on disinfectant. It felt like fire. As best as he could he wrapped the hand in a fresh bandage.

He was certain now that he'd have to dispose of Valerie and her son.

He'd made a mistake taking them to the cabin. He was man enough to admit it. It had been an experiment that had failed.

It was all so obvious now in the fresh light of day: Valerie would never change, no matter how long he kept her at the cabin. And he couldn't keep her there forever. Eventually, she'd be found. And when she was, she'd scream for the police.

He could see her now, bubbling with gratitude, giving Detective Sandoval and that great pig, Lott, big hugs and wet kisses. She'd be oh so eager to cry *Kidnapping!* and to testify at his trial, making up all sorts of vile lies about how she'd been mistreated. She'd sit on the witness stand, just as pretty as could be, with a phony tear in her eye, and the judge and jury would believe every word she said. And then she'd laugh as they dragged him off to prison and locked him away with criminals and perverts.

No, Leonard thought. I won't let her do that to me. The sooner she's gone, the better.

In a way, though, it was a pity. If things had worked out a bit differently, they could have been good together. A couple.

In the kitchen he kissed his mother good morning and began fixing breakfast—extra helpings of bacon, scrambled eggs, and toast. He'd need lots of energy today.

He spread butter on his toast and said, "I want to get an early start on the cabin today."

"Not so fast," Francine told him. "There are a few chores I want you to do first."

"But, Mother, I—"

"Don't argue. You've been neglecting your work around here lately. When you're finished, you can go."

"But—"

"Leonard," she said, silencing him. Then she nodded toward his hand. "That's a pretty sloppy bandage."

Leonard said nothing.

"Maybe you should let me—"

"No," he said quickly.

She frowned at him, and he bit his lip.

"Very well, Leonard, have it your own way."

Chapter

39

THE NURSE CAME IN to remove Greg's food tray.

"You didn't eat much."

"Not hungry." He chewed his lip and glanced at the phone.

"Expecting a call?"

Greg nodded, his expression grim.

The nurse raised her eyebrows. "Is everything all right?"

He met her eyes, then looked away. "I don't know."

The nurse left.

Greg stared at the phone, willing it to ring. It had been nearly an hour since he'd spoken to Detective Gianelli. Surely he'd arrived at Valerie's house by now. Perhaps he was still searching it, looking for some clue. But how long would—

The phone rang. Greg grabbed for it, nearly knocking it to the floor.

"I'm at Ms. Rowe's house," Gianelli said. "And the police are on their way to pick up Leonard Tully."

"My God, then he *did* take them."

"We don't know for sure, yet. But it's a possibility."

"If he hurt them," Greg said heatedly, "I'll kill him."

"Just slow down. If he's guilty of anything, you won't be the one to punish him."

Greg took a deep breath and let it out. "What did you find at the house?"

"Ms. Rowe's purse was on the kitchen counter top. It still contained her driver's license, credit cards, and cash. The dog was out back in the doghouse. He wasn't moving, and I thought at first he was dead. There was a shovel nearby matted with fur and blood."

"My God," Greg moaned, his anger giving way to anguish. "What has he done with Valerie and Matthew?"

"Don't worry, we'll find out," Gianelli said evenly. "I intend to take an active role in Mr. Tully's questioning."

*   *   *

After Leonard had washed, dried, and put away the breakfast dishes, Francine told him what she wanted done—enough chores to keep him busy for two full days.

"I can't just leave the cabin the way it is," Leonard pleaded. He was anxious to get up there and do what had to be done. "The roof's not finished, and if it should rain or—"

"You can't leave your duties here unattended, either, now can you?"

"No, Mother, but the cabin . . ."

Leonard knew how important the cabin was to her, embodying as it did memories of her father and Big Ed. He knew if he kept it up she'd eventually relent. Then he could take care of the real chore at hand.

Finally, she said he could leave if he'd at least do *one* thing first.

And so he dragged the large, heavy old chest of drawers from the rear corner of the shop to the front. He was forced to restack piles of items to widen the aisle enough for it to fit. Francine wheeled her chair to and fro, directing his every move.

An hour later he was done, stick with perspiration. He was anxious to leave. Francine kissed him good-bye.

"Be careful driving to the cabin, dear."

Leonard tried not to run to the back door. He loaded essential items from the tool shed into the bed of his truck: pick, shovel, plastic tarps for wrapping . . .

When he climbed up in the seat his shirt stuck to his back, which was still damp from his wrestling with the dresser. He wriggled his shoulders, not relishing the thought of driving for the next two hours in such discomfort. Better to put on a clean shirt. Besides—and he smiled at this—he didn't want to be unkempt when he faced Valerie for the last time.

He walked in the back door and was about to enter his room, when the front doorbell jangled.

A man's voice, barely audible, drifted through the shop and the kitchen and came down the hallway like an icy wind from Hell. Leonard froze, afraid to even twitch.

"We'd like to speak to your son," the man said. Leonard recognized his voice—Detective Sandoval.

"Whatever for?"

"We have a warrant for his arrest, ma'am."

"Arrest?"

"On suspicion of abducting Valerie and Matthew Rowe. Is Leonard here now?"

"Why no, he already left. What do you mean 'abducting'?"

"Do you know where he went?"

"Of course, I know. The cabin. Now are you going to tell me what—"

"Where is this cabin?"

"Well," Francine said, as Leonard slipped out the back door, his heart pounding loud enough to be heard, "it's a little difficult to find if you've never been there before . . ."

Leonard drove down the alley with his eyes fixed on the rearview mirror. He expected to see policemen running from his house, pointing guns at him.

But there was no one.

He pulled into the street and headed for the highway, trying not to panic, trying to think things through.

His mother would direct the police to the cabin, there was no question in his mind about that. But he felt no resentment toward her. She was doing the right thing. She'd lied once before to the police, going against everything she believed in, and even though it had been to protect him, it had still been lying. Neither of them wanted her to do that again.

On the other hand, the last words he'd heard her speak had been absolutely true: the cabin *was* difficult to find unless you'd been there before. So at least he'd have a head start. Not much, but enough to give him time to clean out the cabin, remove every trace of Valerie and her son.

Unless, of course, the police stopped him before he got there.

They'd probably radio ahead from his house, giving every cop in the state the description of him and his truck. The highway patrol might be lying in wait for him right now. But he had no choice. There was only one route to the cabin. He'd have to hope he could slip past them.

He turned onto highway 85 heading south out of Denver. Traffic was moderate—not heavy enough to hide in, not light enough to allow him to make a speedy getaway should the police spot him.

Then he heard a faint siren.

In his rearview mirror he saw cars and trucks pulling to the side of the road. A highway patrol car rapidly approached from behind, lights flashing.

Leonard knew it was futile to try to run. He slowed the truck and pulled over.

The patrol car sped past him, siren screaming.

Leonard sat there for a moment, forcing himself to breathe slowly, waiting for his heart rate to return to normal. Then he shifted into gear and steered back into the flow of vehicles.

Traffic became heavy and slow. Soon Leonard saw the reason—a semitrailer truck had crossed the double yellow line and smashed head-on into a car and a pickup truck. Police cars, ambulances, and tow trucks blocked the center lanes. Traffic in both directions was being funneled around the mess by uniformed officers.

Leonard drove slowly past a highway patrolman, who barely gave him a glance.

He drove on, gathering speed, smiling grimly.

The traffic accident had been more than a coincidence, he knew. More than a lucky break. It had been Providence. He was being allowed to reach the cabin unhindered. It was up to him to handle matters correctly after that.

His thoughts moved ahead to the cabin. He tried to imagine what it would be like when he arrived. He saw himself chasing Valerie and the boy around the cabin, slashing with his knife, shouting at them, while they screamed and bled all over the place.

Not good, he thought, not good at all. When the police arrived—as they eventually would—he didn't want them to be greeted by blood-smeared walls.

Above all, he wanted to avoid a *scene*.

C h a p t e r

40

VALERIE SAT WITH MATTHEW FOR A WHILE ON THE COT, allowing him to comfort her.

"You'll get us out," he said. "I know you will."

She gave him a hug, trying to build her resolve for another go at the screen.

Then she frowned, staring across the room at one of the unbroken windows. She'd been assuming that all the screens were equally secure. And so she'd concentrated her efforts on a single screen. But why should they be the same? This was an old cabin, and the wood was weathered and dry. Perhaps the bolts or screws holding the other two screens were not as well set.

Valerie gave Matthew a final hug, dragged another chair to the side window, and without hesitation smashed out the glass, sending shards flying. She swung the chair again and again, banging it into the screen. But this screen felt as sturdy as the first one.

She moved Matthew away from the cots, then smashed the remaining window, scattering broken glass everywhere. She slammed the chair into the screen again and again.

Something began to give.

She examined the chair's leg, recalling her previous disappointment. But it seemed as sturdy as ever. Only then did she inspect the screen, running her fingers over its heavy mesh. One corner appeared to be coming loose from the window.

She banged it a few more times with the chair, then rechecked it.

Yes, she could see it plainly now. The screen was bent away from one corner of the window frame. Valerie picked up the chair and slammed it into the screen, her strength renewed. She felt certain now that it was only a matter of time before they'd be free. The question was how much time did they have. Valerie drove the chair at the window, and the leg punched cleanly through, pushing up the lower corner of the heavy screen.

"All right!" she shouted.

Before she pulled the chair out, she wiggled it up and down and from side to side to widen the opening. Her heart was pounding, more from excitement than from exertion.

Thirty minutes more, she thought, that's all I need and we'll be out of here.

Valerie lifted the chair above her shoulders, squared her stance, and . . . she heard the snarl of an engine.

She lowered the chair and watched in horror as Leonard's truck crept from the trees into the clearing, like a beast of prey. It stopped a dozen yards from the cabin, as if it were crouching, waiting to spring. The engine growled once, then fell silent.

Valerie could see Leonard's outline behind the windshield. She stepped back from the window, hoping he hadn't seen her—then realized how stupid that was.

She stood in the center of the room with her arm around Matthew, waiting. She could see the truck through the side window. The door swung open and Leonard stepped out. He stood motionless, staring at the cabin.

Valerie considered barricading them in, but she knew it would be a temporary measure at best. Eventually, Leonard could force his way inside. Keeping him out for a few extra minutes wouldn't make any difference, and the exertion of breaking in might fuel his anger. Better to just wait.

When Valerie heard the scrape of the key in the padlock, she found herself wishing she'd swept up the broken glass that littered the floor. She was certain the sight of it would make Leonard angry. Perhaps if she apologized . . .

Leonard pushed open the door. He stood for a moment in the doorway, a length of cord coiled in one hand. Then he stepped in and set the heavy padlock on the table beside the hurricane lamp. Valerie wondered what he'd do first—berate her for ruining the windows or yell at her to sweep up the glass.

"I . . . I've decided to let you go," he said, staring at her levelly.

"Let us go?" Valerie felt relief wash over her.

"Yes, I—" He frowned, staring at the shattered windows. "The shutters . . ."

Valerie knew he'd get angry now. "I'm sorry," she said. "You forgot to close them." As if that explained the damage.

He nodded his head and gave her a blank look.

"It doesn't matter anymore," he said.

There was something dead in his tone. The hairs rose on the back of Valerie's neck.

"Let me tie your hands," Leonard said.

"Tie my . . . why?"

"I'd like us to take one last walk together in the woods. You know," he said, forcing a smile, "for old time's sake."

"But if you're going to let us go . . ."

Leonard took a step forward. "Please, Valerie, do as I say." His voice held no emotion.

Valerie had not seen him like this before. But she felt certain that he had no intention of letting them go.

"We don't have much time," he said.

"Time for what?" She pushed Matthew behind her, shielding him.

"You know." He stepped forward, holding the cord before him as if it were an offering.

Valerie could see madness in his eyes, and she believed now that he'd come to murder them. Her mind was wild with panic, but her body felt immobilized, as if it had already given up. The effort to move was so great that her bones ached. But she forced herself to back away from Leonard, taking Matthew with her.

"Come on, Valerie," Leonard said flatly. "There's no need to make this difficult."

Valerie pulled Matthew to the rear wall, behind the cots. She tried to quell her panic. She needed a weapon, a way out, *anything*. She fought desperately to think. But there was no escape. Leonard stood between them and the door. There was only one thing left to do.

She swallowed and said, "All right, you can tie me."

Then gently but firmly she put her hand on Matthew's shoulder and pushed him away from her, to her right. He resisted at first, but she held him at arm's length. Then she moved to her left, away from her son, holding her wrists together before her.

"Go ahead," she said to Leonard, her voice submissive.

He smiled sadly and stepped toward her, uncoiling the cord.

She lowered her eyes in surrender.

His hand reached out, touching hers . . . and then she threw herself on him, grabbing him in a bear hug, screaming, *"Run, Matthew! Run for your life!"*

Leonard stumbled backward, thrown off guard by Valerie's aggression, dragging her with him. Matthew hesitated, staring at them, eyes wide in fear and confusion. *"Run!"* Valerie screamed, and Matthew seemed to come awake. He scrambled across the cot and dashed for the open door. Leonard twisted abruptly, swinging his elbows up and outward, tossing Valerie off him, going after Matthew.

Valerie fell to the floor amid shards of glass.

Leonard lunged toward the doorway and grabbed Matthew by the shirt collar. He dragged him back inside the cabin, ripping the boy's shirt. Matthew's screams went through Valerie like stilettos. She looked around frantically for a weapon, then snatched up a long, thin wedge of glass. She hurled herself at Leonard's back and plunged the wedge into his side, slicing open her own hand.

Leonard cried out and swung his fist in a long, backhanded arc, striking Valerie in the side of the head, knocking her to the floor.

But he'd let go of Matthew, who ran out the open doorway.

Valerie scrambled to her feet, dazed by the blow.

Leonard now stood between her and the doorway, staring down in disbelief at the piece of glass protruding from his shirt amid a widening dark stain. He made pained noises, "Ah . . . ah . . . ah," and grasped the sides of the glass with his thumb and index finger, careful not to cut himself on the scalpel-sharp edges. Valerie made a run for the door, dodging between Leonard and the table, just as he gingerly plucked the glass from his side. She saw it come out smeared pink, and then she was past him.

But his hand fell heavily on her shoulder, jerking her back. She grabbed at the table for support, pulling it toward her, teetering the hurricane lamp. Its dull glow shone on the padlock lying beside it.

Valerie let go of the table and snatched up the padlock by the hasp. She let herself be pulled by Leonard, spun around, and swung the heavy lock, hitting him squarely in the forehead.

Leonard grunted and let go, falling backward. Valerie rushed to the door, the lock still in her hand, as Leonard scrambled on his hands and knees across broken glass. He struggled to his feet and grabbed the table for support.

Valerie hurtled through the doorway, pulling the door as she went, slamming it shut. She heard the table tip over with a crash and the sound of shattering glass. She jammed the padlock in place and snapped it shut, then ran from the cabin.

Leonard roared his fury, and Valerie feared the door wouldn't hold.

She looked around desperately for Matthew, finally spotting him across the clearing, standing just inside the tree line.

She started toward him, then changed direction and ran to Leonard's truck. Yanking open the door, she climbed in and reached for the ignition, ready to drive to her son and then speed to safety. The key was gone.

She jumped down and ran toward Matthew.

Suddenly, there was a crackling sound behind her, as if the cabin door had splintered open. She pictured Leonard bursting through, coming after them. She grabbed Matthew's hand, her own slick with blood, and ran into the trees, glancing over her shoulder, terrified that Leonard was in pursuit.

But the clearing was empty. And the cabin door was closed.

Still, something was different about the cabin.

Valerie hesitated, then stopped. She crept cautiously back to the edge of the trees.

The cabin lay in bright sunlight. But there was another light at the window. Yellow, flickering light.

Leonard screamed for help.

Smoke sifted out through the roof, and Valerie clearly heard the sound that she'd first thought to be the door splintering. The crackle of burning wood. In a moment she understood what must have happened—Leonard had pulled over the table and knocked the hurricane lamp to the floor. Spreading oil. Igniting it.

Leonard screamed wildly now, pounding on the door.

Valerie stepped into the clearing, drawn forward by the sight of the burning cabin, while Matthew clung to her, burying his face in her dress. She could feel the heat even from that distance. As she watched, flames leapt from the windows and licked hungrily at the roof, rapidly consuming the tinder-dry wood. She knew that Leonard was trapped, completely and finally.

And now his screaming grew more desperate, high-pitched and insane, like some pathetic animal. Valerie held Matthew tighter, and she thought of Brenda's last days, of Greg lying in the hospital, of Matthew's terror . . . and Leonard's screams did not touch her.

Then she saw him at the window, his face twisted in agony, smoke rising from his hair, yellow flames roaring all around him.

"LET ME OUT!"

And then he was gone from the window, and there were only the flames.

Within moments the entire cabin was swallowed in the blaze. The roof caved in with an explosive crash. Smoke and sparks rose straight up in the still, heated air, and tiny cinders fell back into the clearing, well short of the tree line. One by one the walls toppled and were engulfed in flame.

Valerie stared at the burning ruins. She saw movement within them. For a brief, horrifying moment she expected to see Leonard rise up, blackened and smoldering, coming for them. But it was only charred timbers settling into the dying flames.

Valerie took Matthew's hand.

They turned and walked through the trees, following the faint parallel ruts made by Leonard's truck.

C h a p t e r

THE WHITE LIMOUSINE was waiting for them as they emerged from the hotel.

It was a warm October evening, warm even for Southern California. The chauffeur held the door, and Greg, Valerie, and Matthew climbed into the back. Katherine Stone, the gallery owner, had insisted that they ride in style to Valerie's opening.

"When in Beverly Hills," she'd said, "do as the class-conscious do. I'll send a limo for you at six."

Valerie sat in the middle, with Matthew on her right. He pressed his nose to the window and stared at the passing sights on Wilshire Boulevard. Greg gave her left hand a squeeze. She turned to him, and he smiled.

"You look terrific," he said.

"I'm nervous enough to wet my pants."

Greg laughed. "Everything's going to be great. Katherine Stone loves your paintings and thinks her customers will, too. And I'd say she's a lady who knows what she's talking about."

"I suppose you're right."

"Sure I am," Greg said. He leaned over and kissed her. "And, ah, by the way . . . I have something for you."

He began patting his coat pockets, still facing her. The scar on his forehead, one of the few reminders of his accident, was no more than a faint white line. Valerie looked down at her own fading scar, the one in the palm of her hand. She winced, remembering eight weeks ago, when she'd plunged a wedge of glass into Leonard's side. . . .

. . . Valerie and Matthew had stumbled down the trail, both of them nearly overcome with fatigue. When they'd reached the paved road, Valerie had flagged down the first vehicle that came by. A highway patrol car.

The patrolman took them to a clinic in nearby Sedalia, radioing ahead to the police. While a medic tended to Valerie's hand, the officers listened to her story.

Later that afternoon she and Matthew visited Greg in the hospital. They held each other and wept. Later still, she and her son went to the veterinary clinic. It would take time, the vet told them, but Dodger would recover from his injuries.

During the next day the police sifted through the ashes of the cabin and carried out Leonard Tully's remains in a rubber body bag. His mother, Francine, took the news better than anyone expected. Or perhaps she'd been suffering from shock when she nodded and said "God's will be done." The Denver police questioned her at length about her son. After comparing her answers with Valerie's account of Leonard's confession, they closed the case on the murder of Brenda Newcomb.

In the weeks that followed, Greg was released from the hospital, eventually going back to work in his refurbished print shop—first on crutches, then a cane, and finally with only a minor limp.

Matthew started the third grade. He'd experienced a few nightmares, none recently, and he seemed to have put the episode behind him.

And Valerie resumed painting.

At first it had been difficult to concentrate, her mind still filled with images of Leonard binding her hands, threatening Matthew with a knife, screaming from the window while his hair smoked. . . . Eventually, though, her work took over, and the flashbacks faded.

And Greg asked her to marry him. At least, he'd tried to. She'd stopped him, though, begged him to wait. She wanted to concentrate on finishing the paintings for the show. There was much to be done, and she wanted to devote as much time and energy as possible. She hoped he'd understand. Of course, he had.

Now the limo stopped for a red light.

Greg patted an inside pocket. "Here it is." He withdrew a small, square velvet box and handed it to Valerie. "I wasn't sure where to do this, but the back of a limo seems as good a place as any."

Valerie opened the box. Inside was a ring.

"Oh, Greg, it's beautiful."

Matthew turned from his window. "Hey, cool!"

"*Now* will you marry me?"